FIJIAN LOVE SONG

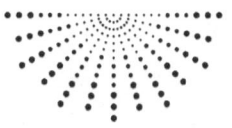

ALISON JOY

DRAGONFLY BLUE ENTERPRISES

Copyright © Alison Joy 2022

First published in Australia in 2022 by Dragonfly Blue Enterprises

alisonjoywriter.com

alisonjoywriter@gmail.com

ISBN

Paperback: 978-0-6487508-5-7

Epub: 978-0-6487508-6-4

A catalogue record for this book is available from the National Library of Australia

Managing editor: Belinda Pollard

Proofreader: Alix Kwan

Cover design by Donita Bundy

Cover images copyright © Alison Young and © kali9 via Adobe Stock

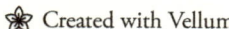 Created with Vellum

AUTHOR'S NOTE

While every care has been taken to understand Fijian customs and traditions, they can vary slightly between provinces/districts. Although I have sought clarification from my Fijian friends, I may have inadvertently made errors and I apologise in advance (and ask for forgiveness) if I have caused any offence or confusion.

PROLOGUE

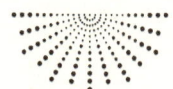

BRISBANE SUPREME COURT, MAY

"*H*ow do you find the accused?"

Caroline Hammond stared down at hands entwined tightly in her lap, her breath held still.

"Guilty on all counts."

Clamping down on the exclamation that wanted to rush from her lips, she fought to keep herself under control.

There was a beat after the announcement before the courtroom erupted.

Behind her. Celebrating. People hugging each other in relief.

The hand of her lawyer, Lloyd Miller, reached over to pat her arm reassuringly.

There was no way she could look up at him or she would burst into tears.

Vindicated.

Finally.

As the court started to clear, she was ushered into another room. A small entourage milled around them, but she couldn't take anything in. Numbness soaked into her body. Her brain became foggy. Something about him being remanded for sentencing, but her part was over. She swayed. The room started to tilt. A male hand made a grab to steady her. Her lawyer?

"Someone get her a seat, please."

"Can we have some water?"

"We need a medic in here."

"I can't leave here in the back of an ambulance," she pleaded with her lawyer. Closing her eyes, she sucked in deep lungfuls of air, trying to right her immediate world.

∼

"Is the car here?"

"Yes, sir."

"How bad is the crush?"

"We've put extra security measures in place."

"And you're sure there's not another exit we can use?"

"Sorry, sir."

"It's going to get chaotic out there, Caroline."

Taking down a well-liked, high-flying CEO would do that.

Flanked by security, Lloyd Miller held tightly to Caroline's arm as they faced the media barrage.

Cameras whirred and questions were hurled.

"Ms Hammond will not be making a statement today," became the mantra.

The crush of reporters surged around them as they struggled to walk the few metres to the waiting black Audi.

Caroline was pushed and jostled until she could manage to climb into the back seat.

Cameras continued to click. The driver blasted his horn. Police cleared the roadway and the vehicle left the courthouse precinct.

CHAPTER ONE

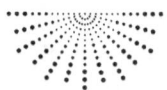

*B*risbane International Airport was quiet at this late hour of the night. One airline check-in counter was open, the rest silent, having been abandoned at a more reasonable time of day. Shops and cafes were closed, tables stacked. A lone cleaner swiped a mop back and forth while a ride-on vacuum sweeper worked its way around the empty concourse.

The line at the check-in counter shuffled along and Caroline shuffled along with it, trying to look as inconspicuous as possible, despite towering over everyone else in the queue.

Beside her, Lloyd Miller wore jeans and a beat-up brown leather jacket. The cap pulled down low on his head obscured his unshaven face. He didn't look anything like a high profile lawyer. But that was the general idea. Arranging to send her out of the country for a few months was the most sensible thing he could do. Caroline hadn't been back to her apartment since the start of the trial. Anticipating the media frenzy, Lloyd had graciously moved her to the guest wing of his palatial home in Brisbane's leafy western suburbs where his wife, Jayne, had enjoyed fussing over her.

Lloyd was counting on the Fijians staffing the check-in counters not recognising her. Unsettled, she waited her turn.

"Next." Grabbing her suitcase handle, Caroline pulled it over, setting it next to her. Lloyd stood off to the side, hands in his jacket pockets. Handing over her passport, she lifted the bag onto the scales. A few questions and she was given her boarding pass, tucked inside her passport.

Leaving the queue, they were joined by a woman in casual dress, hired to escort Caroline to the plane and fend off any journalists who might have got wind of her departure.

Lloyd gave his client a few words of encouragement and a brief hug as she fought against tears.

When no one else had wanted to take on her case, Lloyd Miller had stood beside her, and he and his wife had become good friends. Parent figures, almost. Caroline would not have made it through these last harrowing months without their unwavering support. Most of her friends had fled the scene, abandoning her because she sought to bring down one of the highest profile CEOs in the whole country.

Well, it wasn't just her, in the end. Once she had stood up to be counted, other young women had found the courage to join her. The media had dubbed them the "Sommerfield Seven". And she had become their reluctant leader and spokesperson.

The general public remained divided.

A gaggle of rent-a-crowd opponents of the company had been strident in their views and played to the media contingent who converged daily outside the courthouse. There were others who, no matter what evidence was presented, would never be persuaded that the popular and charismatic Rex Sommer was capable of carrying out the things he had been accused of. Convinced he'd been set up by the women. Even his business partner of thirty-five years, Bruce Field, struggled to make sense of the situation. At least he'd had the decency to meet with the women and hear their stories first-hand, and to offer an apology in private. But the sexual assault claims turned out to be only a fraction of the difficulties the Sommerfield Corporation now faced.

"Excuse me, ma'am, we need to get going," her escort said.

Caroline nodded, swiping away the moisture in her eyes.

"You've got that parcel for Alistair?" Lloyd said.

Another nod. Lloyd had arranged for Caroline to stay at a resort managed by his godson.

He waited while she took the escalator down to the departure area. Turning, she looked up and gave him a brief wave. He lifted a finger in salute and then turned to leave. Gulping back a sob, she steeled herself and followed the other woman, who discreetly flashed her badge at the security checkpoint and gained them fast-tracked passage. At customs, the woman, who had not bothered to introduce herself, bypassed the line-up and waited for her on the other side, talking to one of the border patrol officers as she watched Caroline move through the smart-gate with her passport. If the officer checking her passport realised who she was, he didn't let on.

When they reached the departure gate, Caroline kept her head down, moving away from other passengers who were arriving for the flight to Nadi. Would she be recognised?

There were couples and small groups of friends. Many were Fijians heading home. One group of tourists comprised of twenty or more people wearing identical red t-shirts proclaiming 'Fitzy's 50th' in bold black letters. Heaven help the resort where that raucous crew were headed.

As the flight was called, her minder approached the desk and spoke to the attendant who seemed to be in charge. Within minutes, Caroline had skipped the queue and was walking down the airbridge towards the cabin crew who were preparing to welcome everyone on board. Stowing her backpack in an over-head locker, she settled into her window seat. By the time everyone was onboard she was relieved to find she had the row all to herself. Whether by her lawyer's design or because the flight wasn't full, either way she was grateful. The emergency exit row also afforded her a little extra leg room for the three-and-a-half hour flight.

There was no in-flight entertainment on this short-haul trip, so she plugged in her headphones and chose a playlist, hunkering down to reduce her visibility to anyone walking up the centre aisle.

The evening meal was served, then the cabin lights dimmed. Lifting the armrests, she curled up as best she could on the seat, her head against the side wall, clutching the airline-issued blanket around her to ward off the cabin chill. Although she shut her eyes, there was no possibility of sleep for Caroline. The events of the last few days swirled in her mind like a maelstrom. The cacophony of lawyers' accusations and reporters' questions reverberated incessantly. Focused breathing and other relaxation techniques didn't help her.

The plane touched down in the early hours, a little after two-thirty Brisbane time which meant locally it was 4.30 am. The other passengers pulled their bags down and choked the aisle, waiting to exit. Caroline stayed staring out of the window, waiting for the crush of people to dissipate.

By the time she made it inside the newly renovated terminal and down to the luggage carousel, the suitcases were already on their way around. Choosing a spot away from the crowd of tired travellers, she waited for her bag to appear.

More security screening. Fijian customs. Then she was done. There only seemed to be one flight of passengers to be processed at this hour. The staff looked bored and ready to finish their shift. Walking one way out of the terminal would lead to the resort shuttle buses. The other direction emptied out to the taxi rank.

Pausing to take stock of her surrounds, she was approached by a driver and asked her destination. A fare was negotiated and her suitcase loaded into the boot. The driver opened the back door and she folded herself into the seat. On the drive he asked the usual questions: if it was her first time in Fiji, where she was from. She tried to be polite as she stifled more than one yawn. Away from the airport precinct the early morning traffic petered out. It seemed it was too early for all but the hardiest of locals to be up and about. Sunrise wasn't for at least another hour yet.

Twenty minutes later they were waiting for the go-ahead to cross the temporary bridge onto Denarau Island. According to the driver, the original bridge was in the process of being replaced. When it was first built, no one ever envisaged it would need to withstand the number of vehicles that now used it daily to access the main tourist area. Caroline asked when it would be finished. The driver shrugged and said something about Fiji Time, but she wasn't sure what that meant, exactly.

The taxi pulled up at the darkened port buildings. Fishing her wallet out, she counted some Fijian notes from the money Jayne Miller had given her. Thanking the driver, she walked in the direction he'd indicated she would find the ticket office. The sign outside told her she had time to kill before she could check in for her catamaran ticket out to her island destination. The early morning winter air was nippy, but not as cold as it had been in Brisbane when she left.

There was a small contingent of workers wandering around. Cleaners and security guards. None of them paid her much attention as she pulled the well-worn suitcase past darkened shops, searching for somewhere to sit. Down towards the water she finally found a bench. Offloading her backpack, she dropped onto the seat and hauled her suitcase alongside. Tiredness coiled around her body like a serpent. Insidious and pervasive. Fighting back one yawn after another, she pulled out her e-reader and picked up reading where she'd left off hours earlier.

Soon enough, the sky lightened and the marina started to wake up. White boats of various shapes and sizes waited to take day trippers and other visitors out to the Yasawa archipelago, or to the Mamanuca Islands where she was headed, west of Nadi.

Half a dozen Fijians wearing navy polo shirts with the words Dive Crew emblazoned on the back congregated at the tables outside the nearby, but not yet open, Hard Rock Cafe. From this distance she could just make out their distinctive red turtle logo.

If she remembered correctly, turtles represented good luck. She needed a change of fortune, that's for sure. Maybe she would see actual turtles in the wild while she was here. One of her friends had swum with turtles on a Great Barrier Reef holiday.

Friends. That was a joke. They were few and very far between since she'd decided to stand up to Rex Sommer. Blowing the whistle on a prominent Australian high-flyer had turned her into a virtual recluse, abandoned by those who didn't want to be caught up in the hoo-ha surrounding her every time she ventured outside.

People. Tourists started to congregate in small groups, taking photos of themselves—no doubt to brag on social media. The clock on her phone had bumped over onto Fiji time and it seemed to take forever to reach 8 am. The convenience store finally opened and she grabbed a handful of snacks to take the edge off her hunger. Stowing her e-reader, Caroline donned a pair of sunglasses and joined the line forming at the South Seas Cruises check-in counter. There were several staff working quickly, crossing back and forth behind the counter to process the people queuing. Reaching the front, Caroline gave her name and where she was heading to be checked against the passenger manifest. A girl barely out of her teens served Caroline, rifling through a box until she found a particular envelope. Flicking it open, the girl pulled out a printed aqua wristband, showing it to Caroline before pushing it back inside and handing it over. "You are on the third boat. Departure time is 9 am. Please put your armband on before you leave this area. Do you have luggage?"

Another label was handed over and attached to her suitcase, which Caroline left in a designated area for the crew to pack into one of the metal containers waiting to be craned across to the back of the catamarans.

Passengers streamed out onto the jetty, heading to the various vessels. She pulled her cap down, trying to be as inconspicuous as possible. Another turtle logo—this time green—

adorned the side of each catamaran, along with the words South Sea Cruises in large print.

At the gangway to the third boat, she lined up again and waited to file past the crew member clicking off numbers on his handheld counter. Another check of her wristband as she stepped onto the deck, then she was free to find a seat.

Glancing around, she wondered if there would be a quiet spot where she'd be less likely to be disturbed. Doubtful. The catamaran had hardly left the marina when one of the staff got on the microphone and in a very loud voice called, "Bula, everyone."

The passengers were exhorted to shout bula, which apparently meant hello or welcome, as loudly as they could in return. The crew member didn't think it was loud enough, so they had to try a few more times until he was satisfied with their response. Caroline was over it. There were two hours ahead of her until they would reach Tokalau, going via every other island resort first, and her head was already aching. Rubbing at her temples, she reached into her bag, rummaged around for some painkillers, and downed them with a gulp of bottled water.

The first stop, the small South Sea Island, was not far off the mainland. A number of people disembarked via tender and then the vessel continued on its way. Bounty, Treasure, Beachcomber... the warmth of the sun magnified through the glass window at her side made her drowsy... maybe she nodded off, but she couldn't be sure. There was another announcement but she couldn't make out what was said.

"Excuse me, ma'am." A female crew member nudged Caroline's arm. "This is where you get off the boat." The woman waited until Caroline grabbed her bag and they made their way to the back of the catamaran. There was only blue water in view and she couldn't see an island nearby. The catamaran seemed to have stopped in the middle of nowhere.

CHAPTER TWO

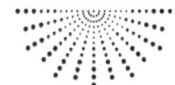

*T*he new section of boardwalk in the resort garden was making steady progress. With sweat rolling down his back, Ryan dropped his hammer and wiped his face, before reaching into a nearby esky for a cold drink and chugging half the bottle. The sun's ascent was reaching its high point and it would be time to head for maintenance work in a cooler part of the grounds. The start had been early—but the crew were working far enough away from the guests that it wouldn't disturb their serenity. Although this oasis was one of Ryan's favourite spots on the island, most of the visitors had a tendency not to wander too far from their bures, the pool, the beach or the restaurant.

Physical work was good therapy, so he escaped the confines of his office as often as he could. There was no gym to help keep him in some sort of shape. The workers also appreciated the boss taking the time to muck in and lend a hand. The office staff were more than capable of running the place in his absence and it wasn't like he was far away—anywhere he went on the island. Surveying the last of the timber as it was lifted into place, he returned to the task at hand, picking up the hammer. Maybe he could sneak in a quick swim before he clocked on for his afternoon shift.

"Hey, boss." Sitiveni was the foreman. A big, solid unit who had played representative rugby back in the day and had the crooked nose to prove it. But now he was a valuable team member here on the island. Ryan would be lost without the older man's practical expertise and work ethic. "Weren't you supposed to pick up a guest off South Seas this morning?"

It took a moment for the words to compute in his head.

"Damn, you're right, thanks for reminding me. What's the time?"

"You'd better get a move on."

Shedding his gloves as he walked, Ryan threw them into a nearby box. He had promised to personally see to this guest and there wasn't going to be time for him to run back to his residence to get changed. Fiji Time didn't apply to everything, especially not the cruise catamarans. Breaking into a jog, he headed down to the small dock at the front of the main resort building, taking the timber steps along the way as quickly as he could, greeting housekeeping staff by name as they pushed loaded trolleys along the paths between bures. Skirting the buildings, to avoid guests seeing him not clean and pressed in his usual work uniform, he pulled up at the end of the dock and grabbed the rope from the mooring post, quickly untying it. Pushing at the side of the tender, he jumped the gap and landed next to Tui, who was manning the outboard motor because resort rules mandated two crew for water vessels ferrying guests.

"Sorry, man, I got caught up with the boardwalk build."

Tui, who was a little like an exuberant puppy, just shrugged one shoulder and started the engine. The boat jerked as Ryan dropped down onto the middle seat. He wasn't going to give a good first impression the way he was dressed, but it was either that or send someone else in his stead and he didn't think that would be the better option. The boat puttered across to the neighbouring uninhabited island. As they rounded the headland, he let out an annoyed huff as he saw the catamaran waiting. Ryan signalled for Tui to open it up and they quickly closed the gap, racing to the waiting craft. Tui manoeuvered the tender alongside the stern of the boat and Ryan threw up a rope to a waiting crew member, who quickly tied it off. Stepping up to the platform, Ryan took hold of the suitcase that was handed to him. He hefted it down into the tender, jumping back to move it to a secure position. Then he returned to assist the guest.

When his godfather had asked him to take on one of his clients from a high profile case, for some reason he had expected her to be older. The woman who hesitated to take his outstretched hand looked to be closer to his own age. Early thirties? Tall and blonde and—from what he could see despite the baggy clothes she was wearing—stunning as well. Model material. He tried to remember if Lloyd had told him anything about the case, but he came up short.

As soon as his fingers closed around hers, a tsunami of electricity surged all the way up to his shoulder. His arm stiffened in support as she tentatively stepped into the boat. Just as her second foot hit the bottom of the tender, the boat rocked unexpectedly and she was thrown off-balance against his chest. Automatically he steadied her against his body. A pop of sweetness hit his nose and her soft hair brushed against his face. He wished she wasn't wearing sunglasses so he could see the blur of her eyes clearly.

"Sorry, are you okay?"

"Um, yeah, thanks." Her head ducked and she turned away. As the guest pulled out of his arms he felt her absence keenly. She gingerly made her way to the nearest seat.

As they motored back to the island, Ryan sat angled at the bow of the boat so he could keep a watch ahead, but still manage to steal surreptitious glances over at the new guest, who slouched in her spot, staring out at the water.

∾

THE PART of Caroline's brain that hadn't completely shut down recognised the man who had helped her into the boat was very good looking. An instant current of energy had swept along her arm when he took her hand. And when she'd been pitched against him as the boat suddenly rocked, his strong arms secured her up against a well-defined chest. Catching a whiff of sand, sun and sweat along with something else she couldn't identify, her jaded senses sprang to life, but she quickly shut them down.

His sun-bleached hair curled over the collar of his work shirt, and the ice-blue eyes that looked at her with concern were magnetic. She discovered it wasn't possible to look at them for longer than a split second, in case he could see right down into her soul. It was surprising he wasn't better dressed—he looked like he had been hard at some sort of physical work. The Fijian man seated near the motor wore dark shorts and a mono-grammed pale-blue polo shirt. Maybe the blond guy had been asked at the last minute to make the trip to fetch her. From her position in the boat she knew he was constantly looking her way. Disconcerted, she kept her own gaze fixed firmly on the horizon.

As the tender turned in at the dock, the man at front grabbed the rope and positioned himself to step up and wrap the mooring line around a wooden pole. A small group of tradition-ally dressed Fijians in bright floral prints seemed to be waiting for them to arrive. Standing carefully, she inched her way to the front and reluctantly reached for the hand held out to help. Her body had the same reaction as before—and she wanted to hold on to his hand for dear life and bat it away at the same time. Her suitcase was lifted out, but her companion took hold of it and wheeled it along behind him. There was a burst of singing from the group at the end of the dock. Some sort of welcome song she guessed, but she felt awkward standing there on her own.

At song's end, one of the ladies broke ranks to walk over and place a string of tiny shells around Caroline's neck. "Bula, welcome to Tokalau."

~

RYAN WAS LEFT to stare after their new guest as an electric buggy whisked her up to reception. Shaking his head, he climbed into his own buggy and took himself back to his house on the other side of the island. He jumped into the shower but his head was elsewhere. He hadn't even introduced himself. Poor form on his part, but she'd stolen his ability to think straight without even realising it. What was her name again? Couldn't even remember that.

Tousling his hair, he left it to dry naturally and pulled out his black trousers and a monogrammed short-sleeved shirt. Adding his name badge to the left-hand side, he grabbed some socks from the top drawer and sat on the edge of the bed, still thinking about the new guest. Feeling guilty about forgetting her arrival, he realised he should reread his emails. Checking his appearance one last time, he stopped at the front door for his black lace-up shoes.

Slipping into his office behind the main reception area, Ryan pulled up the correspondence from his godfather.

Her name was Caroline Hammond and she had been the main whistle blower and star witness in a high profile court case against a well-known CEO his godfather didn't name. The media had been unrelenting and she needed somewhere to go to ground until the fuss died down. It wasn't the first time he had hosted one of Lloyd's clients and, unless the media got wind of her being here, she wouldn't be the last. Ryan didn't mind. It was the least he could do for the man who had taken him into his home while he attended high school back in Brisbane.

Within a few minutes he was deep in work. The responsibility for running the resort on what was essentially his family's island consumed most of his time. Not that he would ever complain about getting to call this slice of paradise home. His maternal grandparents had moved to Fiji in the mid 50s as a young married couple and forged a life for themselves on this small island. Over the years they had built accommodation and established extensive gardens. When his mother, an only child, eventually married, she too made Tokalau Island her home base. His parents' business acumen had built the resort to what it was today. Ryan had transitioned into the managerial role when it became clear his parents would have to follow his grandparents back to Australia due to ongoing health problems. But they visited often to check up on him and their other business interests in the Pacific nation.

As SOON AS Caroline was dropped off at her waterfront bure, she took the Do Not Disturb tag and hung it on the outside of the door. Hardly noticing the elegant white decor, she zipped open her suitcase on the luggage rack and rifled around for her sleepwear and toiletry bag. The thick white towel folded on the end of her queen-sized bed was adorned with an orange and pink hibiscus flower. Moving the bloom to the side table she pulled the covers down before padding across to the bathroom. As she flicked on the light, the mirror reflection told her she looked as bad as she felt. Standing under the welcoming warm shower spray, she reached for complementary body wash and squirted the bottle contents onto her hands. The fresh tropical scent was a welcome change from her usual product and she vaguely wondered if they would sell some in the island shop she'd noticed when she checked in. Changing into a pair of sleep shorts and tank top, she used the hairdryer on her long tresses in a token gesture.

The bed was calling for her. Popping a tablet from the foil strip on the bedside table, she swallowed it down quickly with a swig of bottled Fiji Water, then crawled up into the bed, pulling the covers along with her, and waited for sleep to claim her.

THE DISTINCTIVE RHYTHM of the lali drum disturbed him. Was that the time already? Stretching, Ryan shut down the computer and prepared to do his rounds of the guests as they wandered out to enjoy sunset drinks overlooking the strip of sand in front of the resort. As he mingled with visitors he remembered Caroline, but after checking around was disappointed not to see her among the gathered group. She had seemed exhausted when she arrived earlier so he figured she would be catching up on her sleep. There would be other sunsets to see—equally as spectacular as the one she was missing this evening.

Some of the guests moved inside for dinner, others enjoyed another round or two of drinks, and there were those who took advantage of the balmy evening to walk along the beach. Tokalau was a quiet getaway island, predominantly for loved-up couples, honeymooners, anniversary celebrators and people looking for rest and relaxation. Children weren't explicitly banned from the island, but families preferred to stay at the bigger resorts with more activities on offer. Speaking of which, a handful of guests were making their way to the dock. The resort offered transport twice a week back to the restaurants at the marina in Denarau.

Tui had already moored the bow-rider to the dock and was anxious to get going. He lived for the opportunity to take the boat for a spin and was hustling to get everyone on board, with the seating in the bow filling first. Jesoni, one of the other guys, was also rostered to work the dinner cruise. Whenever there was extra room, as there was tonight, off-duty staff were allowed to join the boat to spend some downtime at the marina. A trio of workers joined the other passengers on board. The bow-rider was also available for hire during the week, to take day trips to various islands in the Mamanucas—inhabited or otherwise. These excursions proved a popular pastime and Ryan was pleased his main business partner had stumped up the money to pay for the twelve-seater and the added extras so it could safely negotiate the trip from Tokalau to Port Denarau at night.

Ryan waited until the boat cast off, then joined guests seated in the intimate resort restaurant overlooking the water. The tiki lights, lit at sunset, danced orange flames in the breeze and the pool lights gave the the blue tiles a satisfying glow. While Ryan enjoyed the resort, he much preferred the solitude of his home, but for now he played the part of relaxed host with consummate ease.

THE POUNDING of some sort of drum roused Caroline from her medicated sleep. Groggily, she pushed hair away from her face and groped around the darkened room for the bottle of water on the bedside table, gulping a mouthful and dragging the back of her hand across her mouth. The doctor had prescribed the tablets before the trial had even started because the emotional roller coaster she'd been on since blowing the whistle on Rex Sommer had quickly taken a huge toll on her health and well-being. While she had been loath to accept she needed help, the tablets at least had been allowing her to sleep a handful of hours. Every time she took a tablet, she reminded herself it was a short-term solution. Maybe being in Fiji on this island would allow her to regain some peace for her mind and soul and, well… everything. That was the end goal. But for now she would take sleep any way she could get it.

Flopping back onto her pillow, she wriggled around trying to get comfortable. Exhaustion still dug its bony talons into her and she struggled to pull herself awake. But why did she have to be awake? There was no agenda. Nowhere she had to be. Hunger didn't even figure into the equation either—her appetite had been one of the first things to fall by the wayside. Maybe the sea air would entice her tastebuds back to life. Cajole the rest of her back to life. Running on empty for so long had become her norm.

She had managed to make it to the end of the trial and BAM! As soon as the verdict had been read out in the packed courtroom her body had pulled up stumps, and she'd barely made it out of there on her own two unsteady legs.

She closed her eyes and random scenes from the last few months swirled together in her mind, like a child mixing every colour of paint together to make a muddy mess. Her head started to spin, her stomach heaved and she stumbled to the bathroom to hurl the meagre contents of her insides down the toilet. Slumping down against the wall, she pulled her knees up as a prop for her elbows, to support her head.

Every day, she questioned her decision to point the finger at her boss. Every day, she wondered if she could have done things differently. Every day, she asked herself if she should have just quit her job quietly. Maybe one day she would see that it was worth what she had endured. Maybe what she and the other members of the Sommerfield Seven went through would save other young women from the same fate. And maybe it would embolden others to make their own stand. But at the moment, if someone asked for advice she would be brutally honest about weighing up the cost for themselves. Because inevitably it would be a high price to pay.

When the room-spin slowed down enough, Caroline literally crawled her way back to the bed and hauled herself onto the top.

Reaching for the foil strip, she pushed another tablet out and gratefully swallowed it, trying to slow her thoughts and calm her mind.

CHAPTER THREE

"*E*xcuse me, Mister Ryan."

He looked up from his office desk, where he was sitting alongside Sitiveni. The head of housekeeping stood in the doorway.

"Yes, Rosi."

"Mister Ryan, some of the staff are concerned for the welfare of the guest in Bure Nineteen. No one has seen her since she checked in two days ago… There's a Do Not Disturb sign on the door and as far as we know she has not come out for food and there has been no room service ordered."

Ryan dropped the pen he'd been holding and it bounced off the edge of the table. Had it really been two days since the woman from Brisbane had arrived? Guilt washed over him. He was supposed to be looking out for her and had allowed himself to get sidetracked with all the work that needed to be done. Sure, he'd thought of her on and off, but as he cast his mind back, he realised he hadn't seen her anywhere around the compact resort.

A sudden fear struck out at him. What if she was too distraught after the trial? What if she had decided her life wasn't worth living, that the stress and harassment were too overwhelming? All these thoughts and more flickered through his brain in a mere heartbeat.

"Sorry, Sitiveni," he told the maintenance foreman, "we will have to catch up later. I had better go and check on Ms Hammond."

Rosi accompanied him to the cabin at the far end of the resort. Along with Sitiveni, the head of housekeeping was a mainstay on the island from when his parents had managed the resort. She lived a dual existence between here and her village on the mainland. Her family had lived here on the island with her while her children were young, going to school on one of the neighbouring islands until they were old enough to make their own way in the world. But now when on-island she mostly stayed on her own.

It was midmorning. He and Rosi detoured via the kitchen for a breakfast tray. It was merely a prop, a reason for him to have access to the room. If Caroline hadn't eaten for a couple of days she might be ready for some food. Then again, maybe she was sick and he would have to summon help from one of the larger islands that had medical personnel on staff.

Ryan knocked on the door. "Room service," he announced. Straining, he listened. No movement. No noise. Nothing. His heart stuttered. How was he going to be able to face his godfather and tell him he had failed to look after Lloyd's client?

Juggling the tray, he thumbed through the bunch of keys Rosi had handed him and unlocked the door, bracing himself for what he might find inside. No horrific smell assailed him. That had to be good, right? In the time he had been in charge, there hadn't been a guest death on the island. It had happened a couple of times during his parents' time at the helm, though.

The head of housekeeping stayed just outside the open door as he cautiously pushed it open. In the semidarkness of the room, he could see a form in the bed. Sliding the tray onto the small table, he approached Caroline. Empty water bottles littered the floor. A foil packet on the bedside table caught his attention. Sleeping tablets. How many had she taken? Had she overdosed? He hoped he was overreacting. Turning his attention to the bed he saw her curled up on her side, facing away from him. The sheet was caught in a tangle around her legs. Was she breathing? He stilled and concentrated on her chest and tried to ignore the sliver of creamy skin showing where her light blue top rode up.

There it was. A breath, and another, and another. Relief washed over him. Returning to the door he rapped on it again, louder.

"Room service." The figure in the bed stirred and twisted, then slowly pushed up, half sitting and half lying. Her hair tumbled chaotically around her as she yawned and seemed to struggle to focus on him, so he took a couple of steps in her direction.

CAROLINE WAS BEWILDERED to see the man who had helped her into the boat standing near the door of her room.

What had he said? Room service?

"I haven't ordered any room service," she managed to croak out, her throat dry and scratchy from sleep.

"Complimentary breakfast is part of the accommodation package."

Suddenly it dawned on her she was dishevelled, and she grabbed at the sheet, hauling it up under her arms. Embarrassed, she ran her fingers through her hair, trying to tame it.

He moved over to the table where a tray of food sat and she eyed it off. Now that sleep was starting to release its hold on her, she was hungry. A Fijian woman in uniform was standing near the door. Maybe she was one of the housekeeping staff. Caroline had lost track of the days. How long had she been here?

"We don't usually intrude on our guests, but when the staff

had not seen you around they became worried. Someone needed to act on their concerns—we have a duty of care to our guests."

"Oh… um… sorry if I've caused any alarm." Caroline wanted to get out of the bed and looked around for her wrap, but couldn't see it anywhere.

He must have sensed her predicament because he headed for the wardrobe, pulled out a white terry towel robe and brought it back, handing it to her. Clutching it to her chest she stood up and quickly shrugged into it, tying it tightly around her.

"Is there anything I can do for you? Would you like me to arrange a doctor to come and see you?"

"Ahhh, umm, no thanks. I'll be okay. The last few weeks have been pretty stressful so I just have to take it easy for a while. That's why I'm here."

"Well, if you are sure you will be alright." She nodded at him. "Why don't you have a shower and freshen up and I will set the food outside for you. Some fresh Fijian sea air will do you the world of good."

"Okay, that sounds good, actually."

Picking up the tray on his way out, he pulled the bure door shut behind him.

By the time Caroline got her head around the fact that there had been a very good looking man in her room and that he had seen her asleep, he was already out the door. It was a good five minutes before she got herself into gear. As she adjusted the flow of water and stepped into the shower, she realised she didn't even know his name. There was a badge attached to his shirt, but she hadn't been close enough to read it and it never occurred to her to ask him. Oh well, she would probably find out in due course. It wasn't like it was a large resort. She was bound to run into him somewhere around the place. And in any case, how many westerners would be working here? Maybe he could introduce her to Alistair. Lloyd had mentioned that he was the manager.

She sighed. The body wash was nearly out already. She hoped housekeeping would replenish her supplies.

The denim cut-off shorts she changed into were her favourite. A well-worn pair. And she teamed them with a light-pink floral blouse. The growling of her stomach needed to be tamed and she rubbed at it self-consciously as she headed for the front veranda, grabbing her sunglasses off the bedside table as she went. Pausing in her doorway she took in the view. Sunlight glinted off the bright topaz blue of the ocean a mere stone's throw from her accommodation. Looking out to the horizon it was hard to see where the smoothness of the water finished and the cloudless sky began. The ubiquitous palm trees all along the beachfront framed the view. There was a hammock strung between two trees down close to the sand. Along to her left some kayaks sat beached above the high-tide line and a middle aged couple were wading in the shallow water carrying snorkelling gear. Breathing deeply, she felt the strain of the last few months ease, just a little.

The guy who had been in her room was on the end of the small timber veranda, leaning with an arm on the railing, chatting to one of the workers in front of her bure. Nodding, he acknowledged her as she slipped into the chair and pulled off the cloche covering her food. The tray before her was crowded with an assortment of breakfast fare. Pineapple slices, papaya, watermelon. A prepackaged box of muesli and a small jug of milk, along with a tub of vanilla yoghurt and a couple of delectable looking pastries, each begging her to choose them first. Picking up the knife she cut the fruit into smaller chucks and devoured it quickly, then moved onto the cereal.

"Hey, how are you feeling now? Any better?"

"Um, yes… I guess." She ran her fingernail under the edge of the cereal box, taking out the inner bag and pulling the edges apart so she could dump the contents into the bowl and add milk. There was movement as he came and sat in the chair opposite her.

"I don't think I've introduced myself yet, sorry. I'm Ryan."

He held out a hand in greeting which she took reluctantly, in case there was another reaction to the contact of his hand on hers. There was. And she dropped her hand as soon as she could, rubbing her palm discreetly, she hoped, on the edge of her shorts. He looked cool and calm, like he belonged on the island with his blond surfer-boy looks. The long black dress shorts he wore showed off his tanned legs and the colour of the shirt intensified the blue of his eyes. She was sure they'd been lighter the other day, but maybe she was mistaken.

"Caroline."

"I'm assuming you are from Australia?"

"Brisbane."

"Is this your first trip to Fiji?"

"Yes it is. From what I've seen so far, this is a beautiful part of the world."

The Fijian woman Caroline took to be one of the house-keeping staff returned to a nearby trolley, pulled a set of sheets from a stack and added clean towels before heading their way.

"Bula, ma'am."

"Bula," Caroline replied.

"This is Rosi. She will be looking after your room today."

"Thank you."

"You're welcome, ma'am." The middle-aged woman stepped up to the veranda, crossed to the open door and disappeared inside before returning a short time later with the stripped bed sheets and wet towels, pushing them into a white canvas bag under the trolley. Lifting a caddy of cleaning gear, she came back. Rosi seemed like the typical well-proportioned Fijian mother Caroline had only ever seen in photos.

"Do you have any ideas what you'd like to do while you're here?" Ryan asked her.

"No not really, it was basically a spur of the moment deci-sion. I guess I'll just have to see."

"Well, the reception staff will be happy to help. You can visit some of the other islands. Do a bit of shopping, visit a tradi-tional village. We can organise day trips on Vitu Levu." When she looked a bit puzzled he added, "That's what Fijians call the main island."

"Thanks. I'll probably just lie low for a while. I'm in need of a huge dose of rest and relaxation for the time being."

"Sure, we're big on that here as well."

HIS GUEST SEEMED UNSETTLED. She certainly threw Ryan for six. The brief glimpse he caught of her vivid blue eyes before she covered them with sunglasses left him wanting to see more. Her fair skin would no doubt darken while she was here, even if she used sunscreen. Her ash blonde hair was brushed and pulled up into a messy bun which caused him to lose his train of thought when she bent forward and he caught a glimpse of the smooth curves of the back of her neck. He wondered how bleached her hair would get in the tropical sun. The scent of the resort body wash floated across the table to him, and he was pleased he had ultimately chosen that particular fragrance when they trialled new samples, because it seemed to suit her. From now on, every time he caught a whiff, he would think of her sitting there eating breakfast in that soft floral blouse. She was gorgeous. After only speaking to her briefly, Ryan knew he was already in so much trouble. What was happening to his system? It seemed to be ready to short circuit with just a simple handshake.

The gentle tug of attraction he felt was threatening to ramp up. Quickly. He decided to cut the conversation short, otherwise he would easily spend the day getting to know her... but there would be time enough for that in the days ahead.

"Well it was nice meeting you. I had better leave you to it and get back to work. See you around, Caroline." He wished she would remove the sunglasses so he could check out her eyes again, to see if they were as deep a blue as he remembered. She nodded at him as he stood to leave. It was all he could do to resist the urge to look back as he walked away.

"Wait a minute." She stopped him in his tracks. "Um… can you just hang on a sec?" Now he had a legitimate reason to turn back. Caroline disappeared inside her bure and returned a short time later with a parcel, which she handed on to him. Recognising the distinctive handwriting on the label, he glanced up to where Caroline stood on the step above him.

"Your manager… Alistair Shaw… is my lawyer's godson, and Lloyd gave me this for him. I was hoping you would be able to pass it on for me."

"Sure. I'll make sure that he gets it, no problem."

"Yeah, thanks. It's mainly a bunch of his favourite Aussie snacks."

"Okay…" He drew the word out.

"What? I saw him pack it up. You know, customs and all that. I wasn't about to carry a parcel I didn't know the contents of… even if I trust Lloyd implicitly… which I do, by the way."

"I guess it's a good idea to be cautious." He nodded sagely as he left.

IT WASN'T hard to shamelessly watch Ryan as he walked away. Broad shoulders were well defined by the stretch of his polo shirt. Although she was tall at 5'10", he would be about half a head taller again. Fijian life seemed to agree with him, and she wondered how long he had been living on the island. Maybe she'd remember to ask him sometime. There wasn't a wedding ring on his finger that she had noticed—not that that was necessarily an indicator of his marital status. And if he was single, he probably had more than his fair share of attention from many a female guest.

"He's a good man, that one," Rosi informed her as she finished in Caroline's bure. "Very good boss. Works hard. But I worry for him being on his own so much. He needs someone special in his life and a family to come home to."

Well, that answered more than one of Caroline's unspoken questions. Rosi said something that sounded like "mothay"—so Caroline guessed it meant goodbye.

"Excuse me, Rosi."

The woman turned back to her.

"How do I say thank you in Fijian?"

"Vinaka." The older woman seemed pleased at Caroline's interest in the Fijian language.

"Okay, well, vinaka then."

Rosi nodded with a small smile, swung the cleaning caddy back into its place and quietly went on her way, pushing the trolley in what Caroline assumed was the direction of the next bure.

She had been so out of it when she first arrived that she had hardly noticed her surroundings. The island was small, she knew that much, but she didn't know much more about where she was staying, happy to leave it all to her lawyer to organise. All she had wanted was to get away from the paparazzi and leave the stress of the trial behind her.

The empty breakfast tray stayed on the table as she stepped down from the veranda. There were no other bures in sight so she walked out a little further. To the right, there seemed to be two or three other cabins stretched along the beachfront—it was hard to tell with all the foliage—and a few more in the opposite direction closer to the main building. She vaguely remembered seeing cabins on both sides of the reception area when she arrived, so maybe two dozen bures all together. They had A-frame corrugated iron roofs instead of the traditional thatched straw that she would have associated with Fiji. Red bougainvillea flowers stood out against the fresh white paintwork and of course palm trees dotted the grounds along with various hedging plants. Grass looked like it struggled to compete with the encroaching sand. The water didn't quite entice her to its edge just yet, but she figured she would be down there before too long.

Turning her back to the blue seascape, she took stock of her accommodation for the next few weeks. There was a regular hinged door alongside a set of glass and timber doors framed either side by a bank of louvres. Two cushioned wooden seats graced the small, slatted table on the veranda and there were two more comfortable looking white wicker chairs on the opposite side. Inside, the high ceiling displayed exposed beams. Under a window sat a white timber day bed with a dark blue mattress, complete with an array of white-and-blue patterned cushions. Next to it were chairs matching the ones outside, and a small coffee table holding a couple of Fijian tourist magazines and a carved wooden bowl containing shells.

The four-poster queen-sized bed in the back corner was topped with more white and blue tonings and a mosquito net canopy, but she wasn't sure if that was needed or just for decorative purposes. There was a small dining table with two chairs as well as a tea and coffee making station beside a bar fridge. The whole day could be spent doing a circuit from the bed to the table to the day bed to the inside wicker and then the outside wicker. No need to leave the confines of her well-appointed room.

RYAN MADE it a point of going back to Bure Nineteen later in the day. The food tray was still sitting on the table. Maybe it was the remnants of lunch. As he walked closer, he saw the Do Not Disturb sign still hung from the front door. Everything was closed-up and quiet. As much as he wanted to knock on the door and check on her welfare again, he respected Caroline's wishes to be left alone. For the time being, anyway.

The pretty blued-eyed guest had been on his mind most of the day. He just couldn't get her out of his head and he didn't quite know why. Intrigued, he wanted to get to know her better.

He knew the rules—no fraternising with the guests—which

he often used to his advantage to ward off unsolicited advances from female visitors to the island. But if ever there was a reason to pull rank as manager and forget the rule even existed, it was now. Sighing, he collected the tray and walked back to the kitchen to hand it on.

CHAPTER FOUR

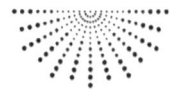

"*R*oom service."

The knock on her bure door roused Caroline from the twilight zone between sleep and alertness.

Groaning, she rolled over and checked the time. Eight-thirty in the morning, which meant it was only six-thirty back home. You'd think she'd have been in Fiji long enough to adjust to the time zone.

"Coming," she called. Whoever was knocking didn't presume to come in. Yesterday was probably an anomaly and, yes, justified when she thought about it. The staff had been concerned about her welfare, not having sighted her for a couple of days.

As she slipped the robe over her shoulders, she wondered if perhaps Ryan was the one bringing her breakfast again. In her not-quite-awake state, she couldn't be sure. It was definitely a male voice. Maybe it was just wishful thinking on her part. To be honest, she wouldn't mind seeing those ice-blue eyes again. Okay, and the rest of him.

Padding to the door she resisted the urge to fling it open. Taking a deep breath, she casually turned the doorknob.

"Hey there. Good morning, Caroline." Ryan gave her a warm grin that almost had her fanning her face and she couldn't help smiling back at him.

"Fancy seeing you here," she said.

"Your breakfast, madam." He waved the tray with a flourish.

"But I didn't order any." This conversation sounded familiar. Was it the same one they had yesterday?

"Compliments of the management."

"Oh, I see, then you had better thank the management for me."

"Sure, I can do that. Where would you like this?" He tipped his head slightly to one side, regarding her as he waited for her decision.

Caroline indicated for him to set it on the outdoor table.

"Let me know if I can get anything else for you," Ryan told her as he slid the tray down.

"Okay, thanks." Caroline felt awkward. What should she say next? Would he sit again if she asked him? That would be presumptuous. He probably had other guests to see to and she shouldn't keep him from his work. Ryan straightened up and locked eyes with her. Just briefly, but it was enough for her to get a decent fix of that delicious blueness. Could his eyes be ice-blue and warm at the same time? She grabbed at the door to stop herself leaning forward to get the tiniest bit closer to him. *This is ridiculous,* she scolded herself. *I just got here. I can't take up with a staff member.* There were probably rules about staff not having relationships with guests, no matter how much her brain said she was interested.

~

RYAN WAS ALMOST MESMERISED by her. Not just her face and those stunning eyes. All of her.

There was a hum of awareness or connection or whatever

you wanted to call it. Subtle but compelling. And he thought she felt something as well, because she seemed to sway forward just ever so slightly before she caught herself and pulled back. Flashing her a grin, he gave her a casual two fingered salute. "I'll leave you to it. Enjoy." Turning to leave he felt her gaze on his back... so he may have added a bit more swagger to his step.

⁓

THE DEPARTMENT HEADS gathered in the small boardroom to give their weekly updates. The staff he had in place were, in his opinion, second to none. Some, like Rosi, had been mainstays here since he was young.

Ryan took notes from where he sat and added their reports to the pile next to him. They ran through the agenda and he thanked them for their time.

He grabbed a coffee, headed into his office and tried to settle in. But his attention span would give a fruit fly a run for its money. Paperwork was always a challenge, but today his usual resolve to stick it out deserted him. He couldn't even muster up an inducement to keep him at his task.

The grounds staff probably needed him to check in with them.

Outside, he paused to scan the beach. Aha, the perfect distraction. Wandering along the sand, he stopped where one of the men was currently near the top of a palm tree, spiked shoes dug into the side of the tree, anchoring him while he used a machete to bring down coconuts and then pruned some of the fronds. On any tropical island, coconuts were an occupational hazard and they had to be safely removed to prevent them injuring a guest or worse. A worker on the ground retrieved the fallen coconuts and put them in a wheelbarrow to take back to the kitchen. The palm frond offcuts were piled nearby.

The worker finished the job and dropped the machete to

hang from a cord around his waist, then climbed to the ground with practised ease. The three of them talked briefly as the machete knocked the top off one of the coconuts. The worker pulled a packaged straw from his pocket stash, unwrapped it, then pushed the white cylinder into the coconut. He handed Ryan the drink and gestured towards a nearby bure. Ryan looked where the man was indicating. Caroline was sitting out the front of her bure reading. Ryan grinned his thanks at the worker.

"Bula." As he caught her attention, she dropped the electronic device she was reading on her lap and flashed him a sweet smile that warmed his insides. She wore navy shorts and a blue-and-white striped sleeveless shirt, tied at the waist. Her hair was in a high ponytail and she looked a little more relaxed than she had been.

"Bula. Back so soon?"

"Just doing the rounds of the workers."

"So, what exactly do you do around here."

"A bit of this and a bit of that. Whatever needs doing, I guess. Here you go. Fresh off the tree. Literally." He pointed back to where the worker was in the process of scaling another palm tree.

Caroline took the coconut from his hands. Was he imagining it or was she avoiding his fingers? He took a step back, just to be on the safe side, when he really wanted to get closer and see if he could catch a trace of her perfume.

"I've never had fresh coconut water before." She took a sip, and he could tell she wasn't sure of the taste but wasn't about to admit it. "Looks like he's had a bit of practice doing that." *Good diversionary tactic.*

"Yeah, I guess most Fijian guys learn the skill early on."

"What about you? Do you get up the trees as well as part of your bit of this and bit of that?"

"I have been known to climb the odd tree now and then, but I prefer to leave it to the experts."

"Fair enough. I guess it comes more naturally to the locals."

"Have you had a chance to see the gardens yet?"

"Gardens? I didn't realise you had any."

"Happy to give you a tour a bit later when it cools down. I'm on my way back to the office, but I'll be looking for an escape late afternoon, so how about I come and find you then?"

After Caroline agreed to a garden tour it was all he could do to stop himself doing a fist pump as he walked away. He felt like he was sixteen again and the pretty girl he was crushing on had agreed to go out with him. He hadn't felt this way since... well, since Lucy. This afternoon couldn't come soon enough for him.

The sooner he knuckled down to work, the sooner he could skive off for an hour or so. It wasn't easy to put the new guest out of his head but if he wanted some time with her later that's what he would need to do—even if he was checking the time regularly. Nope, he'd have to set an alarm and just put his head down to work.

Instead of taking a buggy for their garden tour, Ryan decided to walk, to give himself as much time with Caroline as possible. On the way to meet her, he stopped to chat with various staff members and guests. One beautiful day rolled into the next around here, but he wasn't naive. Life for most Fijians wasn't anywhere near as privileged as his situation on Tokalau Island. Sure, his family had worked hard over the years, but they still had advantages that the locals didn't have.

The island was a quiet haven and that was the way the guests liked it. The staff were friendly with beaming smiles of welcome. Whenever Ryan travelled back to Australia to visit family or on business, it wasn't long before he felt the tug of Tokalau calling him back. Other managers and corporates could keep their big city living. As far as he was concerned, the advantages tipped the scale firmly in favour of Fiji life.

Caroline wasn't outside when he arrived at her bure. But before he could take the first step, the door opened. Had she been watching and waiting for him? She was wearing a different outfit. Long pale-blue shorts, a navy tank top, and slip-on shoes.

Vacation-cute. That was the thought that popped into his head as she pocketed the room keys and joined him.

And… her hair was down. He barely restrained himself from reaching over to slide his fingers through its thickness.

~

"How big are the gardens?" Caroline asked as they walked along a signposted track behind the bures.

"About six acres' worth."

"That's sounds like a lot of work to keep up."

"Yes, there's a team of gardeners as well as a maintenance crew."

The green corridor ahead of them looked inviting. A small thatched-roofed open-sided bure straddled the entryway to the garden.

Her companion stood back and gestured with his outstretched arm for her to go ahead of him.

"Oh my," was all that she could get out as she took in the tropical paradise in front of her.

It reminded her of an open garden she had seen once, back in Brisbane. Balinese themed. Lush and green.

This was all that and more. It was another world, away from the beach views, and just as stunning.

Layers and textures of green fringed the area. Gravelled pathways wound their way around the foliage.

Which way should she go first? To the right. No, to the left. The edged path was about two metres wide. There was a boardwalk up ahead and it looked like there could be a water feature as well. She wished she had thought to bring her phone to take photos.

~

RYAN WAS ALWAYS thrilled when someone saw the gardens here at Tokalau Island for the first time. Caroline's reaction made all the hard work by his family and staff over the many years seem worthwhile. Walking alongside her, he answered her questions about the plants that grew in the area.

"Okay, these are the easy ones like frangipani," she said. "One of my favourite flowers, by the way." He'd tuck that bit of information away in case he needed it. "Hibiscus, bougainvillea on the arbours. And is this red one ginger?" She pointed and he nodded. "What is the national flower of Fiji?"

"Unofficially, that would be tagimoucia."

"Sorry, what was that?

"Tahng-ee-mow-theea."

She repeated it a couple of times.

"It's a red-and-white flowered plant."

"Are there any here in the garden?"

"No, they only grow in the highlands of Taveuni which is about three hundred kilometres from here. The name of the flower means sleeping tears because legend has it—and it varies slightly—that a princess had given her heart to someone but her father wanted her to marry another man, so she ran away to the mountains and, exhausted, she fell asleep crying… and her tears turned into the red and white flowers."

By now they were both leaning on the boardwalk railing overlooking the lily covered pond.

"Next time you see a fifty dollar note, have a look because it has a picture of tagimoucia."

CAROLINE WASN'T sure which part of the gardens she liked the best, but to be honest maybe she enjoyed having a very attentive tour guide more. From what Ryan had shown her so far, red seemed to be a popular flower colour in Fiji. Apart from the obvious hibiscus, there were small clusters of star-shaped sinu flowers. Kakala with their rounded petals were often used in graduation and wedding garlands, according to her guide. The fragrant white blooms of Tahitian gardenias were also a prominent feature in the gardens. There was a new section of boardwalk under construction at the far end.

Mini bures containing hammocks looked inviting, and she was sure she would be back here on a daily basis. She dropped down on to one of the many wooden benches that dotted the landscape and closed her eyes. A light breezed teased her face, cooling the sun's warmth on her skin.

~

RYAN STRETCHED an arm along the back of the bench seat, hoping he wasn't being too presumptuous. It was impossible to tear his gaze away from her up-turned profile.

"Do you ever get called Callie?" he blurted out—not sure why that thought had forced its way out of his mouth. "I think it suits you better." Caroline was too formal and stuffy to his way of thinking.

She opened her eyes but didn't turn in his direction, instead fixing her gaze somewhere other than in the garden.

"Not in years," she admitted. "That was what my grandfather called me, and it died when he did."

Her wistfulness tugged at his heart. "I take it you had a special relationship with him?"

"My mother's father. He was the one person in my family that looked out for me. That I could go to for anything. He patched up my skinned knees and my first broken heart. I miss him so much. He's been gone a dozen years or more. I really could've used his advice in the last couple of years, that's for sure."

"Do you have any siblings?"

"Two younger sisters. Much to my father's disappointment. You'd think in this day and age most men would be over the need to have a male heir, but not in our family. My mother actually had a couple of miscarriages along the way. Both boys. It was like her body couldn't be pregnant with males. I should've been the second child. It was boy, girl, boy, girl, girl. Eleanor is twenty-six and Tania is twenty-three. I'm thirty-one in case you were wondering and… our father is rather… indifferent to us. Don't get me wrong, he's provided for us and everything, but it's like he can't relate to us."

"And your mum?"

"They divorced six years ago. She has remarried and moved to the States with her American husband. Don't hear from her much. Dad has had a string of lady friends since, but nothing serious."

~

CAROLINE LEANED FORWARD, elbows on her knees, palms pressed together, tossing a sideways glance in his direction.

For some reason she felt she could talk to Ryan more freely than she had been able to with anyone since her grandfather.

Maybe it was the vibe of acceptance she sensed. Like he was interested. Like he cared. Really cared, even though he hadn't said any words to that effect. And if he wanted to call her Callie, she'd actually be okay with that. The little she knew of him so far demonstrated traits that her beloved grandfather had possessed in bucket loads.

"You can call me Callie if you like. I don't mind." His raised eyebrow was question enough. "No, really. But enough about me for the moment. What about your family?"

~

WELL, he had to confess at some time. It might as well be now.

"I also had a good relationship with my grandfather. I was

named after him, by the way, but I go by Ryan. So, I'm Alistair Ryan Shaw."

It took a few beats for it to register with Callie. "What, wait a minute. You're telling me that you are Alistair? As in, Lloyd Miller's godson? As in, you manage the resort?"

"Ahh, yeah."

"I thought you would be older."

"If it's any consolation, I thought the same about you."

"You could have told me who you were earlier... like when I gave you the parcel."

"Sorry, I know I should have, but sometimes people treat you different because you are the boss. It's nice to just be Ryan without all the other stuff that goes along with it."

"I actually get that."

He wondered if it was something to do with the court case, but didn't think it was appropriate to ask.

"What about the Shaw family? Do you have siblings?"

"Yeah, I have three of each. Older sisters and younger brothers."

"That's a good-sized family."

"Well, there wasn't a whole lot for my parents to do here back in the day," he joked.

"You grew up here, then?"

"Basically, except for high school and uni. My grandparents moved here in the late fifties and started from scratch. My mum was an only child because Nan was advised not to have any more kids. Mum lived in Australia for a while, then she and Dad moved back after they married and helped run the place. Eventually they took over and, well, now it's my turn."

"None of your siblings live in Fiji?"

"No, they are scattered around Australia."

~

CAROLINE LISTENED AVIDLY as Ryan talked about his family and growing up in Fiji. It sounded idyllic. But there had been many challenges along the way. If she remembered correctly, there were old photos on display up in the main reception area. Maybe she could check them out some time.

"Anyway, I need to get back for happy hour," he told her, getting up. "You are welcome to stay here. The solar lights are due to kick in soon or you could come and join me for sunset with the other guests."

As much as she wanted to spend more time with Ryan, there was a good chance that a number of the guests on Tokalau would be from Australia, so there was a risk she could be recognised and found out by the media back home.

"Thanks for the invite but, no, I'm going to take a pass. I'll walk back with you though."

～

RYAN GAVE HIMSELF A MENTAL KICK. Callie had been lying low since she arrived. Of course she couldn't run the risk of being found out by other guests. All he knew was what Lloyd had told him in the email. In time, he hoped she would feel comfortable enough to tell him her story.

"What does the name of the island mean?"

He started guiltily. "Sorry, I didn't catch what you said."

"Tokalau... is there a meaning to the word, you know, like beautiful place or calm waters?"

"Nothing quite so lyrical, I'm afraid. It means east. The island is east of Malolo Island."

"Am I allowed to be a little disappointed without offending you?"

He laughed. "I'm not easily offended." By the time they reached her bure, he was going to have to scramble to get changed in time to mix and mingle with the guests. "I'll have to catch up with you tomorrow."

"Sure."

The cute wave she gave him made him want to forget the guests and happy hour and just stay here with her, to enjoy the sunset from her bure, with her standing alongside him, so he could breathe in the soft scent of her along with the evening breeze.

But, duty called... and sometimes it sucked.

CHAPTER FIVE

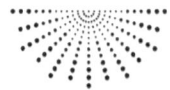

At first, Caroline didn't see the piece of paper tucked under her plate. Plucking it out, she unfolded the resort-monogrammed page.

A complimentary massage. That actually sounded divine. Was it something Lloyd had arranged as part of the accommodation package? All she had to do was call reception and book a time for someone to be sent down to her room. Mobile massage.

The breakfast tray had arrived with a wink and a smile from Ryan again. It was a nice way to start the morning and she had to admit she kind of hoped it would be a daily thing. Doubtful, though. There were other guests. He would be busy, so she shouldn't get her hopes up.

The attention and gentle flirting were doing wonders for her battered heart. But she was sure if he found out who she was and what she had done back in Australia, he wouldn't be able to back off fast enough. That's what her last boyfriend had done. The fallout from her going to the police and setting the whole thing in motion had been the death knell to their relationship. The public scrutiny had been intense and he'd wanted none of it.

Collateral damage. Unintended consequences. There had been a lot of those.

While she ate breakfast, Caroline made her choices for both lunch and dinner. She set the room service order on the tray and left it on the outside table for collection. Eating in her bure was the best choice for her. It was a little lonely, but her own company was preferable to the possibility of being recognised.

Finally, she got around to unpacking. There was no need to live out of her suitcase. The heavy brown wardrobe was short on coat-hangers, so she would have to ask for more. Thankfully, she wouldn't have to be pressed and immaculately turned out every morning—not that she was a slob at heart.

The laptop could just stay in its case for the foreseeable future. The thought of writing her side of the saga, which she knew she must, made her stomach churn with nausea. Not enough distance yet. Who knew how long it would take for her to be able to piece together the maelstrom of thoughts into some sort of coherent form.

There was a collection of word-search puzzles. A pack of cards for solitaire—old school. Some adult colouring books. These were stacked on the bottom shelf of her bedside table. As well, there were games on her phone. More books on her e-reader than she could ever hope to read. And, according to the resort info guide, there was a rec room that might have some jigsaws to fill in time if needed.

A rap on her open door raised her eyes from the almost empty suitcase.

"Oh, hey Ryan." Dang if her heart didn't do a little happy dance when she saw him leaning against the door frame in bright red board shorts and a snug fitting khaki t-shirt. A pair of sunglasses had been pushed back onto the top of his head, making him look like a fellow guest rather than one of the staff members.

"Hey yourself... the tide's out. Just wondered if you were interested in a little reef walk. It's one of the activities we offer to guests." Was he offering to take her or was he expecting her to join other guests?

"Um… I'm not feeling particularly social to be honest."

"That's okay. This is strictly one-on-one. I've been stuck inside all morning so I was looking for some fresh air and thought I'd see if you wanted to tag along."

Instead of jumping up with enthusiasm, she tried to look as though she was giving serious thought to the request.

The hopeful expression on his face won her over.

"I guess that would be nice. Thanks for thinking of me."

The grin that enveloped his countenance was so cute.

"What will I need?"

"Sunscreen and a hat. Sunglasses. I grabbed a couple of pairs of aqua shoes on the way out, so I'm hoping a pair will fit you." He held out a pair of hot pink shoes and another of fluoro yellow.

It was then she noticed Ryan was wearing a black and red pair on his own feet. A water canteen hung from a strap looped across his chest.

"Okay, give me a few and I'll be with you."

"I'll just wait outside." He took one large step down the stairs and was gone from her line of vision.

FEELING PLEASED WITH HIMSELF, Ryan found a shady spot nearby to wait. Before long, she joined him and he handed over a bamboo pole that was almost as tall as his six-foot frame. When the staff took guests out at low tide it was typically just in front of the main resort building. But they were heading a little further around the point where they would be less likely to run into other people.

Chatting casually, they waded into the shallows, with Ryan demonstrating how to use the pole for extra support. Before he realised it, they had walked a hundred metres or more, stopping as he pointed out the different marine life. Spiky sea urchins, underwater flower anemones, spotted sea cucumbers. Some rather large clams. And shells. Lots of shells. Tiger cowrie, cones, conch.

"Do Fijians use the big shells to blow through?"

"Mostly just for the tourists. You know, instead of a dinner bell, they use a conch—or a davui, as we say. They were traditionally used to announce the arrival of a chief or special guest to a gathering. Not so much now, but at the funerals of chiefs, they would have men blowing conch shells."

"I guess they could sound really sad at a time like that." He nodded as they picked their way over the slick rocks.

Callie was not as surefooted as he was and slipped a few times, catching herself with the pole.

Scooping up a blue starfish, he gently deposited it on her flat palm.

"Can you take a photo for me?" She pulled her phone out of her pocket with her free hand and held it out for him.

Their fingers brushed, he made sure of it. Just so he could see if there was still a tingle of electricity to be had. There was. She had to have noticed it too—her head snapped up. Tugging the phone out of her fingers, he held it while she tapped in her passcode.

Stepping closer, he zoomed in on the starfish in her hand, then pulled back to include her upper body in the frame as well.

There were the beginnings of a smile, so he pulled out some corny line that actually made her laugh—a full-on chuckle that had him laughing along with her as he tried to take a string of photos. Oh my goodness, he was instantly hooked on that delightful sound. Now he knew he had a mission. To make her laugh. As much as possible.

The last little while had probably been a drought for her in terms of laughter and fun. Hopefully he could change that.

WHEN CAROLINE HAD INITIALLY ASKED how long they would be out on the reef, Ryan told her thirty minutes. An hour and a half later, they were still wandering around. "We'd better head back before we get cut off by the incoming tide," he informed her.

"Thirty minutes huh?"

"What can I say? Fiji Time." He grinned at her and she couldn't help but smile back.

Ryan took the pole from her as they walked back to her bure and said goodbye.

Lunch was arriving as she toed off the hot pink shoes and laid them in the sun to dry.

"Bula, Ms Caroline."

"Bula."

"Where would you like this tray?"

"Just on the table there. Vinaka."

Mid-afternoon, a buggy pulled up outside her bure and a youngish woman in a traditional hibiscus-print skirt and top alighted. She proceeded to haul out a folding table and carried it over to the bottom of the steps.

"Bula, ma'am. I'm here for your massage."

Caroline stood aside as the masseur set up in her room.

The younger woman had a flower behind one ear as many female workers on the island did.

"I've been meaning to ask someone about wearing flowers. Isn't there some particular meaning behind it?"

"Yes ma'am. If you wear a flower on your right ear like this"—she gestured—"it means you are single. And on the left side means you are spoken for."

The worker waited for Caroline to situate herself on the table then started the massage.

An hour later, Caroline was thoroughly, physically sated. Every part of her body had relaxed under the soothing touch from the expert fingers of the massage therapist. The tightness around her neck and shoulders had melted away. How had she not noticed how much tension had been trapped there? Now, if there were only a way to massage the tension out of her thoughts, then she would really be on the way to restoration.

"Vinaka… vakalevu." *Thank you very much.* She hoped she had gotten it right.

"You are welcome, ma'am." The soft lilt of the response added to Caroline's sense of wellbeing and a whooshing sigh of contentment left her lips as she was left alone again.

Despite her medication, steady sheeting rain woke Caroline in the middle of the night. In time, she hoped to be completely free of the tablets, but for now they were a lifeline to sanity. A cooling breeze swept over her warm skin as she stirred. The thrumming rhythm from the open heavens lulled her back to sleep.

By morning, it was still raining. Caroline peered out of the bure. An umbrella was propped up alongside the door. One of the staff must've dropped it off earlier. A buggy splashed past, plastic sides rolled down as it transported guests and their luggage back to the main building. Fancy having to leave the island in this weather.

Pulling her feet up underneath her on the chair, Caroline sat on the small veranda, sipping on a cup of herbal tea. Rain cascaded off the edge of the roof overhang. Puddles had grown overnight and covered the ground every which way. The bright blue waterscape had leached its colour to a dolphin grey that matched an equally dismal sky. Still, the weather here seemed bearable with the promise of sunshine following close behind.

A buggy pulled up close to her bure and a navy rain jacketed figure stepped out then leaned into the back for a covered tray.

"Good morning, Callie." Ryan joined her under cover and set the tray down in front of her.

"I don't envy you having be out and about in this." She pointed in front of her.

"It's not so bad." He flicked the hood back and shook his head, sending a spritz of water droplets into the air, then raked his fingers through to settle his hair back into some semblance of order. The monogrammed jacket he was wearing stopped mid-calf and his shoes were sodden. They chatted for a few minutes, Ryan leaning back on the veranda rail, before he announced he should get back to it. "What are you planning for today?"

Caroline shrugged. "The usual, I guess."

"I can bring you back a jacket in case you find you're getting a little cabin fever." He paused at the top of the steps.

"I'm good. I'm sure you have plenty of things to do other than run around after me."

Ryan just shook his head as he pulled the hood back into place.

LATER IN THE DAY, Ryan was again at the wheel of the buggy, taking lunch to Bure Nineteen. Any excuse to spend a little more time with Callie. Clutching a white plastic bag in one hand and balancing a food tray in the other and a rain jacket over his arm, he was thankful when she rescued the tray to set it down while he draped the jacket over the railing.

"Here, I thought you might like to do a jigsaw."

Callie pulled the box out of the damp bag. A tropical island sunset was on the box.

"I have it on good authority that, finished, it will just fit onto the coffee table." He nodded at her open door. As much as he would've liked to have offered to help her with the jigsaw so he could hang out with her, it probably wasn't a good look for the other guests.

CHAPTER SIX

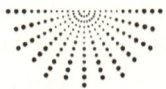

"I'd like to get off the island. I've been here a month already. It's my first time in Fiji so it seems crazy not to have a look around when I've come all this way. Who knows if I'll ever come back here again?"

That comment rocked Ryan, as he realised he didn't want Callie to leave and not come back. Even though he was still getting to know her, he liked what he'd discovered. Callie made him feel... more alive than he had felt in such a long time. It was an overused line, he knew, but honestly that was exactly how he felt. She was only supposed to be here for a short time and he wasn't looking for a casual fling, so he didn't have a clue how things would play out.

"Have you thought about what you'd like to do?"

"I've had a look at a few brochures Rosi left for me. What I'd really like to do is just pretend to be a local. Jump on a bus and see where I end up. Some village somewhere."

"You know you can't actually just turn up at a village unannounced?"

"But I've seen photos of people visiting villages."

"Yes, but those ones are specifically for tourists. You can't just rock up to a village without an invitation."

"So how can I get an authentic taste of life in a typical Fijian village?"

"How about you just leave it with me and I will organise a day trip for you."

~

CAROLINE WAS DRESSED AND WAITING, backpack at her side, when Ryan arrived, casually dressed in long khaki shorts and a snug fitting white t-shirt. Ryan was so... she was at a loss for words. Cute was an understatement. Good looking, handsome, gorgeous. She mentally scrolled through a list of words to describe him in a nanosecond, and none of them seemed to do him justice.

Stopping at the bottom of the steps, he threw her a grin that quickened her pulse. Caroline couldn't stop herself smiling back. Today was going to be a good day. She just knew it, despite the internal havoc he was causing in her midsection.

Over one shoulder, Ryan was toting a well-worn backpack that looked like it had been on many adventures.

By comparison, her pristine pack was carrying the usual sunscreen, insect repellent and water as well as an assortment of other bits and pieces and a light jacket in case it got cool while they were out and about.

"Ready?"

She was so ready, but tried for what she hoped was an air of nonchalance, casually standing and reaching for her bag. Caroline fell in beside him as they walked to the dock in front of the resort where the tender was waiting. They would meet up with the South Seas catamaran for the trip into the port at Denerau.

Tui reached up to take her hand as she stepped carefully down into the tender and decided where to sit.

"Bula, Miss Caroline."

"Bula, Tui."

The Fijian's wide grin displayed a couple of missing teeth. He was becoming one of her favourite staff members on the island. He seemed to have a variety of roles around the resort, including designated driver of any watercraft. Caroline chatted to him as Ryan stepped in beside her.

Copping a not-unpleasant eyeful of his muscular legs, her eyes strayed all the way down to his casual slip-on shoes before sliding off to the horizon. Ogling was probably not a good idea, but it was hard not to at this close range. Grabbing at the side as the boat tipped a little, she felt Ryan take his seat behind her. Ignoring the wave of awareness rolling over her at his proximity, she looked ahead as the boat motored towards the looming catamaran. Tui made a wide turn before coming in to position the tender alongside the back of the catamaran. Ryan brushed past her, setting off a involuntary reaction on her right side. Maybe she admired his backside as he climbed across to the catamaran and waited for her to join him.

Disappointingly, one of the crew members grabbed for her hand to help haul her up onto the deck. Pulling her cap down low, Caroline followed Ryan into the main lounge area. He motioned for her to follow as he headed for a vacant seat on the starboard side.

There was a mixture of passengers—couples and families heading back after their vacations. Some of the women and girls had their hair tightly plaited. A couple of the younger brothers also sported plaits. There were faces and arms flushed with sunburn, and fussy babies who'd had enough of ferry travel and were not hesitant in letting everyone else on board know about it. One of the female crew took it upon herself to relieve one of the mothers of her grizzling child and within minutes the youngster had settled, giving the harried mother a short reprieve.

Malolo and Tokalau were at the end of the Mamanuca run, so it was only forty-five minutes back to Denerau.

As soon as the catamaran approached the marina, Ryan motioned for her to follow him, apparently keen to get ahead of the crush of passengers who would be trying to disembark.

When they became separated in the line-up, he waited to the side until she managed to get to him. Leading the way, he strode along the dock, weaving around straggling tourists who pulled at their suitcases reluctantly, realising their holiday was almost over.

He'd been prepared to drive her anywhere she wanted to go, but she wanted to travel like a local. Ryan took a left and headed to the taxi rank.

"This isn't quite what I meant about local transport," Caroline told him as the taxi headed north out of Nadi.

"All in good time."

She watched the local scenery pass for half an hour until they pulled up at The Garden of the Sleeping Giant. "What is this place?"

"Just wait a sec." Caroline followed as Ryan walked to the ticket area, but they seemed to know who he was and waved him through.

The cafe area wasn't particularly busy but the number of white high-backed cane chairs lining the perimeter indicated it was a popular place.

A foliage-covered timber walkway led to lush gardens opening up into a green vista. They strolled at a leisurely pace around the area, with Caroline stopping to take photos on her phone every few minutes. The walkway crossed a crowded lily pond and Ryan headed to a vine covered archway at the foot of a set of stairs. Once at the top he paused to allow her to survey the surroundings. Caroline could visualise garden parties and weddings in this picturesque setting.

Her body zapped to life when Ryan's arm brushed against her. "How big is the garden?" Maybe if she asked some questions she could dull the effect he was having on her nerve endings.

"About twenty hectares."

"I'm not sure why, but I'm getting a feeling of deja vu. It's so weird."

"Not weird at all." He grinned at her, white teeth contrasting with his permanent Fijian tan.

A sensation gripped her lower body and she had to will herself not to buckle at the knees. Focus! The garden needed her attention, not the good-looking guy next to her.

"The gardens at Tokalau take a lot of inspiration from these ones," he said.

"Why is that?" She cast him a half glance before looking back at the view.

"In the sixties there was an American actor by the name of Raymond Burr."

"Oh, he was *Perry Mason*, wasn't he?

"I'm surprised you know who I'm talking about. Most people our age wouldn't have a clue, even though it's a big deal here."

"My grandfather loved that show. He was always watching reruns of that and… what was the other character he played?"

"*Ironside*, the wheelchair detective."

Caroline nodded. *Keep looking at the view. The garden view not the guy view.*

"Well Raymond Burr lived in Fiji for a number of years and established these gardens. My grandparents became good friends with him and spent a lot of time here gathering ideas to implement back on Tokalau Island. The main thing here, though, are orchids—that was his passion. There are a couple of thousand different varieties."

RYAN TOOK the giant timber swing alongside Callie's. Pushing off with one foot she moved back and forth, seemingly content to enjoy a gentle ride. He was content to watch her swing, eyes closed, face to the sunshine. Peaceful. Beautiful. Almost carefree.

The swing slowed and she jumped off, sticking the landing with a flourish.

"Bravo." He laughed as he joined her for the walk back. The timber boardwalk was a little uneven in places and he used it as an excuse to brush against her. More than once. Enjoying her reaction and his.

Something involuntary was going on here between the two of them. What it was he wasn't sure, but he wanted to explore it further. Maybe he should concentrate on the walkway. Yeah, that was a good idea. It was a reminder of the maintenance work waiting to be done in the gardens at Tokalau.

No, the work would wait; he wanted to enjoy his time with Callie.

THEIR DRIVER WAS SLOUCHED BACK in his seat, arms folded, dozing, by the time Ryan and Caroline made it back to the carpark. He woke with a start when Ryan spoke to him, yawning and rubbing his eyes as his passengers climbed into the back.

On the trip into Nadi, Ryan told his companion a little about Fijian culture. When the riotously bright and colourful, intricately carved Hindu temple close to town caught her eye, Ryan explained it was the largest of its kind in the southern hemisphere. Indian migrants had come to Fiji to work in the sugar plantations and nowadays about forty percent of the population was Indian.

Closer to town, Ryan asked their driver to drop them off in the main street. Tourists didn't tend to venture into Nadi itself. Most were happy to stay exclusively at the resorts on Denerau. Callie was strikingly good looking and totally oblivious to the attention they were attracting. Teenage girls giggled as they passed by, and the head of every male crouched in every other doorway turned to follow their progress. Several men started to cross the street towards her but he steered her out of the way. Callie wasn't in any danger, but he was still wary.

Someone Ryan knew called out from just inside a shop and he paused to chat for a minute or two before continuing, stopping after a few metres when he realised Callie was no longer beside him. Turning back, he saw she'd been waylaid by a tall Fijian and engaged in earnest conversation. Sighing in annoyance at himself for forgetting to forewarn her, he jogged back to the couple.

"This man has been very helpful and has offered to show me where to buy locally made souvenirs," she told him.

"I bet he has," Ryan muttered under his breath before challenging the man in Fijian. The guy's eyes widened and he held his hands up as Ryan tugged her away along the footpath.

"That was a bit rude of you, don't you think?"

"Sorry Callie, that guy was a tout. He's paid to cajole gullible tourists into visiting the overpriced shop he works for and gets a kickback for every customer he brings along. There are other places to go if you are keen for some souvenirs. See that green building up ahead?" Callie nodded. "Jack's is the biggest and most popular souvenir shop. More like a western department store. Or if you want to support smaller enterprises, just tell me, I've got a little local knowledge."

CAROLINE FELT a little embarrassed she hadn't known she was being set up. She'd be more careful in future. The air conditioning in Jack's was a welcome reprieve from the sticky humidity outside but it was disconcerting to be followed by overly attentive salespeople. Ryan didn't seem to mind wandering around the store with her, approving her choice of a hibiscus print dress and making some suggestions for other purchases.

Back outside at the local handmade markets, vendors competed for sales by telling Caroline she was their first customer of the day. It was hard not to feel sorry for them and buy from every single market stall, but Ryan had already warned her before they set foot in the area. Having him alongside to negotiate and hustle her away if necessary was a relief.

Nearby food markets bustled with locals selling all kinds of fruit and vegetables. Some were recognisable, others were not. They purchased a pudgy bunch of bananas to eat later. Caroline watched as a man wielding a machete pulled a small peeled pineapple out of a display case containing ice, and deftly sliced thin wedges out of the flesh before offering it to her. A pineapple popsicle? Grasping the stalk handle wrapped in a plastic bag she nodded and said, "Vinaka" as Ryan handed over money. Her pace slowed as she slurped the ice cold fruit.

A few stalls over, Ryan stopped and cast an eye across the produce before picking up some sort of plant root. He waited for it to be wrapped in newspaper and placed into another bag. He shoved the parcel into one of his backpack compartments as he thanked the middle-aged man presiding over the stall.

Outside the markets, there was a herd of carrier vans in a dusty paddock, basically utes with a covered tray. Underneath green canvas canopies, bench seats ran the length of either side. The drivers had congregated in a bunch, waiting for fares. Ryan told her once a van had four passengers it would leave.

Wheeled food carts holding perspex display cases painted red or blue lined the edge of the road, but Caroline couldn't see what food they were selling.

The bus depot was a sight to behold. Rows of buses angled in along a central platform. Green and white, blue, purple and white, yellow. Old buses in varying states of repair that looked like they should have been retired in the seventies, alongside sleek new air-conditioned coaches, and everything in between. Each bus had a sign in the front window announcing its destination. The depot teemed with people, weaving in and out, sitting waiting with bags of shopping piled at their feet or hauling themselves onto buses. It seemed that this was the preferred mode of transport for most Fijians.

A ticket booth—or more aptly, a ticket cage—for one of the bus companies had times and prices painted on every side. Caroline got separated from Ryan but his tall blond frame was easy to keep tabs on. He towered over most of the locals. Keeping her eyes on his back, she weaved her way through the throng of people, dropping her pineapple stick into its bag for later when she wasn't in danger of having it jostled out of her hands.

There were a few people ahead of Ryan in the queue at the main ticket box, but he didn't seem to mind and spoke to those around him who were keen to strike up a conversation. His ability to speak fluent Fijian always seemed to surprise the locals until they realised he was a long-term resident. Lots of sidelong glances in her direction had her wondering if she'd been recognised, but she doubted anyone here would know who she was. She did stand out from the locals, so she supposed that was the source of their interest.

Catching up to Ryan, she stood alongside him, not saying much as the line inched towards the counter. Finally, with tickets in hand, he put a hand at the small of her back to guide her to where they needed to board their bus.

"We still have about twenty minutes, so we can either grab a seat now or wait till closer to the time."

"I think I should do a bathroom run before we get going." They backtracked to a rest room where Ryan handed her a coin to pay the attendant for toilet paper and to enter the washroom.

"Here, you'll need this." He pulled a bright turquoise geometric print sarong out of his bag and held it out to her, answering her question before she had a chance to ask. "In a village you either need to wear a long skirt or a sulu like this."

Taking the sulu without comment, she walked inside the amenities.

All things considered, the toilet wasn't as bad as she had feared it might be. She attempted to tie the sulu around her waist, but wasn't doing a very good job of it. A grandmotherly type took pity on her and quickly wrapped and tied the cloth for her.

"Vinaka."

The classic old-style bus had rolled-up canvas instead of

windows, to allow the breeze to flow through. Ryan presented their tickets and waited for her to board ahead of him. Everyone on the bus seemed curious about the two white people. Caroline found a seat towards the back and swung her bag off her shoulder so she could slide across to the window. The little guy in front of her peeped the top of his head over the back of the seat and ducked down again. Caroline pushed her bag down between her leg and the side of the bus as Ryan settled beside her.

"Where are we headed?" she asked.

"We're going to visit Rosi in her village. It's her time off. She works three weeks on and has a week at home. Technically she could commute every day, but like many of our workers she prefers to use the onsite staff accommodation."

"How far away is it?"

"By bus, a bit over an hour. We are headed the back way, because it's the scenic route."

The driver finally climbed into his seat, started the engine, and reversed the bus out of its allocated space. It was a tight squeeze and Caroline was surprised he didn't scrape the paintwork in the process.

All at once, loud reggae music blared from the speakers. On closer listening, Caroline realised it was the same songs that were popular on the radio at home, just with a unique twist. Eyebrows raised, she turned to Ryan who just shrugged his shoulders.

"It's the local version of what the rest of the world is listening to." He shot her a grin that had her shaking her head.

"It's different, that's for sure."

CHAPTER SEVEN

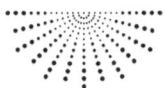

*T*he bus headed east along Queens Road past green, rolling hills and blue skies scattered with fluffy clouds. White-painted school buildings came into view, but school was finished for the term. Houses dotted the roadside, framed by palm trees, orange bougainvillea or banana plants. Lowset houses, highset houses. Painted pink or blue or some other pastel shade. Besser brick boxes, concrete structures or homes cobbled together with whatever materials were at hand. Corrugated iron mostly, plywood, sugar sacks. Tin roofs, thatched roofs and washing. Always washing. Strung up between two forked tree branches, precariously leaning poles or between palm trees. Shorts and shirts hung alongside brightly coloured dresses and skirts.

Kids ran out to wave at the bus. Others played under hoses, half undressed. Skinny horses ran in roadside paddocks. Stray dogs searched for food. And then there were the bus stops seemingly in the middle of nowhere. Dubious constructions that barely provided shelter from the sun, let alone the rain.

The bus turned off the main road and trundled down what Caroline assumed was "the back way". Ryan leaned around her to point to the landscape, his body warmth caressing her. She almost swooned as his hand skimmed the back of their seat, brushing against her back. The winding road showed off picturesque water vistas at every turn. In the distance she could see thatched houses with million dollar views and was surprised there wasn't more resort development. Speaking of resorts, the bus pulled up near one at Momi Bay to let some workers exit. Ryan told her it was the only other resort on Fiji apart from Likuliku near Tokalau that had bures right out over the water.

"I'm surprised there aren't more of them," Caroline said.

"They'd be at greater risk if a cyclone comes through."

The bus driver reversed the coach so he could make the turn back onto the road.

The little boy in front of her had his head out of the window, enjoying the breeze in his face. Caroline returned his huge grin. Ryan started playing peekaboo with the little sister who kept poking her head above the back of the seat.

The bus would stop and people seemed to be getting on and off at random. Heading off to who knew where, with no sign of any houses.

Caroline wished she could get the driver to stop so she could buy fruit from one of the roadside stalls they passed.

The bus turned off onto yet another side road and crossed an old wooden bridge before coming to a halt in the middle of a village. "This is our stop."

Caroline hoisted her backpack in front of her as she followed Ryan to the door, careful not to bump any passengers on the way, echoing Ryan's "vinaka" to the driver as she climbed down. Ryan had told her she wasn't to wear her backpack in the village as the shoulders were considered sacred, and she had already tucked her cap away—only the village chief was permitted to wear a hat.

Just one man was waiting to board the bus and it soon rumbled on its way. Ryan was already embracing the smiling Rosi, who had been standing off to the side with an assortment of other locals. Rosi was wearing a bright hibiscus print skirt and a matching top. The older woman hugged Caroline as well and led the way to her home.

It was a concrete house with a front veranda. Caroline walked along a plank over a hollow in the ground and across to the doorway where Ryan was shucking off his shoes. Pulling her own shoes off, she glanced up to see a group of people sitting at the far end of the veranda as she followed him inside.

The floor of a large central room was covered with a woven pandanus mat. On one side of the room were two curtain-covered openings which might be bedrooms. The doorway on the far side led to a breezeway and a kitchen area beyond that.

Ryan pulled the wrapped plant out of his bag and presented it with a flourish to Rosi, who accepted it gratefully and hurried away.

Caroline stood awkwardly next to Ryan for a few minutes before they were ushered back outside to the waiting group. Rosi joined them, gesturing for Caroline and Ryan to sit cross legged in a circle with the others while she took her place near a large carved wooden bowl. Rosi seemed intent as she slowly pounded a section of the brown root Ryan had given her, placed the pulp into a cloth bag and then put it back into the bowl. It was probably something she had done time and time again over the years. One of the teenagers poured water over the bag and a brownish coloured liquid started to fill the bowl. Rosi rolled and squeezed the bag and the water grew darker in colour.

Ryan leaned over close to her ear. "This is a traditional welcome ceremony. Everyone takes turns drinking the kava."

"But it just looks like muddy water," she whispered, hoping no one else could hear.

"Sorry, but it's considered rude not to participate."

The coconut cup was dipped repeatedly in the kava and presented to each person in turn, starting with the handful of older males in attendance. It looked like it was going by age or seniority.

Before accepting the cup, the recipient would clap their

hands once and say "bula", drink the cup in one gulp and then clap three times and say something that sounded like ma-tha. Caroline was puzzled at the faces some of the younger ones pulled as they swallowed the drink. Must be an acquired taste. The jangle of her nerves grew stronger as she watched the cup being passed back and forth, hoping she didn't embarrass herself or Ryan. There was just the glimpse of a grimace from him as he tipped the cup to his mouth and swallowed.

Then it was her turn.

"Low tide," Ryan told Rosi, winking at Caroline. Rosi smiled and held out the partially filled cup.

Ryan prompted her to clap and say bula before taking the cup between her hands.

Oh goodness, she thought, staring at the liquid, summoning up the courage to swallow it down. Everyone was watching and waiting.

Lifting the cup to her lips, she closed her eyes and drank, trying not to gag. Was this what it was like to drink dirty water? Her eyes watered and her mouth tingled as she handed the empty cup back, hoping she didn't throw up. She didn't think she'd be taking up kava drinking while she remained in Fiji. Ryan reminded her what to do next, giving her a reassuring smile.

Finally, the ceremony was over. Ryan tugged her to her feet and she hobbled ungracefully to get the circulation flowing again.

"You okay?"

"I will be when I get some feeling back in my legs."

Her companion chuckled. The grin he sent her way didn't help her legs regain their strength and she had to plant her feet firmly on the concrete floor before she wobbled further.

"Hope you are hungry," Ryan told her as some of the group went inside the house and others left to go back to wherever they had come from in the village. "They have been waiting on us for lunch."

"It's, like, after two o'clock. They must be starving."

Rosi and a couple of teenage girls came back into the room and set saucepans and other containers on a table pushed up against the back wall. One of the girls handed Caroline and Ryan a plate and the two of them approached the table.

∾

RYAN WASN'T sure how Callie would react to the food that was on offer. It was different to what she ate back on Tokalau.

Her eyes widened momentarily when she saw a number of whole fish in the first pan.

"Here, I'll break a section off for you." Scraping back the fish skin, he forked some flesh onto her plate.

There was chicken on offer as well. It looked like a chow mein, and she scooped some up with a generous serve of gluggy rice, adding noodles and vegetables. Ryan squirted a stream of tomato sauce on her cassava. "Trust me, you'll thank me for it later," he said when she looked less than impressed. Taking a glass of orange liquid, he handed it to her. "It's Tang. A powdered drink. You might appreciate it to wash the food down."

∾

CAROLINE RETREATED to the side of the room and sat on the floor next to Ryan, their backs up against the wall, carefully setting her glass alongside her, aware that she was being watched.

"Why aren't they eating?" she asked him.

"We are the guests. They will eat after we have finished."

It was bad enough to have to try and eat unfamiliar food, but to eat while everyone else was watching was disconcerting.

Apart from some whispered conversations happening on the other side of the room it was mostly quiet. Maybe they were shy of their guests. She could relate to the feeling. It was a little over-whelming.

Taking a mouthful of the chicken she nearly choked on a bone. Turned out the dish was full of them, so she ate very cautiously.

Across the room was a huge pile of woven mats covered with mounds of pillows. Caroline leaned closer to Ryan.

"Can you explain what all that is about?"

"Rosi's daughter is getting married soon, so all the mats are for her new home. It's traditional to give the bridal couple pillows." At a quick count there were over twenty pillows with brightly coloured cases of hot pink, purple or lime green. They all seemed to be heavily machine embroidered with the couple's names, flowers and other motifs.

She almost said, "You're kidding," out loud but managed to stop herself in time. She knew from Ryan's raised eyebrows he'd read her mind.

Caroline caught a glimpse of a woman sitting cross legged on the ground just outside the back door, working her way through a pile of dishes, hand-washing them in a small metal bowl. The kitchen across the breezeway held an old gas oven and little else apart from a wooden cupboard and row upon row of bottled water, neatly lined up against the far wall. A small amount of light crept in from a narrow set of louvred windows, the curtain tied in a large knot.

Afterwards the younger members of the family took them on a tour of the village. Caroline felt like a pied piper as more and more children joined the entourage. The visitors were a source of great interest. The big white Methodist church building stood out proudly, with its narrow arched windows and blue-painted doors. But like most buildings here it could probably do with a new paint job. A small shed sheltering a wooden vessel out the front of the church caught her attention. It was a much larger version of the one back at Tokalau. Curious, she turned to ask Ryan about it.

"That's a lali drum. Every village has one… and most of the resorts. It's the equivalent of a church bell calling everyone to worship, and also lets the villagers know what time it is. Each village has its own rhythmic pattern that they beat out at set times every day."

Residents were out on their verandas or in doorways, waving as the group passed by. Word about them had spread. They walked along the middle of the single lane road through the village. No one seemed concerned about vehicles. There weren't any concrete footpaths here and white-painted rocks lined either side of the road, defining drainage culverts for vehicles to avoid.

A long timber building on wooden stumps seemed to be a community centre.

Just on the edge of town was a narrow-gauge railway track. The group stopped and appeared to be waiting for something. Before long an open-sided rail car packed with half a dozen big Fijians in shorts, high-vis vests and heavy work boots trundled out from the greenery, picks and other implements crowded into a rack at the back. They laughed and waved as they puttered by.

"Sugar cane is one of the main crops around here," Ryan said. "It goes from here to Sigatoka and then by a slow train to the mill at Lautoka which is about half an hour the other side of Nadi."

The road headed uphill to the right, over a timber bridge showing signs of recent repair. Caroline walked well away from the edges as there were no guard rails to prevent a drop into the brown water of the river five or more metres below. She prayed that no truck would come barrelling around the blind corner, as she didn't want to jump into the water from this height.

The group cut across the road and up a steep pinch of dirt track through a gate, then continued up another hill to where the local school was perched. Several low white buildings trimmed with blue stood on the far side of a timber playground that looked like it had been recently painted. It was quietly eerie. Deserted. The school bell hung forlornly. No noisy children playing and laughing and talking. No teacher calling them to line up for class. Caroline peered in the louvred windows. Timber chairs stacked at one end of each room. Chalkboards still adorned with messages about having a safe vacation.

Between the trees in the distance, Caroline could see water, grey and smooth.

She was surprised to learn that the school had dormitories for children who lived too far away to travel to and from school every day. Rows of bunk beds were jammed close together. Mattresses stripped of linen. The rooms empty and silent.

The children fanned out and ran here and there, giggling, singing and chasing each other. One of the girls slipped her hand into Caroline's and smiled shyly up at her. Another walked alongside, dragging a stick in the dirt. Ryan was in deep conversation with a group of boys who had gravitated to him. A boy had been throwing a football around and it sparked an impromptu game. Fiji was well known for playing seven-a-side rugby. They ran around for about fifteen minutes before Ryan called it quits.

"You feeling your age, old man?" Caroline teased as he flopped down on the grass where she was sitting with the rest of the group.

"Argh, I'm so out of shape," he complained, wiping his face on the sleeve of his shirt.

Caroline eyed him off. Out of shape? No way in the world. But she wasn't going to tell him that. In case he got the wrong idea.

Ryan leaned back on his hands, "So, what do you think—"

"Of your rugby skills?" she jumped in before he could finish. "Not much, to be honest."

"Hey!" He bumped against her and it was more than just static electricity that jolted her.

She laughed at his indignation.

"I was going to say, what do you think of the day in general… visiting the village?"

"Yeah, it's been good. Thanks so much for organising it."

"You are welcome," he replied, getting to his feet and waiting for her to scramble up beside him.

It was a beautiful afternoon and Caroline felt a sense of peace and wellbeing wash over her as the entourage headed back down the hill. One of the girls started to sing, another joined in and before long the whole group was singing... in parts.

Caroline thought the tune sounded familiar. "Why do I feel like I've heard this before?" she asked Ryan as the English words to the gospel song rang out.

"The Fijian Rugby Sevens adopted it as their team song a couple of years ago and it's become part of their game ritual. It's called *E Da Sa Qaqa, We Have Overcome.* You've probably seen a huddle of big Fijian guys belting this out in harmonies on the news at some point."

"I'm not sure what it is about Fijians and singing but I literally get goosebumps every single time."

"And here I thought it was your proximity to me that caused your reaction," he joked, nudging her.

"Ha ha, you wish." Caroline didn't want to admit that his proximity did in fact cause a reaction in her body.

To the left, rich emerald grass carpeted a courtyard area, with houses on three sides. Leaving the road, the group meandered past different houses, winding in and out, still singing. Caroline waved and greeted people as they came to investigate the noise. Everyone seemed very friendly.

The kids continued to lead them through the village. Along well-worn tracks and sometimes-narrow spaces between houses, over plank bridges stretched across muddy gullies, to the river where fishing nets were piled in a heap on a platform waiting to be tossed out into the water from nearby dinghies.

It was time to be on their way. One of the young people phoned for a vehicle to take them up to the main highway.

They said their goodbyes as a carrier van pulled up outside Rosi's house. Caroline clambered aboard awkwardly and found a spot to sit on the bench seat running along the side, tucking her backpack on the floor between her legs. A spare tyre sat chained in place on the floor near the cabin. Ryan scooted in alongside her and a couple of villagers jumped in for the bumpy ride. Caroline grabbed the support bar as she jolted into Ryan, who extended a hand to help steady her, while he and the others chatted away in Fijian and she wished she could understand what they were laughing about…

The bus stop on the side of the highway amounted to no more than a rough, slapped together wooden structure that would have been condemned back home. Caroline cast her eyes down the highway expecting a bus to lumber along from Suva any minute. There was however a vehicle flashing its headlights in the distance. As it got closer, one of the girls flagged the minivan to stop on the road shoulder and spoke to the driver through the open passenger window.

"When a hire vehicle has spare seats and is willing to stop and see where you are headed, it will flash its headlights so you know you can pull it over." It looked like the van was almost full of people. There was some negotiation before the driver pulled back onto the highway without extra passengers.

"He wanted more money than was fair because we are white," Ryan explained. "But there will be another vehicle along soon."

"You aren't taking up the challenge to haggle?"

"No, I'll leave it to the experts."

"I would have assumed you were an expert by now."

Ryan just shrugged as another van pulled up alongside.

After a bit of back and forth, a price was agreed upon and someone inside the van slid the door open. Ryan indicated for her to go ahead of him. She felt self-conscious as she ducked to step in, finding the only spare seat behind the driver. She slid over as far as she could to make room for Ryan, but it was a tight squeeze. The heavily patterned Indian-style upholstery was protected by clear plastic seat covers. The driver had a photo of what she assumed was his family on display along with a couple of small plastic Hindu gods glued to the top of the dashboard. While the taxi van was in better shape than many of those she had seen on the roads today, there wasn't any air conditioning and only minimal breeze from a partially open window. The left side of her body pressed up against Ryan quickly became hot and sweaty. She wriggled uncomfortably to try and put a sliver of space between them to allow some airflow.

RYAN HOPED that now Callie had tried the various forms of local transport she would be happy for him to drive them in air-conditioned comfort in future. There hadn't been any need for him to travel this way for a long time, and to be honest he much preferred to drive himself.

The taxi van dropped them off at the bus station and then they had to find a bus to take them to the marina. There was no ferry this late in the day, but Ryan had arranged for Tui and one of the others to meet him. Both men were stretched out asleep in the back of the boat. Ryan called out to wake them as he held out a hand for Callie to climb aboard.

The day had been long and tiring. Callie was fading fast. She sat, eyes closed, with her elbow propped on the edge of the boat, her hand supporting her chin.

Ryan scowled at Tui when he opened the throttle and Callie jerked out of position. She readjusted herself and settled again.

Deliberately leaving a space between them, Ryan leaned back, folding his arms behind his head, breathing deeply and trying not to Callie-watch, something he had struggled with all day. Trying not to watch her and failing. Seeing how she reacted, what made her smile, what pushed her out of her comfort zone. He had enjoyed spending the day with her and getting to know her better.

Not surprisingly, Tui decided to show off for anyone who

might be watching from the beach as they arrived back at the island, with the boat making a couple of passes before doing a wide arc into the dock.

The boys tied the boat off and waited while their boss and his guest gathered their bags and off-loaded.

~

"THANKS FOR TODAY," Caroline told Ryan as he walked alongside her up the path past the main building. "It was full-on, but I had a good time."

"You're welcome. Let me know if there is anything else you'd like to see while you're here. We could do the mud pools and hot springs, or we can zip-line. Maybe we could visit the sand dunes near Sigatoka or do some island hopping."

"I'll think about it. Right now, though, I need a shower. See you around." Caroline left Ryan and took the well-worn track to her bure. Rummaging through her backpack she found the room key and slipped inside her room, flicking the light on and peeling clothes off on her way to the bathroom. Washing off the dust from the day, she stood under the warm water and reached for the body wash and then grabbed the shampoo, taking her time to clean up. After drying off, she pulled on her new dress.

The hair dryer from under the vanity got a brief workout before she decided to let her hair dry off naturally. Unpacking her backpack, she sorted through her purchases and started rear-ranging her belongings.

A knock on the door caused her to look up. She recognised the voice that called, "Room service."

Really? She hadn't been going to bother about room service, but her stomach let her know its opinion as she opened the door.

"Hey there, I thought you might be as famished as I am, so I ordered up some food from the kitchen. I hope you don't mind." He grinned at her.

"Um yeah, thanks."

"Out here okay?" He gestured to the table and when she nodded, he set the tray down, pulled out a seat for her, shook out a linen serviette and draped it over her lap. Condensation had already formed on tall glasses of pine-coconut cream he plucked off the trays. Then he removed lids from the plates with a flourish. Burgers and fries, a small dish that looked like it might contain a traditional dessert, and another with what was probably the Fijian version of mud cake.

Without asking, Ryan took the other seat and pulled a plate towards him.

"What?" he asked at her expression. "Do you want me to eat elsewhere?" He made to leave but she reached for his arm, her fingers enjoying the sensation of his cool skin and the underlying muscle. Maybe she held on a fraction too long, because he looked down at her hand.

"No, it's fine."

Resuming his seat, Ryan winked at her before tucking into his burger. He had showered and changed. His damp hair was tousled and she didn't need to lean in to get hint of the beach vibe scent he had going on. Clearly off duty, he wore denim shorts teamed with a natural coloured t-shirt that bore a distressed ocean wave print, and well-worn leather beach sandals on his feet.

Although she had been with him all day, Caroline still felt self-conscious as she pressed down on the top of her burger before slicing it in two. There was just no elegant way of eating one of these in public.

RYAN CONCENTRATED on the ocean view as he ate his burger, aware that Callie was nibbling away, no doubt trying not to make a mess of her plate and herself. Her just-washed hair cascaded in riotous waves down her back. The salt air and humidity combined to make her seem carefree and... extra enticing, especially with the hibiscus print dress she was wearing. They were quiet for a while. A glob of dressing had landed at the corner of her lips and he fought the urge to lean over and lick-kiss it away, just before she wiped the serviette across her mouth. Picking up a fry, he wondered if she would let him feed her. Mmm, probably not. She reached for her own serve of fries, licking the salt off her fingers, totally oblivious to the fact that her actions were as sexy as...

"Sorry, what did you say?" he asked guiltily as she disrupted his slightly salacious train of thought.

"The dessert." She pointed. "What is it?"

"Cassava cake."

She picked up a spoon and lifted some to her luscious mouth. He. Was. In. So. Much. Trouble. And when she sighed in that cadence, he thought he was going to need a cold shower.

"Can I try some of this one as well?" she asked, positioning her spoon over the mud cake.

"Be my guest," he managed to get out, swallowing hard and looking away from her. But of course he lasted less than a second before his gaze flicked back to her. "You have a bit of a sweet tooth, I take it?"

Nodding, she swallowed the mouthful. "Yep." She dived in for another spoonful.

"Looks like I'm going to have to play dirty to get my fair share." Her eyes widened as he grabbed her wrist and manoeuvered the spoon towards his mouth. There wasn't much resistance on her part and the little nose-scrunch she gave as he succeeded in getting the spoon into his mouth made him grin. Her giggled response caught in her throat as his gaze settled on her. Blue eyes sucked him into an eddy of emotion, need and desire. Did he imagine it, or did she lean forward as if to invite him to taste the dessert from her lips?

"Bula!" a couple walking past her bure called out in their

American accent, and the moment evaporated. Biting her lip, Callie looked away from him, waving to the interrupters.

CAROLINE WAS sure Ryan had been about to kiss her. The thrill of anticipation that sparked through her was crushed when the older couple decided to be friendly. Ryan leaned back in his chair, arms crossed, not making eye contact. The cold drink in front of her looked good about now, and she reached out to take it with a hand that gave away her heightened emotional state. After gulping down a few mouthfuls, she grasped the glass with both hands to keep it steady as she looked everywhere but at her dinner companion.

Catching movement out of the corner of her eye, she saw Ryan stand up at the railing and rake a hand through his hair.

"Hope you enjoyed the food. I think it would be best if I get going. You can finish both of the desserts. Someone will call past later for the tray." As he made his way from the small veranda, she kind of wished for a backwards glance of regret but there wasn't one. Now that she was on her own, Caroline stuffed the remains of the sweet dishes into her mouth.

Swallowing down the disappointment of what might have been.

CHAPTER EIGHT

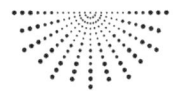

*S*ince they'd visited Rosi's village, it seemed that the older woman had become even friendlier, if that was at all possible. Although quietly spoken, Rosi was keen to teach the Australian guest a few Fijian words. For her part, Caroline enjoyed the few minutes they got to talk every day Rosi was working on the island.

Village life was easier to envisage now that Caroline had been there and seen it for herself.

"How are the wedding preparations going?" Caroline asked.

"Good, good."

"I'm interested to know what happens in a traditional Fijian wedding. Can you tell me what it's like?"

Rosi appeared to think for a minute. "You can come to the wedding and see for yourself."

Caroline was surprised. Maybe Fijian weddings were a lot more relaxed than back in Australia. "Oh no, I couldn't do that." She didn't imagine there would be other white people there and she didn't want to be the odd one out.

"Yes, you can. It would be an honour to have you there. You could come with Ryan."

"He's going to the wedding?"

"Ryan is like one of the family."

The next time Caroline encountered Rosi, the woman pulled a tape measure out of the pocket of her uniform.

"I will take your measurements for the clothes." Rosi talked her into wearing a traditional outfit after telling her Ryan would be doing the same. Maybe she would be less conspicuous that way. Wielding the tape measure, Rosi quickly wrote down the measurements in a battered spiral bound notebook, promising to bring the clothes back with her when she returned from her week off.

The women agreed on a price and Caroline handed over a number of notes which Rosi pocketed gratefully.

RYAN PICKED up Callie in the buggy and headed towards his side of the island, planning to take his own boat from his private dock into Denerau enroute to the wedding.

Pulling up, he heard her soft exclamation as she took in the building with its wide timber veranda.

"This is your place?"

"Yep. You can come and check it out if you'd like to. We have time."

Callie nodded.

Ryan grabbed her overnight bag and motioned for her to go ahead of him up the handful of stairs, almost slamming into her when she stopped suddenly to look up at the high pitched roof. "Come on in."

Callie stopped again to admire the large open plan living area.

"Oh Ryan, this place is amazing. I can't believe you get to live here."

Built by his parents some distance from where his grandparents had lived on the island, it was where he had grown up. Where he had looked forward to coming back to for school holidays, often times with a friend or two who had been equally impressed at their schoolmate's home.

Ryan took stock of the interior of his house, imagining it through Callie's eyes. Beautiful local timber floors. High ceilings with exposed beams. Large, comfortable lounge chairs. The fourteen-seater dining table. The huge kitchen that had been the heart of the house, the scene of many family get-togethers over the years, although these days it didn't get much use. He guessed he did take it for granted.

On the far side of the room, he pushed the massive concertina doors open. The back entertainment area was one of his favourite places in the house. A spot to sit and relax and take in the peace and solitude, and the golden sand and turquoise waters that wrapped around the bay beyond the house.

CAROLINE HAD NEVER SEEN anything so breathtakingly stunning in all her life. The house was magnificent, and the view! She hoped Ryan realised how blessed he was.

He invited her to look at the rest of the house and she had to restrain herself from running room to room like an excited five year old.

"Oh my goodness." Her jaw was going to get gravel rash from constantly hitting the ground. Honestly, she almost cried when she saw how beautiful the master bedroom was, with its white painted ceiling and outer walls that consisted of windows and banks of timbered louvres opening up to more of that idyllic view. Fancy waking up to that vista every day of your life!

RYAN LEANED up against the door frame as Callie walked around his bedroom, forcing himself to stay put as if he were superglued in place. He tamped down all the errant thoughts that crowded his head. The white cotton mid-length sleeveless dress she was wearing had a small blue floral all-over print. It was nipped in at the waist and the rounded neckline was modest.

Callie seemed as enamoured with this room as she had been with every other room in the house. Not as much as he was enamoured with her, though. He was pleased she liked his home base so much—as if it might mean tacit approval of him as well.

~

TURNING SLOWLY AROUND THE ROOM, Caroline faltered when she saw Ryan watching her from the doorway, feeling the heat from his gaze warm her cheeks. "Um, I really like your place, Ryan. You are fortunate to be able to live here." She wasn't sure how she would get past him and out the door. As if he sensed her confusion, he stepped back into the hallway.

Ryan cleared his throat. "Time for us to get going, I think."

Did she imagine it, or was his voice a little huskier? Oh man. She jammed her hands into her dress pockets out of harm's way and all but scurried out of the house.

Retrieving her overnight bag, Caroline pulled her sunglasses out of a side pocket and hoisted the bag over her shoulder. Ryan was just ahead, toting his own bag down to the small dock at the back of the house. At the end sat a sleek, dark-blue trimmed boat named *Shaw Thing*. Caroline wasn't familiar with boats, but it looked like you could walk around to the front.

She waited while Ryan took their gear aboard then stretched out his hand towards her. Wishing she was confident enough to get aboard under her own steam, Caroline accepted the help and almost slipped out of his grasp when a pulse of electricity shot all the way up her arm. Ryan didn't flinch, so maybe it was her overactive imagination. Moving undercover to the steering wheel, Ryan started the engine. Once it warmed up, he untied the mooring lines.

Moving carefully, Caroline walked to the rear of the boat.

There was a bench seat across the back near the motors and another behind the cabin, so those passengers would have their back to the driver. If she sat out there on her own she would feel like she was being chauffeured, but Ryan called her up to where he was sitting at the wheel. He gestured to the seat alongside his own as he plucked sunglasses from his top pocket.

Shaw Thing headed around the bay and turned in the direction of Port Denerau. The skipper... captain—or whatever Ryan's title should be—had settled back and seemed relaxed as the boat motored along. Wearing navy shorts, boat shoes of course and a plain white short-sleeved button down shirt, he looked right at home behind the wheel. The breeze toyed with his hair and ruffled it gently. She was almost enticed to stretch over and run her fingers through its thickness. Instead, she folded her hands tightly on her lap, trying to keep her attention on the water views to her left, but inevitably her gaze swung back to her companion.

There were other vessels out and about. Tourist boats, mainly. Catamarans, sailing boats, and others similar to *Shaw Thing*. Some were obviously in a hurry to get wherever they were going, and for others the journey was at a much slower pace. As if they had all day to get somewhere.

It only seemed like fifteen minutes instead of forty-five before Ryan slowed the vessel to enter the marina at Denerau, turning towards a long jetty with vessels docked on both sides and eventually pulling in to a berth alongside a much larger boat. Caroline waited until *Shaw Thing* was tied off before slipping from her seat. Her companion was already heading below deck and she hesitated before following, curious to see what was there. Tucked up in the bow of the boat was a cushioned area that she guessed could be used as a bed. Before that on either side were padded bench seats with a small table in the centre. There was a compact kitchen area and a door she suspected led to a tiny bathroom. Surprisingly, it didn't feel claustrophobic.

Ryan had hold of a bag in either hand and waited for her to finish inspecting his boat.

"Well, what do you think?"

"I don't know the first thing about boats but it looks pretty good to me. I guess I'd need to see it in action with other people on board."

"Are you angling for an invitation for a day out cruising somewhere?"

"Oh, not at all. I just don't know anything about the practicalities of this boat, or any boat. I've nothing to compare it to."

"Fair enough. Are you ready to get going?"

She nodded and followed him back on deck, careful not to hit her head on the way out.

Caroline tried to take in her surroundings and keep up with Ryan at the same time. They walked out of the marina and across the road to a fenced, gravelled car park. Then through a side pedestrian gate and along a row of cars before Ryan stopped at a silver Toyota sedan.

She gave him a quizzical look and he explained, "I keep a car here on Vita Levu for when I need to travel for business. Local transport isn't always convenient or reliable."

Ryan cranked the air conditioning up to cool the car quickly as they headed out of the parking lot. The wedding was to be held in the groom's village to the north of Suva, a three-hour drive away. Caroline wondered out loud how Rosi and her family would get to the wedding.

"They have hired a bus, so they will leave in the early hours tomorrow to make the trip in time for the wedding."

"That doesn't give them much leeway if the bus happens to break down."

"Yes, but they wouldn't be able to afford the cost of a hotel."

Grateful they were travelling a day ahead and staying in a hotel for a couple of nights, Caroline settled back into the passenger's seat.

THIS PART of Fiji was known as the Coral Coast. About halfway to their destination, Ryan pulled into the Warwick resort for a lunch break. The Bula Brasserie faced the ocean and it was easy to see why the buffet was so popular.

They were escorted to a table close to the massive concertina doors. Dark timber fans spun lazily overhead. There was a huge array of choices on the buffet: soups, appetisers, various mains. There was even a live cooking station, which today featured pork shoulder cooked lovo style.

"That's slow cooking in an underground oven," Ryan told her when she asked. "It's the Fijian equivalent of the Maori hangi." He handed her a plate from the stack at the end of the counter and they made their selections.

There was no urgency to be in Suva. Lunch was relaxed. Conversation flowed easily. Ryan was keen to see what dessert Callie would choose. Banana in coconut cream with sago pearl was the one that won out, but he could tell she was tempted to go back for a taste of some of the others on offer.

SIGHING, his travel companion settled back in the car.

"So how are you enjoying the pace of life here in Fiji?"

"Admittedly, it's taken some getting used to. 'Fiji Time' is something else entirely. After the crazy stress of the last eighteen months it's a welcome reprieve, believe me."

"Lloyd didn't tell me much about what happened other than you were the star witness in a high-profile court case."

She was quiet for a minute. "Yes, I was."

"I'm interested to hear your side of the story, but I understand if you don't want to talk about it." Ryan shot her a sideways glance, but she had her head turned, gazing out of the side window. After a few minutes the silence started to wear on him. The casual relaxed conversation they had enjoyed since leaving Tokalau this morning had vanished, tempting him to turn on a local radio station to fill the air with something other than awkward nothing.

Another sigh, this one laced with resignation. "Do you pay much attention to what goes on back in Australia?"

"Not usually. The resort as you know has limited access to the world at large. People come to detox and leave their everyday behind."

"Have you heard of the Sommerfield Corporation?"

Ryan started to shake his head but then he vaguely recalled something he heard in a business meeting. "Wasn't the CEO up on sexual assault charges?" Ryan wasn't sure he liked where this conversation might be headed. Was she about to say she was a victim of Rex Sommer? The instant churning he felt in his gut needed to be tamped down somehow. But, if she had been assaulted...

"That was the court case I was involved with. I was Rex Sommer's PA. I suspected what was going on behind the scenes. But I didn't have more than a shred of evidence and that wasn't enough. So I started to write stuff down. Who was coming and going. Anything I noticed that was a little off...

"When the first woman had the courage to come to me and confess what had happened, I was shocked. Then the next one approached me. I had to go to the police and that started a major criminal investigation... and I was the chief informer.

"It was happening right under my nose and I didn't pick it up. I failed those women, Ryan. It should never have happened on my watch. I feel like I was an accessory to the abhorrent behaviour of my boss."

At the anguish in her voice, he reached over and placed a comforting hand on hers. "I think you are being too hard on yourself. He was obviously clever at covering his tracks, so it's no wonder you didn't have a clue what was going on. As soon as you found out, you went to the authorities, so you did the right thing."

"If I had known earlier, maybe I could have prevented the others being preyed upon."

"But you didn't know."

"I feel like I should've, though. I was his PA! There was never any hint of anything untoward in his boss/employee relationship. Nothing that would have alerted me."

"You were his veneer of respectability, I guess."

"Yeah, that's what the judge said. Didn't stop all the trolls and haters accusing me of enabling his crimes, though."

"You were absolved of any wrongdoing though?"

"I was just..." She smacked her hand down on her thigh in disgust. "Guilty of being blinded by his charm and brilliance."

CAROLINE FELT the crushing weight of guilt ease a little, relieved to talk with someone who wasn't basing his opinion of her on media sound bites.

Talking in the car while Ryan drove was better than having him focus solely on her. If she kept her face averted to the side window, maybe he wouldn't see her fighting back the tears. Of anger. Regret. Frustration. You name it, the tears were there. Fumbling around, she managed to find a couple of crumpled tissues to dab her eyes.

"The hardest part..."—she gulped—"was my so-called 'friends' deserting me. Not only that, but my family has disowned me. My father is firmly in the 'women were making it up just to destroy him' camp and Rex Sommer is innocent."

"The court found otherwise, though."

"Not a whole lot of comfort at times, to be honest... I only hope, down the track, my sisters will understand that I did it for them and other young women who might find themselves in a similar position. But the toll on me and the others has been horrific. We did what we needed to… and the court believed us."

~

RYAN WAS angry that Callie had been judged by the general public and found wanting. It didn't matter what she did, people would always find a way to criticise and condemn her actions. It hurt him to see her so wracked with guilt.

"Hey, thanks for telling me. I know that it can't have been easy to trust me… but I hope it has helped to be able to share your thoughts with a listening ear."

Callie kept her eyes fixed on the view outside the car, obviously not keen to have him see her meltdown. The rest of the trip was quiet.

Ryan tried to process what he'd heard. Maybe he should get onto the internet now he was on the mainland and check out the news reports for himself, to get a better handle on what she was coping with. If it were him in that situation, he was damned sure he wouldn't want to set foot back in Australia for a long, long time. On Tokalau Island she would be able to rest and recalibrate, and he would do all in his power to help her recover from the ordeal.

The car pulled up under the stone portico of a hotel just this side of Suva. The friendly porter opened Callie's door before Ryan had a chance.

"Bula, ma'am. Welcome." He opened the hotel door for her. The valet arrived to take care of their bags.

~

CAROLINE WAS EMOTIONALLY WIPED out from the conversation she'd had with Ryan. Falling back on her bed, she lay with her arm over her face. He'd asked if she was interested in meeting up for dinner. But she felt too raw and vulnerable, so she opted for room service and sitting on her small balcony.

Thoughts swirled around her head and she couldn't help but wonder what Ryan thought of her disclosure. She had chosen not to make eye contact, not wanting to see his reaction in case she saw something she couldn't cope with. His words had been reassuring, but were they genuine? She hoped so.

CHAPTER NINE

Caroline stood in front of the mirror and adjusted the outfit. It was called a chumba, if she remembered correctly. An ankle-length skirt and a hip-length blouse with short sleeves, both in a vibrant purple hibiscus print. Purple, because it was the colour scheme for the wedding and the guests would dress accordingly. It wasn't compulsory by any means, but it seemed like a good idea.

Her hair was bothering her though—she had no idea what would be appropriate. Most of the Fijian women she had seen so far had short hair. It was bound to be rather warm today with no air-conditioning, so leaving her thick hair down was not going to be a good idea. A simple plait seemed too informal for a wedding and something elaborate would feel over the top. In the end, she pulled her hair back into a sleek bun.

Satisfied, she packed her small cross-body bag and crammed a few other bits and pieces into her day pack to leave in Ryan's car.

Propping the room door open, she placed the breakfast tray on the floor outside and added the "please make up my room" sign on the handle before grabbing her things.

The plan was to meet Ryan downstairs at nine-thirty.

"Callie."

Or maybe she would just meet him here.

Did she see a momentary frown as Ryan walked along the corridor towards her? Goodness, she hadn't expected him to go all-in with a black sulu and leather sandals instead of black trousers and matching shoes. And he wore the outfit so well, for a westerner. But she guessed he'd spent most of his life here, so wearing a traditional outfit would be second nature to him. The short-sleeved shirt he had on was made of the same purple patterned material as her outfit.

The two of them seemed to attract attention as they made their way downstairs. Lots of bula greetings. Wide knowing smiles and nods. Was it because of the matching outfits? Did the staff approve of their attire? It seemed like it.

The doorman was quick to reach the door ahead of her.

"Vinaka."

The drive to the little Methodist church where the wedding ceremony or Tevutevu was to be held took less than an hour. Ryan parked on a side road nearby. As they walked to the church grounds, a packed bus pulled up. The locals from Rosi's village spilled out and joined the throng of people streaming across the potholed bitumen driveway into the old, off-white church building. A handful of people waved to Caroline in greeting and Ryan talked to one or two as they joined the wedding guests.

Caroline felt out of place. It was no wonder. She and Ryan were the only two white people. Her companion put a hand at her back to guide her into the church, greeting people on all sides as they walked with an unhurried pace.

"Here." Ryan motioned for her to go ahead of him. She slipped into a pew and he sat on the end next to her.

The church interior was predominantly white with exposed beams. Brown timber pews on either side. Brown panelling across the front behind the altar. White material had been draped across the altar rail and tied with purple ribbon. The pulpit was draped in white. Several mats similar to what she had seen at Rosi's house were piled on top of each other in front of the first pew.

Caroline tried to take it all in, but felt the eyes of everyone in the church on them. Hopefully, once the bride arrived everyone's focus would be elsewhere.

~

RYAN HAD KNOWN they would attract attention; it was par for the course for him at functions like this. But he could tell that Callie was uncomfortable. There wasn't anything he could do to put her at ease, although he had warned Rosi not to treat him and Callie as VIP guests.

Even though it was July, a handful of old ceiling fans spun slowly. Every window was open, but there was little if any breeze in the sanctuary. Many of the woman were using woven hand fans, and more than one male mopped his forehead with a handkerchief.

As the bride made her way barefoot down the aisle wearing a short-sleeved white blouse and a voluminous skirt, Caroline leaned closer to Ryan. "Can you tell me what she's wearing?"

"Melaia's outfit is a tapa, made of mulberry bark. The colours are traditionally black, white and brown and the pattern symbolises where it was made."

"What's the significance of the plaited cord she's holding up as she walks?"

"Not sure if you can see from here, but that's a whale's tooth on the end. A tabua. Fijians use them in important ceremonies."

Caroline hoped to be able to sneak a closer look at the outfit later to inspect the intricate designs. The bridesmaid, if that's what she was called, wore a tapa with different pattern combinations, as did the best man.

"What about the groom?" she whispered.

"That's Tomasi."

"His outfit looks a bit like a mat."

"Pretty much. It's called a ta'ovala."

The teenage ring bearer was also wearing a ta'ovala, but his had a more elaborate collar.

The minister started talking. Caroline didn't understand a word, but she got the general idea. It wasn't that different to a church wedding back home. A choir off to the side sang with the usual Fijian harmonies. Closing her eyes, Caroline let the words wash over her as they gave her a sense of peace. For now, at least, all was right with her world.

A couple of men gave speeches, maybe on the sanctity of marriage or a welcome to the family type of thing. Then Rosi and a group of village women gathered behind the almost-newlyweds and sang. Caroline rubbed at the goosebumps on her arms. Fijian singing was something else, and the sheer beauty of it caused a stream of emotion to bubble up. She hastily pulled out a tissue to wipe away some errant moisture from her eyes. A firm hand closed over hers and gave her comfort.

At the end of the ceremony, Ryan and Caroline lined up with everyone else at the door to congratulate the bride and groom.

People milled about. The reception lunch was to be at the church hall next door and before long a couple of open-backed trucks arrived, loaded with men and large pots of food. It took two adults to heft each of the biggest pots Caroline had ever seen. Another two carried the carcass of an animal trussed up in woven banana leaves. Maybe it had been cooked underground.

Caroline found a spot in the shade where she could people-watch. Selfies were the order of the day.

"Why are there groups of people all wearing clothes with the same patterned material?" she asked Ryan, counting one group of about twenty adults, teens and kids all decked out in variations of the same material.

"Every family member wears the same pattern, so it's easy to see who belongs together."

"Oh." Callie looked down at her outfit and then at him.

HE RAISED an eyebrow as she apparently realised the significance of what he'd just said… and her face flushed. He had been surprised when Rosi had made them matching outfits. Maybe she was trying to get a not-so-subtle message across that the two of them should be a couple.

He would be more than okay if they were a couple. He was grateful to his godfather for arranging for Callie to come and stay on Tokalau. And even though the last couple of years had been horrific for her, he would never have met her otherwise. Now that Callie was in his life, he didn't want to see her go back to Australia. He wondered, not for the first time, if there could be something between them and if she would ever consider moving here. Permanently.

But he was getting way ahead of himself. That had happened with Lucy, and he should know better than to get his hopes up and head down the "what if" track again. *Back off, Shaw!* He reprimanded himself for the thoughts that were gallivanting out of control in his mind.

NOW SHE KNEW the significance of the outfits, Caroline was surprised that Rosi hadn't made Ryan's outfit to match her own family, seeing as he was considered "one of them". Maybe she didn't want Caroline to feel left out. It was logical to make her and Ryan matching outfits seeing as they were the only white people in attendance. They were together, but not really. People would no doubt assume they were.

Oh… now that she thought about it, that was probably why they scored all the knowing looks at the hotel this morning. Maybe… maybe they should be together. Could they be? Sometimes when she caught his gaze, she was sure she could see something more than just casual interest there. The intangible pull of connection she had felt from the get-go had strengthened over the time she had been on Tokalau Island.

As they talked, one person came over to ask for a selfie with them and that started a procession. Before long there was a line-up of people all waiting for the chance to have a photo taken.

"Look, the bridal party have returned." Ryan pointed to the cars pulling up.

The bride stepped out in a white dress with a dark purple floral pattern. Her attendant had the same material, except it was a lighter purple in the same pattern. Tomasi's shirt was the same material as his new wife's and they both wore flower garlands called sasusalu. The happy couple posed for photos with, it seemed, every guest, so it was a while before they made it into the hall.

Surprisingly, the crowded hall wasn't all that far removed from country church halls back in Australia. A canopy of purple material had been strung across the ceiling. Pillars had been covered with purple, and a myriad of purple balloons were strung across the width of the hall. More balloons had been arranged into an arch behind the cake table which held a three-tiered cake similar to what Caroline would see at an Australian wedding, including a western-style bride-and-groom topper. Dark purple fondant flowers trailed down the front. A pile of simply wrapped gifts had been artfully arranged on the floor in front of the cake table.

Long tables were being loaded with all manner of traditional food. At one end sat a row of silver bain-marie containers, serving spoons at the ready. Frangipani fairy lights stretched the length of the table edges. The bridal table was covered in white satin cloths and draped purple netting. Purple satin hung from the curtains behind the bride and groom on either side of an elaborately patterned bark cloth—a masi. Caroline assumed the mats from the church were the ones that now covered the floor in front of the bride and groom. On either side, adjacent to the head table, were a line of tables with older men on one side of the hall and women on the other. A long food line quickly formed and snaked around the edges of the building.

Women and children sat in groups crowded on the floor, chatting and laughing. There were hardly any men to be seen. Were they eating outside? "Um, Ryan are you even supposed to be in here?" Caroline asked him.

"Don't worry, I'm not going to leave you here by yourself. We can be inconspicuous and sit up the back."

After waiting in the line-up to fill their plates with food, they gravitated to the rear of the hall, where Ryan managed to commandeer a couple of well-used wooden chairs. Caroline set her drink cup underneath her seat and balanced the plate on her lap.

Later, there were speeches. The cake was cut and the laughing newlyweds tried to feed each other.

Everyone seemed to be leaving. "So, is that it then?" she asked.

"No, there is another ceremony. The bride will dress in another traditional outfit and be escorted by family members to her husband's house. It used to be that the older women would sit around the outside of the house overnight and check the bed sheets in the morning to see evidence that the bride was a virgin." Ryan grinned as Callie choked on her drink, colour sweeping across her face. He gave her a few pats on the back. "They don't tend to do it these days though."

"Just as well. I can't get my head around that," she finally managed.

CHAPTER TEN

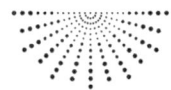

*R*yan wanted to suggest dinner together, but it had been a long day and despite the air conditioning in the car Callie seemed to have wilted in the humidity. She didn't say much on the drive back to the hotel, seeming to need some time to process the sights and sounds of the wedding. They made tentative plans to catch up at breakfast and he left her at the door to her room, wishing her a good night's sleep.

By the time Ryan had showered, he didn't feel like staying in his room. Wandering down to the lobby and out to the pool deck, he stood leaning on the railing overlooking the darkening bay. There were a handful of sail boats anchored a couple of hundred metres across the water near Labiko Island, one of the small land masses that led to this area being called the Bay of Islands. Although it was still early, the pool was empty. Maybe everyone was inside enjoying dinner.

A cooling breeze wafted over him, and Callie was on his mind. When she had told him what she had gone through back home, he had felt like he needed to be some sort of avenging hero, wading into battle with her to help make it right. It wasn't possible, of course. Thankfully, she'd had a good legal team headed by Lloyd. But it saddened him that she was on her own without the support of family and friends. He wished he could've been in the courtroom with her to help shoulder the load.

CAROLINE WAS TOO restless to call it a night. The shower had invigorated her enough that she decided to head outside for a bit. Maybe she could find a sun-lounge in the pool area to enjoy the quiet after the noise and colour of Rosi's daughter's wedding. It was nice that Rosi had taken time to come say hello and thank them for attending. She seemed pleased with how everything had gone. To Caroline, the wedding was familiar and foreign at the same time. But she was glad she had taken the opportunity to go, even if it meant wearing matching clothes with Ryan. Recalling the look on his face when he had first seen her in the outfit made her smile, now she knew what it meant.

Family huh? She had never given much thought to having a family of her own. She had been consumed with her career— and where had that gotten her? The career, and the lifestyle that went with it, went up in spectacular flames not long after she realised she had to blow the whistle on her employer.

Ryan hadn't judged her when she'd told him what had gone down at work and the subsequent court case. The more she saw of Ryan and the more she got to know him, the more she liked. A breath of fresh salt air after the choking staleness of the life she knew back home.

Dropping onto a lounge, she swung her legs up and leaned back, closing her eyes. A few deep breaths later she felt herself starting to relax. It had been a very stimulating day. All the delicious and vibrant colours of the wedding guests' clothes and the Fijian singing resonated somewhere deep within her.

RYAN WALKED BACK along the deck, his attention caught by someone lying on a lounge on the other side of the pool. Was it Callie? Had his thoughts somehow conjured her up?

Skirting the end of the pool he slowed his step. Yes, it was Callie, eyes shut, looking peaceful with her hair flowing over to one side. The inbuilt magnet she possessed pulled him closer as if he didn't have a choice. But he didn't care.

He zeroed in on her face. Could he risk a kiss? Ever since the missed opportunity after dinner the other week, he had been looking for another chance. Maybe if he just... he licked his lips in sweet anticipation and moved as close as he dared. A sneaky attempt might earn him a sock to the jaw if he scared her, so he cleared his throat.

~

CAROLINE OPENED ONE EYE. "Ryan?" Scrambling up, she stood face to face with him.

"Hey," he said, "you still needing to unwind from the day too?"

"Yeah, I'm tired but I wasn't ready for the four walls of my room just yet."

"Wanna walk a bit with me?"

She nodded.

At the end of the pool deck, Ryan held his hand out for her to step down onto the grass.

Barely hesitating, she put her hand into his and sighed inwardly at the rush of sensation that rolled across her body from their joined hands.

"Watch it, there's a drop down," he told her.

When she landed on the grass beside him, she half expected him to let go of her hand. But he didn't, and she happily entwined her fingers with his as he brushed his shoulder against hers. Weaving in and out of the palm trees that edged the property, they wandered past the accommodation block and around the far corner of the building, exchanging quiet remarks about various aspects of the wedding ceremony.

"I had a lovely day," she assured him. "Thanks for letting me tag along."

"To be honest, it was much more enjoyable having you along. And you saved me from becoming the centre of attention for every unmarried woman under the age of fifty."

"What… no… really?" She laughed. "In that case, I'm glad I could be your bodyguard."

He arced around and took her other hand in his. "It was hard though, because there was something I really wanted to do… but that would have taken away from the bride and groom's special day." He stilled in front of her, his eyes seeking hers in the shadowed light.

Caroline fervently hoped that what she saw in his face was an echo of what she'd been wishing for.

"Oh," was all she could manage as he took a step closer. She tried to suck in a discreet lungful of oxygen in case she didn't come up for air for a while.

HE WAS PLANNING on making this moment last as long as possible. The first kiss. Hopefully, the start of something much, much more between them. Letting go of one hand, he gently brushed the back of his fingers across her cheek as her eyes fluttered closed. The pad of his thumb traced the curve of her bottom lip and her mouth parted in invitation, which he accepted.

Skimming a hand around the back of her head, his fingers relished losing themselves in the texture of her silky hair as his lips met hers with care and reverence. The light kisses he bestowed quickly exploded into a need for a deeper connection. Planting his other hand on her back, he pulled her closer, taking her lips with a firm urgency that she returned, her hands leaving a heated trail as they swept up his chest and around his neck. Her fingers worked their magic against his skin and a growl of pleasure flew out from deep within him as he re-positioned himself to touch, taste and smell her satiny skin.

His lips took leave of her mouth and wandered all around her face. Dropping kisses at will on their unhurried way to explore her neck and down to her collarbone. The shiver of delight that rippled across her skin caused him to pause as he took in the effect of his kisses. "Should I stop?" he whispered close to her ear which elicited another shiver. He couldn't help but grin against her cheek at the small shake of her head before he moulded her body closer to his as his hand roamed her back.

ANY SHRED OF rational thought flew out of Caroline's head the instant Ryan's lips met hers. The firm caress of his lips sparked a sense of something new and exciting that she hadn't experienced for a long time. Maybe never. It was raw and elemental and oh so very seductive. Pressed against his athletic frame she returned his kisses with an intensity that shocked but didn't surprise her at the same time. At times she had wondered if she had anything more to give, but Ryan coaxed the embers of emotion into a blaze of warmth and want. Clinging to him as he swept her along, she never wanted him to stop. The moan of frustration that escaped her lips when he took a step back didn't embarrass her in the slightest and she tugged him back for more.

KISSING CALLIE WAS a revelation that he'd unconsciously hoped for but didn't expect... and it stunned him. It was like his life had been in a holding pattern, waiting for her to drift into his orbit, and he was damn sure he would do everything to keep her there. Unbeknown to him there had been a

Callie-shaped void in his life, until he kissed her and felt the space fill with her presence. There were no guarantees, he knew that. But he was desperate to see where this might lead. Hugging her tight against his body, he rubbed his cheek against her hair, getting heady from the lingering scent of her perfume.

"Hey there." He looked into the softness of her eyes. The shy smile she bestowed on him was at odds with the heat and passion she had just shared with him. "I think we had better call it before we get carried away."

A first she shook her head… then nodded, reluctantly.

THERE WAS no answer when Ryan knocked on Callie's door the next morning. They had made plans to eat together, in between a plethora of sweet kisses outside her room before he bade her goodnight. Maybe she was already down at breakfast. Grinning to himself he headed down the stairs and into the large open dining room. Pausing, he scanned the area and saw no sign of her, then remembered there was another dining section around the corner.

Ah, there she was, drinking a tall glass of juice as she gazed out at the water view. Weaving his way around the tables, he never took his eyes off her. Her hair was styled up in a messy bun and she had a relaxed beach vibe going on in a long flowing sundress.

"Good morning, beautiful." She turned at his greeting and he leaned down for a brief cheek kiss before pulling out the seat opposite her.

That smile captivated him. "Good morning yourself."

"Did you sleep well?"

"Hmm, yes, once I got to sleep." She paused, obviously unsure if she should continue. "There was so much from the day swirling around in my head. Not to mention… um…" She trailed off, her face flushing with more than a hint of embarrassment.

Ryan leaned closer to her. "You mean you were reliving my kisses?" he suggested cheekily, even though he had done the same thing.

Their eyes locked and he barely stopped himself from diving right into their blueness. "Something like that," she admitted quietly. The space between them diminished as he pressed his lips gently against hers and tasted the sweetness of fresh-squeezed orange juice. Seconds would have been on the cards if they hadn't been inconveniently interrupted by a staff member, who placed a plate of bacon and eggs in front of Callie. Ryan drew back reluctantly.

"Here you are, ma'am. I hope they are to your liking."

"Vinaka."

"And sir, would you like any eggs?"

"Yes please, I'll have the works, thanks. Bacon, eggs over easy, hash browns, tomato."

"Sausage, sir?"

"Yes, why not. I'm particularly ravenous this morning. And could I have some coffee as well?"

"Yes sir, I will send someone over shortly."

"It was all those calories I burnt off last night." His words were barely audible, but it was enough to make Caroline blush. Again.

That sexy little grin he shot her? Oh, my goodness. It would be safer if she concentrated on her food. Seriously.

A short time later, his plate arrived, and he reached across for the salt, his fingers accidentally-on-purpose brushing against her bare arm, tingling her skin. Her eyes flicked to his and held, her breath catching in her throat. Did he have to look as though he wanted to eat her for breakfast as well? And if he tried, would she let him? Probably. It was too early in the day for the intense look he was sending her. Wasn't it?

Pulling her eyes back to her plate, she studiously avoided the man across from her.

Ryan Shaw was all things good and was pulling her slowly and inextricably into his life. And she was not of a mind to resist.

～

"Vinaka, Mr Shaw. Thank you for visiting with us again. And Ms Hammond. We hope you enjoyed your time and will come back to see us soon."

The porter hurried to open the car door for Callie before loading their luggage into the boot. The staff beamed and waved as they pulled out of the hotel driveway.

Once they were underway, Ryan leaned over and grasped her hand with gentle pressure. Turning her palm over against his, she returned the pressure and watched as he pulled their joined hands to his mouth so he could plant a kiss on the back of her hand. Caroline sighed to herself as he brought their hands down to rest on his thigh, his thumb caressing her skin. That small act of connection thrilled her and she left her hand in place.

Caroline wanted to know what life was like for Ryan and his siblings growing up on Tokalau. He regaled her with many a tale about what they had got up to.

"It certainly sounds like you had an idyllic childhood."

"I loved my family and, yes, we had a great time growing up, but it was still a shock to the system when we were sent back to Australia for high school."

"Boarding school?"

"No, actually. I spent my time with Lloyd Miller and went to Brookfield Grammar with his sons. He's a close friend of my dad."

"Your godfather, right?"

"Yes… so his family got to stay on Tokalau in exchange for hosting me."

"What about your brothers and sisters?"

"The girls stayed together with one of Mum's relatives. And the younger boys lived in a share house with a bunch of other expat kids. Each year, a different mother took a turn to live back in Australia as the house parent.

"That must've been full-on."

"You're not wrong. Lots of testosterone in one small house."

In Denerau, Ryan put his car back into the holding area and they left their gear on board *Shaw Thing* before enjoying lunch in one of the many small restaurants that lined the boardwalk.

Some of the staff seemed to recognise her companion. "Do you come here often?"

"On and off, I guess. I'm usually way too busy… or I should say, I don't make the time. But then it's much more fun when you have someone to share food with."

"I expect you would have no shortage of female guests ready and willing."

"Yes and no. There is always plenty of interest, I'll admit, but also an unwritten rule about fraternising with guests. Which has got me out of more awkward situations than I care to admit."

"Yet here you are with me."

"You are a delightful exception to that rule, I must say."

"I sense there's a 'but' in there somewhere."

"Look, Callie, to be honest, I've not met anyone quite like you and I'd like to spend some more time together but… I can't be seen to be dating one of the guests."

"Oh, I see." Caroline was crestfallen. It looked like this thing that was developing with Ryan was over before it had begun. It was probably for the best though. A holiday romance would have been nice, but Ryan still had to live and work on Tokalau. "So, this is it, then?"

"No, not at all. I'm determined to make something work. We will just have to be discreet about it."

"It's a small island, Ryan. I don't see how that is possible."

"I'll make it work, you'll see."

~

AFTER LUNCH they strolled hand in hand around the shops. Ryan was happy to wait for Callie as she checked out the retail outlets. Taking some of the merchandise bags from her, he indicated a nearby ice cream kiosk. "Would you like some New Zealand ice cream?"

"Kiwi ice cream here?"

"Why not?"

"Seems a little incongruous."

"Actually, there's a lot of New Zealand products in Fiji."

The queue wasn't very long. Ryan chose the classic hokey pokey in a single scoop and Callie opted for a mango sorbet.

Ryan headed for a nearby table, but Callie had other ideas. "What's that noise I can hear?"

"Sounds like dancers."

"Can we go watch?" Over the years Ryan had seen plenty of traditional dancing so it didn't hold the same appeal for him, but to Callie it was new. Tourists had filled white plastic seating on either side of a checkerboard performance plaza. They snagged a spot underneath a tree, dropping the bags at their feet. Ryan pulled Callie back and she relaxed into him. Taking the last bite of his ice cream cone, he wrapped both his arms around her, leaning his chin on her shoulder. Her hands came to rest on his arms, and he closed his eyes to memorise the sensation of her pressed against him and the light scent of her hair product.

CHAPTER ELEVEN

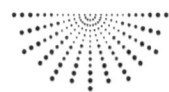

*T*he no fraternising rule was more for his benefit than
for any of the other staff members. It had come into
effect after Lucy.

Back when he had been in his early twenties, that girl, a
regular visitor to the island with her older parents over several
years, had caused him no end of heartache. Ryan had been
smitten with the dark-haired beauty and was soon at her beck
and call. He always seemed to be counting down the days till her
next visit, stealing away to spend as much time with her as possible, neglecting his duties. According to his father, Ryan's
behaviour didn't set a good example for other staff members,
especially if one day he would take over as manager.

But her whispered promises turned out to be empty words.
When it all came to a crashing end at the news of her engage-
ment to her boyfriend back in Australia, the "Lucy Rule" had
been invoked, and it had given him a chance to glue the frag-
mented pieces of his heart back into place.

Once he had stepped into his father's shoes, he put his head
down and continued to keep any female guests at arm's length—
which wasn't always easy, but he didn't want to run the risk of
getting caught up again. He even avoided any romantic entan-

glement among his ex-pat friends. There was too much on the line.

But now with the inevitable benefit of hindsight, he didn't think he had really loved Lucy after all. His ties to Tokalau had been much stronger than his ties to her. He hadn't been ready to throw it away to be with her.

Understandably, he was wary about getting involved with a guest again, but Callie was different. In every way. And he was prepared to throw what little amount of caution he had into the Fijian breeze.

Rosi was always telling him to take time out to smell the frangipani, and now he had a very pretty blue-eyed reason to justify that. And maybe he could combine a little work along the way... like today. The hiking trail on the eastern side of the island needed to be checked, so he decided to make it a day out for the two of them. And by putting a chain across the start of the track with a "closed for maintenance" sign, they wouldn't run the risk of being caught out by other guests.

He'd told the head chef he was extra hungry when he grabbed some food from the kitchen and stowed it into his backpack before setting out for their rendezvous spot. Callie was already waiting on the far side of the garden, leaning up against the old banyan tree that he and his siblings had once used as their secret hideout. The tree house was still there, in need of repair. But the tyre swing was long gone. This place held great memories. He hoped, in time, if he ever had a family here on Tokalau, they would create some more. A vision of Callie in a long, flowing dress holding a youngster by each hand as they wandered towards the tree made a welcome intrusion into his mind.

"Hey, Ryan." Her voice broke into his daydream.

"Morning, Callie. You ready to get going?" He could smell the sunscreen she had used and almost leaned in to give her a kiss, but thought better of it.

"Yes, looking forward to it." She grinned at him. The knee

length shorts she wore were teamed with a natural stonewash t-shirt and running shoes. Her hair, tied into a ponytail, had been threaded through the back of her cap. Very cute. She fell in beside him as he led the way.

"Were those your initials carved in the tree back there, by any chance?"

"Yeah, along with my sisters and brothers. It was our preferred play area, growing up."

They reached the part of the track Ryan had cordoned off late yesterday. He held up the chain for Callie, she ducked underneath, and he twisted under to follow.

The signposted trail was wide enough for them to comfortably walk side by side as it wound around through the vegetation. There was a set of wide, timber-edged dirt steps to negotiate, but they would have to climb even higher to enjoy the view.

"We'll do the whole circuit," Ryan told her. "Across the top here, and then back along the beach track. I'll be checking the signage and the railings and anything else that might need maintenance work. Like this tree, for instance."

An uprooted tree had fallen just off to the left, and its canopy was blocking part of the path. It was too heavy for two people to shift. A crew would have to be sent up with a chainsaw. After taking a couple of photos on his phone, he made some notes. They manoeuvered around the foliage and kept walking, chatting, until they reached a track that led down to the beach.

"I'm just going to duck down here to check if there's anything I need to be aware of. Then we'll keep going. You can tag along if you want or just sit here and take in the view. I won't be long." He indicated the timber seat.

"Nah, I'm good to go." They descended another set of stairs with handrails either side, followed by more winding track.

Less than ten minutes later they were at the bottom, where another set of stairs led to the beach track. One of the handrails was a little loose, so Ryan added it to his job list. Callie walked over to the edge of the track to survey the vista from this angle. Every spot on this island was picture perfect. Ryan pulled her in for a selfie before they climbed back to the top of the ridge.

Further along was a wooden viewing platform. "Oh Ryan, this is spectacular." She waved her arm around the expanse. "Where is the resort from here?"

Standing behind her, Ryan turned Callie slightly to face the direction of the resort. Leaning in, he rested one hand on her shoulder and stretched out his other arm. "Over that way."

"What about your place?"

Ryan turned her further around. "That ridge-line is in the way—but over there."

After inspecting the woodwork, they stepped back onto the trail and followed it to the end. A signpost at the top gave the distance back to the resort in either direction. Down yet another set of stairs, they set up lunch on a shaded picnic table. Callie took her drink over to the water's edge, yanking off her shoes and socks and wading into the water to cool her toes. The flat rock nearby would have been an ideal spot to sit if only the noonday sun hadn't fried the surface. Ryan waded in beside her.

"I still can't believe this is your island and you get to live here."

"Well, technically it belongs to the whole family, but yes, I am blessed to call this island home."

CAROLINE LEANED her elbow on the table and dropped her chin into her hand as they lingered over lunch. Ryan's animated tales of some of the more memorable guests who'd visited the island kept her laughing. The man obviously enjoyed his job. The responsibility of overseeing the family legacy didn't seem to weigh too heavily on him, although Caroline was sure it would have its challenges. She wondered if he ever felt lonely in that beautiful house, all by himself. From talking to Rosi, she didn't think he'd been married, and he'd never given any indication of a girlfriend in his recent past. She wondered if the no-fraternisation rule had come about after a personal experience that went south, but thought it rude to ask. They were still in the initial stages of getting to know each other.

Gathering together the remnants of lunch, Ryan stuffed them into his backpack. Accepting his outstretched hand without hesitation, Caroline was tugged closer as he took a step forward and leaned down for a kiss, tossing his cap aside and knocking hers askew. Her hands landed either side of his waist, grabbing at his t-shirt to keep herself upright under the knee-buckling kisses that were coming her way. One of his hands held her face with infinite care while the other stretched across her side, exploding each and every nerve ending into the stratosphere.

RYAN HAD GIVEN up waiting for just the right moment to kiss Callie. He couldn't wait another second. Her kisses grounded him, yet sent him into orbit at the same time. Kisses like none he had ever experienced before. Every cell of his body reacted to her nearness and yelled for him to pull her even closer and deepen the connection.

The indistinct sound of a jet ski slapping the water registered somewhere in his brain. Then another. The sound intensified and with it came cheering and catcalls. They'd been sprung by a passing jet ski tour out of one of the neighbouring islands. Callie's eyes widened as he broke it off, glancing in the direction of half a dozen watercraft as they sped along just out from the shoreline.

He wasn't sure if her face was flushed from embarrassment or the noonday sun. Or just maybe it was because things were heating up between them. Very quickly. As much as he was reluctant to acknowledge it, the jet ski interruption probably stopped him getting carried away, and he knew Callie hadn't been far behind him. Pulling her in against his side, he waved an arm in acknowledgment to the procession of jet skiers. Callie stepped back, straightened her cap, and shoved her hands in the pockets of her shorts as she started walking along the track. A couple of strides and he'd caught up. Even though she was shaking her head, there was a hint of a smile playing around her mouth.

"I'm not sorry, by the way." Her step faltered at his admission. "Callie." He grabbed her arm and she stilled, mumbling something.

"What was that?"

"I'm not sorry either."

A grin split his face as he pulled her into a hug before letting her go again.

IN THE MORNING, Ryan arrived with her breakfast tray as usual. He only stayed a few minutes before going on with his workday. As much as she was craving the touch of his lips on hers, she knew that she would have to wait for a private moment, settling for some heated eye contact in the meantime. They hoped if he delivered breakfast trays to other bures, it would deflect any suspicion that something was going on between the two of them.

Caroline set her e-reader aside and took a seat, pulling the lid off her food at the same time. The crisp white napkin immediately caught her attention. There was a slip of paper tucked into its folds. Plucking out the note, she unfolded it.

Meet me in the garden behind the hut on the left side of the pond at 4pm. Bring a swimsuit. Ryan

Intriguing. But four o'clock was still so far away. Now she just needed to keep herself occupied until then.

Lots of reading. A chat to Rosi when she arrived to clean the room. A walk along the path that led to the lookout on the western side of the island. A long lunch. Some meditation and contemplation. A nap.

Callie wasn't sure what to wear. She rifled through the bag of returned washing and pulled on a pair of cut-off jeans over a swimsuit and fished out a t-shirt from the cupboard. Dressed, she stood in front of the bathroom mirror trying to decide how she would style her hair. A plait was the final choice. Her bag held a towel and some spare clothes, a light jacket and a water bottle; she had no idea where they were going so choosing the contents of her bag had to be an educated guess. If anyone asked, she was just going to sit and enjoy the garden for a while —she was there regularly so it shouldn't raise suspicion.

Telling herself to relax and walk slowly, she ambled across the garden, a flutter of anticipation building at spending time with Ryan. There was no one about as she took the left-hand path around the perimeter, until she came to the hut in question. The note said behind the hut. There was a small gap in the foliage. She squeezed through.

Ryan sat waiting in the buggy for Callie's arrival. A little early, he knew. But he didn't want her to get there and not see him.

It felt a bit high school-ish, sneaking away from work, but he had started his day earlier and worked through lunch, so he didn't feel guilty clocking off for a couple of hours. His most trusted staff members, Rosi and Sitiveni, knew what he was up to. He had to be accountable to someone for his planned mini leave of absence. Rosi seemed more than a little pleased and smiled knowingly at him.

Finally, he noticed some movement on the other side of the bushes and Callie slipped through the gap toting a bag. Every time he saw her, he felt a tremor of giddy emotion. That sweet smile flipped his stomach in the best possible way. As she got in alongside him, he started the buggy before leaning over for a kiss that she returned as if she was parched and he was quenching her thirst.

"Hey there," she whispered against his mouth as he struggled to find some words, any words, but her kiss had chased them away. "Missed you."

"Mmmm, missed you more."

"So what's this all about?"

He blinked. What was what about? Oh right. His plan. "I thought we could take a run over to one of the other islands to escape for a couple of hours."

"I'm in."

"How would you like to try some stand-up paddleboarding?" He turned to focus on driving them back to his place.

"Sounds great," she enthused.

Once back at his house, he helped her board *Shaw Thing*, and she went below deck until they were well away from Tokalau.

"Hey, we're clear," he called and she popped her head up, smiling at him before coming to sit alongside him.

This afternoon they could pretend to be a couple of tourists.

APART FROM A COUPLE OF DUNKINGS, Caroline soon mastered the basics of stand-up paddleboarding, thanks to Ryan's expert tuition. She suspected he would be good at most water sports he put his hand to, and she quickly felt at ease. No doubt her muscles would protest tomorrow. Maybe she could fit in a massage.

Scooting her board into the shallows, she carefully put one leg into the water to touch down, Ryan alongside her. Flipping the board onto its side, she hefted it up and waded out of the water. The attendant took the board from her and she unclipped her life vest, peeling it off to hang on one of the pegs on the storage rack. Ryan held out a hand for her and they walked to the nearby hut for a cold drink, then headed back to Tokalau.

The pattern was repeated regularly over the next couple of weeks. It was like Ryan wanted to show her all that Fiji had to offer and he was working from some sort of checklist of all the things to do in the Mamanuca and Yasawa islands.

Jetski… tick.

Parasail… tick.

Kayaking… tick.

Swim with manta rays… tick.

Even if they couldn't sneak off the island, they always found a window of opportunity to spend time together. Their favourite spot was tucked away in the garden. An undisturbed spot they claimed as their own. Just swinging lazily together in one of the hammocks.

On some of Ryan's days off they headed to the main island and did touristy things. They zip-lined, went to the mud baths, the Sigatoka sand dunes and even did a glass blowing class at a place called Hot Glass in Korotogo on the Coral Coast. The paperweight she ended up with was going to be a treasured memento of her time here in Fiji. He took her to a Rugby Sevens game between a couple of local teams. They also managed to attend a Sunday church service on the main island, with Caroline giving her wedding outfit another airing. Ryan was dressed similarly to the local men: black trousers with a white shirt rolled up at the sleeves. After listening to the singing at the wedding, Caroline was keen to hear more. Although she didn't understand what the minister was saying, it was still an enjoyable experience, especially as the villagers invited them to join them for the community lunch afterwards.

With every passing day she was falling for Ryan just that little bit more. All the stress and trauma of the last year and a half was melting away. She slept without the need for medication. The feeling of belonging filled her with a sense of peace and contentment. Ryan valued and cherished her—and she hadn't felt like that since her grandfather passed away.

"You seem much happier these days," Rosi observed with a grin after catching him whistling on his way to his office.

"You would be right."

"Miss Caroline has put a spark in your eyes that I've not seen for a long time."

"Mm-hmmm." Ryan grinned as he powered up his computer.

"It's good to see you taking time off and enjoying life. Getting out and about instead of holed up here on Tokalau."

"I've seen the light, Rosi," he joked.

"That's good to hear, and Miss Caroline looks like she is thriving on all of your love and attention."

Ryan paused, looking up at the older woman as she stood in the doorway of his office. Rosi fixed him with a steady gaze. The Fijian knew him better than most.

"She's had a tough time back in Australia for the last couple of years, so yeah, it's a good thing."

"I'm hoping there will be a tevutevu before too much longer."

"Rosi, I appreciate your optimism but I'm not sure that Callie is ready to go down that track yet."

"I see the way you look at each other. It's only a matter of time, and then I will get to look after another generation of delicious white babies."

Ryan shook his head. He would like more than anything to fulfil Rosi's wish for more babies to hold and cuddle.

His and Callie's, if he had his way.

CHAPTER TWELVE

a helipad had been constructed between the resort and Ryan's house after his business partner came on board, and that's where he was now, waiting for his friend to arrive. The tell-tale thwack of rotor blades reverberated as the dark blue Davis Air helicopter touched down. As usual, Jake Davis was at the controls.

Headset removed, Jake spoke to his co-pilot before exiting, grabbing a couple of suitcases from the back, and manhandling them over to where Ryan stood alongside one of the larger buggies. Jake shook hands with him briefly then returned to the helicopter to assist his pregnant wife, Matisse, before unbuckling the harness for his young son and pulling him out into his arms.

Once clear of the rotor, Jake gave the co-pilot the all clear and the helicopter powered up, lifting off the concrete pad before circling the island and heading back to base.

Jake's frequent visits had petered out after Leo arrived on the scene almost three years ago, but they still caught up a couple of times a year when Jake came to check on his investment. Jake hefted one bag after another into the back of the buggy.

"Travelling light and travelling with a toddler don't seem to go together," Jake joked.

"Hey Ryan, good to see you again," Matisse said as she made her way over to the buggy.

"Hi Matisse." He leaned down and kissed her cheek. "You look like you're doing well." And she did. The loose-flowing white embroidered blouse she was wearing complemented the long pale denim shorts. Her hair was pulled back into a simple ponytail and she was as radiant as he had ever seen her.

Ryan wondered if Caroline would look as radiant when it was her turn to be an expectant mother. He was sure she would make a great mother. It was just a gut feeling he had. And he was wishing he could be the father of that child. Shaking the image out of his head, he walked around to the driver's seat.

Matisse climbed into the front of the buggy while Jake and Leo took the back. There was hardly time for small talk before they were pulling up outside Ryan's home. Last time they were on Tokalau, Matisse had been in the early stages of pregnancy and wracked with morning sickness, but now she was thriving.

Jake set Leo down inside the door and the little guy spied the basket of toys Rosi had pulled out of storage. He started hauling out everything to drop onto the floor. Matisse sighed as she eased herself down on one of the large, cushioned sofas.

"Can I get you guys a cold drink?"

"Yeah, that would be great," Jake said as he pulled the suit-cases through to their usual bedroom.

Ryan returned holding a tray with ice-filled glasses of fresh pineapple and coconut juice.

"Thanks, Ry." Matisse sipped gratefully at the drink.

"So how was the trip?"

"Yeah, not too bad all things considered. I was borderline for being allowed to travel, though." She patted her stomach.

"How much longer? Jake did mention it, but that was a while ago."

"Thirty-five weeks."

"Not long now, then."

"I'm so ready for this one to be born. It seems like I've been pregnant forever this time around. Maybe because I have a toddler to chase after."

Jake joined his wife on the couch and the three adults sat and chatted while Leo played among the toys he had scattered around himself.

"So, Ryan, any news to report on the personal relationship front?"

Trust Matisse, he thought. He was hard pressed to know who was keener to see him matched up: Matisse or Rosi. Not even his parents were dropping hints that they were keen for grandchildren from him.

"Well, as a matter of fact…" he trailed off, turning the drink glass in his hands.

"Go on."

"There's someone who I'm seeing at the moment."

"And…?"

"And her name is Caroline and you can meet her tonight because I've invited her to dinner."

"Oh, this sounds promising. What else?"

"How about you wait and find out tonight?"

Leo loved "Uncle Ry" and they spent quite a bit of time together after the little guy woke up from his nap. He took the toddler by the hand and they walked around the garden. Jake and Matisse appreciated him stepping up so they could have some time to themselves. The boy picked up sticks and pebbles and other treasures as they went and gave them to Uncle Ry, whose pockets were filling fast. Leo picked flowers with some help and carried them back proudly to give to his mother.

CAROLINE HAD a pile of discarded clothes on her bed, unable to decide what to wear. Meeting Jake and Matisse was a big deal. Ryan had filled her in a little about their friendship. Chewing on her lip, she crossed her arms as she surveyed her choices, hoping she would be able to make a good impression. In the end, a high-necked, sleeveless, tiered midi dress in beautiful tropical blue tonings won out. She pulled on a pair of strappy low-heeled sandals and hoped she wasn't overdressed—they were staying in tonight. Her hair was left hanging loose.

The salt-kissed and sun-drenched look she had acquired over her time in Fiji was a nice change from the polished sophistication that had been de rigueur in the corporate landscape she used to inhabit. If she never had to return, she would be happy. Not for the first time, she wondered if there was a chance she could find a place here in Fiji. The languorous lifestyle of Fiji Time held enormous appeal. No wonder it was a popular holiday destination.

A few sprays of her favourite perfume and she was ready. Swinging the key ring, she picked up her small cross-body bag, pulled the door shut and sat in a wicker chair to wait for her ride.

RYAN LEFT his guests for the short drive to the resort to pick up Callie. As he pulled up, he saw she was waiting. Before he had a chance to get out, she had bounced down the steps and hurried around to get in next to him.

"Hey there." He glanced around to see if any guests were in the vicinity before leaning over to give Callie a light kiss on the cheek. "You ready for this?"

"I hope so… It's not quite as nerve wracking as it would be meeting your parents, but I'm still nervous."

Ryan turned the buggy back in the direction he had just come.

"Relax, honey, it will be fine, you'll see. They can't help but love you."

Within a few minutes of walking into Ryan's lounge room, Caroline felt right at home.

"I hope you don't mind if I don't get up?" Matisse said, rubbing her stomach.

"No, not at all." Caroline joined the other woman on the lounge. "Pleased to meet you. I'm Caroline, but you can call me Callie."

Ryan looked at her from across the room where he was standing with Jake, seemingly a little surprised that she had asked Matisse to call her Callie. Was he jealous that she was going to allow someone else to call her by the pet name he'd been using? Maybe it was about time she shed some of the formality of her life back home. Callie seemed to fit the lifestyle here better than Caroline.

"How long have you been here, Callie?" Matisse wanted to know.

"Oh, a little while. I'm fortunate to have an extended visit."

"Long service leave?"

"Something like that." Caroline couldn't keep her eyes from straying to Ryan and Jake. They could almost be brothers, or cousins at least. Similar height and build and even their face shape, except Jake had dark hair and eyes and Ryan was the blond haired, blue eyed surfer. And the way Jake was looking at his wife made Caroline want to fan herself. She wondered if anyone would look at her seven-months-plus pregnant with the same desire she saw in Jake's eyes. She was glad she wouldn't be trying to sleep in the room next to them tonight.

It wasn't long before the two women were chatting away like old friends. Ryan was more than pleased that Caroline, or Callie as she had asked to be called, seemed to take to Matisse and vice versa. The laughter and good natured teasing directed his way was more than welcome. The cute dress she was wearing hinted at a more relaxed lifestyle. One that she seemed to be embracing wholeheartedly.

He wondered if she would consider this lifestyle on a permanent basis. She brought him something almost intangible that he hadn't realised he'd been missing. His life had been made so much richer these past few weeks with her. He was dreading the thought of her going back to Australia. The stressed-out, exhausted woman who had first arrived on Tokalau was nowhere to be seen.

~

"How do you like Tokalau?" Matisse asked her.

"It's stunning."

"You know, I've been trying to persuade these two," she gestured to her husband and Ryan, "to make Tokalau a wedding destination and build a waterside chapel."

"Oh goodness. Yes! That's a great idea." Caroline caught the unspoken interplay between Matisse and Jake. The indulgent smile he gave his wife as he raised his glass in her direction.

"Jacob's parents hold weddings on their property in Cape Otway. So it's not an unknown proposition."

"Lots of work though," Jake reminded her.

"What do you think of the idea, Ryan?" Caroline wanted to know.

Ryan took a slow drink, apparently contemplating his answer. "Haven't really crunched the numbers. There's a demand, for sure."

"You could rent out the whole resort to wedding guests," Matisse continued. "Your numbers would be capped at, say, fifty, so that wouldn't be too overwhelming. Maybe build a larger bure for the bridal party to get ready…"

Caroline suspected that this conversation had happened on more than one occasion.

Matisse pulled her phone out, typing into the search bar. "Look, these are some of the other chapels around Fiji."

The women started debating the merits of the various buildings.

~

RYAN LOOKED AT HIS FRIEND. "Looks like they'll be busy for a while. We should go and get the barbecue fired up."

Jake crouched down on the floor where Leo had been stretched out playing with toy cars and got his son's attention. "Hey buddy, Uncle Ry and I are going outside to start cooking the food. You can stay in here with Mummy or come out with us."

Leo waved him away, content with his game. Ryan went into the kitchen and pulled the meat out of the refrigerator where it had been marinating, and directed his friend to grab the utensils and serving plates before they went out to the barbecue.

"Callie seems lovely."

"Yeah, she is."

"You seem quite taken with her."

"Not going to deny it."

Jake was looking at him intently. "You've got it bad, bro."

Ryan raised an eyebrow at his friend. "You think?"

"The question is, of course... what are you planning to do about it?"

"Nothing much. If it's purely a holiday romance for her, she goes back to Australia and I get on with my life."

"Or you could follow her there."

Folding his arms, Ryan shook his head. "Not likely. You know I'm the third generation to live here. I can't see myself living anywhere else."

"Well, she could always move here."

"Look, you know I've been down that track previously. I'm more than a little reluctant to get my hopes up. But I guess you never know. It's probably too early in our relationship for one of us to contemplate moving countries."

"Yeah but at least it would take you less than half a day to get there."

~

"I THINK this one appeals to me the most," Caroline decided. "I like the freshness of the white walls, and the timber shutters don't overpower the room. The woven mat down the aisle is a nice touch and I like the simple elegance of the individual white timber chairs."

"We'd have to come up with something to make it uniquely Tokalau, though."

"Shouldn't be too hard," Caroline said.

"So many beautiful spots in the gardens for photos, and I think we could add to what's already there. Like a giant swing."

"Maybe we're getting ahead of ourselves a little. They haven't agreed yet."

"Oh, I'm sure between the two of us we can convince them it would be a good idea."

Leo wandered over, climbed up between the two women and leaned into his mother's side. Matisse swept her finger through his dark hair as he sized up Caroline. Leo seemed happy to have another adult to wrap around his finger and Caroline was more than happy to oblige, playing "round and round the garden" on his palm. Once she started, other childhood rhymes came back to mind and she kept Leo entertained for at least twenty minutes. The little guy was such a cutie. Caroline had never given much thought to having a family of her own. But now?

"So, Matisse," Caroline said as Leo decided he'd had enough and slid off the seat to go back to his cars. "Ryan mentioned you're an artist. Would you happen to have photos of any of your work you could show me?"

"I can do better than that. There's a couple up in the reception and dining areas, and every bure has a painting as well."

Caroline remembered the impressionist seascape on the wall over the bed of her bure. The colours and textures had drawn her in.

"Hey, Ry," Matisse called out to him through the open door. "Have you found a place for that painting we gave you for your birthday?"

"Still sitting in my office." He came to the door briefly. "I haven't made a decision yet. Maybe you could make a suggestion while you're here." Ryan returned to cooking the meat.

"So does that mean the paintings in the shop are yours as well?"

"Yes, some of them are. Which reminds me, I brought a small stash with me to add to the stock. I can show you later."

THE BUGGY PULLED up next to Caroline's bure.

"Well, what do you think of my friends?"

"They're an amazing couple. I really like them."

"I'm pretty sure they like you too."

"And Leo is adorable to boot."

"We'll see how adorable you think he is when he's throwing a tantrum."

"Oh, come on, he's just at that age. The terrible twos."

"He can test the boundaries, that's for sure. I think he's had at least three melt downs in the short time he's been here."

"I don't blame the kid. I had a few of those myself when I first arrived." She could sort of joke about it now, but she hadn't been in a good head space when she arrived. It was mainly thanks to Ryan and the relaxed lifestyle that she had gradually found a way back to some sort of equilibrium. "Maybe you can work some of your magic on Leo like you did on me." She bumped against his arm.

"Is that what you're calling it?"

Caroline nodded slowly, caught in the moment as he slid across the seat and backed her up against the thin arm rest.

"How about I just use some of that magic now," he whispered, his breath warm against her cheek. One arm reached around her shoulders while his free hand cupped her cheek softly. The pad of his thumb started to smooth the curve of her lips which parted at the gentle pressure. As soon as his lips made contact with hers, she sighed and wrapped her arms around his neck, urging him as close as he could get in the confined space. He groaned, but she wasn't quite sure if it was a reaction to her kiss or if he'd bumped the steering wheel in his eagerness to get closer to her.

Putting one hand on his chest, she pushed him back a little to ease herself into a more comfortable position without breaking the kiss. The whimper she made when he came up for air was silenced by a trail of heat he kissed across to her ear and then deliciously down her neck. He reclaimed her lips, and his arms pulled her flush up against the strength of his chest.

Clutching at his shoulders, she returned his passion, nipping at his bottom lip and drawing it into her mouth. The night melted around them as they lost themselves in the embrace. The gentle island breeze helped keep her rapidly-rising body temperature in check.

Ryan eased away from her and moved reluctantly back to his side of the buggy. She felt the loss of contact keenly, but she knew it was the right thing to move out of the danger zone.

"Um, I think I had better say goodnight." It seemed like he couldn't help himself and he leaned over for another lingering kiss. "I'll just stay here," he rasped. "Otherwise I won't be able to stop at your door."

Caroline nodded wordlessly as she found her bag on the floor of the buggy and fumbled for the key. Pausing at the door, she turned and gave him a little wave then went inside, waiting to close the door until he started the buggy and drove away.

CHAPTER THIRTEEN

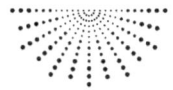

$\mathcal{M}$atisse was still up when Ryan returned from taking Callie to her bure. The slow pace he'd taken on the way back had given him time to try and get his head together.

"Bubs is very active tonight. I thought I'd wait and see if things quieten down a bit." She gestured to the seat nearby and he dropped into it, expecting to hear her verdict on his date.

"So that was Caroline."

"Yep."

"Not your average holiday-maker, I gather."

"No, I don't suppose so." He wasn't sure where this conversation was headed.

"Why didn't you warn us it was Caroline Hammond?"

"What do you mean?"

"Mate, everyone back in Australia knows who Caroline Hammond and the Sommerfield Seven are," Jake told him as he walked into the room and came over to sit next to his wife.

"I didn't think it mattered, to be honest."

"How did she end up here in the first place?"

"It was Lloyd's doing."

"Your godfather, right?"

Ryan nodded. "He's her lawyer. It's not the first time he's sent clients here to lie low."

"The paps have been looking everywhere for her."

"Yeah, I heard. I'm hoping she will be safe enough here for the time being. I trust my staff implicitly."

"I honestly don't like your chances, Ryan." Jake leaned forward to emphasise his point. "Fiji is a popular holiday destination for Aussies. All it will take is for someone to spot her out and about in Denerau or wherever, and the paparazzi will be swarming the place."

"We've been lying low. Away from the usual tourist hot spots." Well, mostly, he thought.

"She seems to be doing okay though, considering everything she went through," Matisse commented. "It was pretty nasty at times."

"Yeah, she was a mess when she first arrived, that's for sure."

"Looks like you've been just the tonic she needed, mate."

"I hope I'm more than just a tonic, Jake."

Matisse looked at him knowingly. "I'm pretty sure you are much, much more than that."

Ryan wasn't sure if she expected him to respond. Was he more than just a tonic? He hoped so. Sometimes when Callie looked at him, it was like there was this almost overwhelming sense of... he wasn't sure what. Something intangible. A connection that made him want to settle down and make a life with her at the centre.

RYAN HELD Callie's hand as she stepped onto the boat. The outfit she was wearing was causing his brain to short circuit. A flirty little red ruffled skirt that showed off her long legs to perfection. It wasn't as if he hadn't seen her legs before; she wore shorts most of the time. But somehow this particular outfit set his pulse racing and she seemed to have no idea of the effect she was having on him. Just as well he would be at the helm and she would be sitting behind him. Far enough away so as not to distract him.

He tossed a tiny life jacket to Jake, who had to convince the toddler to wear it. Eventually, Jake won him over, and he adjusted the straps and set his son down, putting a red bucket hat on the toddler's head. Leo still had to acquire his sea legs, and staggered about like a little drunk. Matisse stowed their gear and pulled on a wide-brimmed hat as she settled herself on the starboard side of the bench seat that ran across the back.

As soon as everyone was ready, Ryan untied the mooring rope and jumped across the gap onto the deck, dodging Leo, as he made his way into position and turned over the engine. They weren't venturing too far away today. It was the perfect spot. One of any number he could take them to visit.

Puttering along at a leisurely pace, a sense of calm and peace washed over him. Trying to be philosophical, he reasoned that if he and Callie were meant to be an item, then it would happen. And if not? Well, he would just have to deal with it. Zoning out a little, he jumped a mile when she put a hand on his shoulder.

"Sorry, I didn't realise you hadn't heard me."

"Um, yeah, I was away in my head somewhere."

"Matisse spotted dolphins off to the right at about two o'clock."

Ryan slowed the boat and followed Callie's outstretched arm.

Sure enough, there looked to be a pod of about eight or nine of the marine mammals frolicking off to starboard. He angled the boat to make it easier to follow their progress through the smoothness of the blue water.

"Can you swim with the dolphins?" Callie said.

"Yes, quite a number of resorts promote ocean-going tours as an activity. There are a couple of areas where the dolphin pods are non-migratory so you are pretty much guaranteed they will be there to snorkel with."

Her arm brushed his and the faint smell of her perfume,

intermingled with sunscreen, floated his way. He had to catch himself before he leaned in for a deeper breath. They watched the animals for a good ten minutes.

Jake had been pointing out the dolphins to Leo, but whether the little guy understood was debatable. His friend joined him at the wheel.

"Do you mind if we have a turn to steer. He's getting a bit restless and the distraction might be good."

"Sure." Ryan swapped places with Jake, who sat with Leo on his lap. Ryan stood to the side so they could talk.

Callie popped up with Matisse's phone to take some photos for her friend, but she was having trouble getting the toddler to look in her direction.

Crossing behind her, Ryan called Leo's name and made enough of a distraction to attract his attention.

CAROLINE WAS hyper-aware of Ryan as he stood behind her, cap spun backwards. The sound effects he was making had the desired effect and Leo looked their way long enough for her to grab a handful of decent shots. "Thanks."

"You're welcome." His hand rested briefly on the small of her back as he stepped around her. Even though his hand was barely there, it still tantalised her. It was all she could do not to follow him and beg to be taken into his arms.

Inhale slowly, girl, she told herself. *Back away from the man.*

Turning around, she walked to Matisse and handed over the phone. Matisse tucked it safely back into her bag as Caroline sat down beside her. Giving herself something to do, she made a pretence of pulling off her cap and adjusting the band at the back before re-threading her ponytail through the space.

"Ryan is looking particularly hot today, my friend," Matisse said.

It was true that the organic cotton t-shirt he was wearing

stretched just nicely across his chest. And Caroline had a new appreciation for males wearing hibiscus-print board shorts. Okay, just this one. But there was no way she was going to admit that, so she just shrugged and grabbed a bottle of Fiji Water from the nearby esky and twisted off the lid.

"You two would make the cutest couple, and just think of the beautiful blue eyed babies you would make."

Caroline started coughing as a mouthful of water went down the wrong way.

Matisse slapped her on the back. "What? I'm just stating the obvious."

"You must've had too much sun already this morning."

"Really? Sun or no, I can see the way he looks at you. He can't take his eyes off you, and you're no better when you think no one is watching."

"Just don't even go there, please." Caroline wasn't prepared to examine her growing feelings for Ryan too closely. There wasn't much point in getting involved. Her life was back in Australia and he was firmly ensconced here in Fiji.

Thankfully, Jake and little Leo came over at just the right time and the conversation moved on. Leo was handed off to his mother so Jake could help position the boat just offshore from a small palm-fringed island as Ryan killed the engine. The anchor went into the water. Ryan climbed over the side into knee-deep water and reached up to take the chairs as Jake handed them down.

"You ladies can hang tight for a minute until we get set up," Ryan told them.

Matisse set Leo onto the deck while Caroline gathered up some more gear to hand to Jake after he shucked off his shoes and got into the water.

The two men waded ashore. The crescent shaped beach on the tip of the island was deserted except for a thatched roof shelter which stood sentinel above the high tide mark.

Quickly setting up the chairs and depositing assorted paraphernalia onto the pale white sand, they returned to the boat. Ryan climbed aboard and Caroline grabbed one of the esky handles with him on the other side, grunting as they hauled the cooler to the low section near the motor. Jake by that time had joined him and they grabbed an end each and swung it down to carry it across to the sand.

Next trip, Jake took Leo in one arm and Matisse followed with some difficulty as she lowered herself off the back of *Shaw Thing.*

Caroline grabbed towels and whatever else she could, to pass on to Ryan as he waited. After a quick scan around the deck, she strung her beach bag over her shoulder and eased herself into the water, tucking up her skirt as Ryan waited for her to catch up.

"I guess you know all the best spots to hang out," she commented as they waded ashore.

"Comes with the territory."

"Does anyone live here?"

"No. There's three hundred islands that make up Fiji but only about a hundred are inhabited."

"Wow, I didn't realise there were so many. How come there's a beach hut, though?"

"For day-trippers like ourselves. Quite a few of the uninhabited islands have them."

By the time they reached the beach, Matisse was already sitting back under the shade. Leo had been released from his life jacket and had plopped down, skimming his hand through the sand at his mother's feet. Jake sat one side of his wife and Caroline took the other chair. Ryan moved his seat alongside Caroline and positioned it at an angle so they could talk more easily.

The conversation picked up from where they had left it last night. Caroline felt like she had known Ryan's friends for years instead of only a few hours.

"So how did you two meet?" Caroline wanted to know.

Jake and Matisse exchanged smiles as if to see who wanted to tell the story.

"Well, as you know I'm an artist and I was still coming to terms with a scooter accident I'd had a couple of years earlier in Bali. You see, my fiancé died in the accident, and I was still trying to process the loss even though physically I had recovered."

"That must have been a dark time for you."

"Yes, you can see it in the paintings I did in the aftermath… anyway, I was looking to get away from my support networks in Sydney for a bit and found an old logging cabin for rent in Cape Otway which was on Jake's property."

"But there had been a mix-up at the real estate," Jake interrupted, "and it wasn't ready to be leased, so I was surprised to turn up to find someone living there. I thought a backpacker had broken in again."

Caroline was soon invested in the story and leaned forward, arms on knees, taking it all in, listening as they described their love journey.

Even though it obviously ended in marriage, while she was listening to their story Caroline found herself willing Matisse and Jake to realise they were meant for each other.

"And, well, here we are," Matisse finished, rubbing her baby bump.

Ryan heard a small sniff and could tell Callie was struggling to keep it together. If he'd had a handkerchief stuffed into the pocket of his board shorts, he would've offered it to her. Even though he had heard it all before, the whole incident at Johnson Creek still made the hairs on the back of his neck stand to attention.

"Now that's been told, I think it's time for a swim," he said, by way of a distraction.

"Um, yeah. Sounds good." Callie got to her feet.

Taking off his sunglasses, Ryan dropped them onto his chair and peeled off his shirt, tossing it on top.

Callie kept her head down as she stepped out of her skirt and untied the crop top, folding it before setting it down on her chair and adding her sunglasses to the pile. The navy and floral halter-neck top she was wearing with high-waisted bikini pants couldn't help but draw his attention. He was sure he hadn't seen it before, guessing she had bought it sometime when they were in Denerau. He liked that she didn't feel the need to wear the bare minimum. There was merit in leaving something to his imagination... and his imagination was having a field day. She headed down to the water's edge, twisting her hair up into a bun as she walked.

To his left, Jake was pulling Matisse to her feet, helping her slip off the dress she was wearing over a black tankini. Scooping up Leo, he grabbed his wife's hand as they strolled down to join Callie.

Standing in the shade, Ryan took a few deep breaths of sea air. Observing. He could do this. Casual friends. Nothing serious. He wanted it to be serious though. Couldn't deny it.

The others had waded into the water and Callie had already shallow dived under and wet her hair. Hoping he appeared more nonchalant than he felt, Ryan sauntered over to join them.

Caroline could feel Ryan watching her as she made her way down to the water. If anyone would've accused her of adding a bit of extra sway to her hips as she walked, she would have vehemently denied any such knowledge. It was hard enough to keep her hands to herself when he was wearing that cream coloured t-shirt. But now he'd stripped it off, she had to move well out of his way before she succumbed to the over-whelming desire to run her hands over his muscled chest. Not that she hadn't seen his naked torso before, but today it, or rather he, seemed more magnetic.

Maybe it was a hormone thing. Being emotional, after listening to Jake and Matisse tell their story. That had to be it. Maybe the cool water would douse her ardour. Nope. Ducking under the water again, she surfaced with a determined stroke and swam away from the others, parallel to the shore. After about fifty metres she rolled onto her back and floated, her hands moving gently beside her, closing her eyes against the glare of the mid-morning sun.

As soon as her eyes closed, her thoughts ramped up another level. Images of Ryan crowded into her mind's eye, teasing her. The way he looked at her that set her pulse racing and her temperature climbing into the danger zone. The way he held her firmly, yet with an infinite tenderness. The way his lips sought hers, causing delicious sensations to course through her body. The strength of his body pressed against hers. The feel of his hair as she pushed her fingers into its thickness. Inhaling the unmistakable tang of Fiji from his body. A seductive combination of sun, sand, sea and a hint of citrus that spoke of lazy afternoons swinging in a hammock strung between two palm trees, tall glasses of fresh pineapple juice, and not a care in the world.

He was a soothing balm after her soul-destroying battle with the Sommerfield Corporation, and she would always be grateful to her lawyer for arranging for her to come to Fiji. Lloyd Miller had known what she needed. Little by little she had felt herself come back to life, like a patch of parched, cracked ground after receiving steady soaking rain.

Did Lloyd have an inkling of the likely effect his godson would have on her? Maybe even subconsciously he was trying to do a little matchmaking. Caroline found it hard to believe Lloyd wouldn't have known that her head would be turned by Ryan. A ploy to help her push the stress of the last year and a half out of her system?

Living on Fiji Time held more and more appeal by the day.

Especially if that time included Tokalau Island and Alistair Ryan Shaw.

Not for the first time, she debated if she should join the ranks of other ex-pats and live here permanently. So enticing. After all, what did she have waiting for her back in Australia? No job. A cramped apartment. Deserted by friends and abandoned by family. The ire of some of the general public, who refused to believe, despite evidence to the contrary and the jury's decision, that Rex Sommers could ever be guilty of the crimes of which he was convicted. It would take more courage than she currently possessed to go back to the glare of public life.

Oh, but Ryan didn't need her drama. She should stay away from him. Maybe she could find a bolt-hole on another island somewhere. There would surely be opportunities to work at any number of the resorts dotted around the nation of Fiji. And she should write that book about her experiences. The truth needed to be told.

~

"Aren't you going to swim after her?" Jake asked Ryan, nodding in Callie's direction.

"She looks like she needs some space to think."

"Yeah, I'm sure you've given her plenty to think about," his friend teased.

"Probably," Ryan conceded as he deliberately turned his back on where she was swimming and headed in the opposite direction.

As he concentrated on every stroke of his arms and every kick of his legs, he hoped it would allow him to temporarily banish thoughts of the blonde-haired beauty who had captured his attention from the word go. As far as he was concerned, she was gorgeous inside and out, and he relished having her in his arms any chance he got. The way she pressed into him, and the soft little mewl she made just as he took any kiss deeper, and her eager response. The way she threaded her fingers through his hair and urged him closer, as if that were possible.

Stopping to tread water and catch his breath, Ryan noticed splashing behind him and realised Jake was catching up to him. He looked back further. As far as he could tell, Callie was still swimming, and Matisse was watching Leo sitting at the edge of the water. Once Jake reached him, Ryan set off again, and before long the two of them were in sync, matching stroke for stroke. Although Jake pushed him, Ryan knew he was the better swimmer and would outlast his business partner. As if in tacit agreement they both stopped at the same time and paused, before swimming back at a more leisurely pace.

By the time they swam back, the two women were already out of the water and dressed. Callie was setting out food on the folding table while Matisse rocked back and forth with Leo on her hip. Ryan trudged out of the water with Jake and followed him up to the shade hut. Grabbing a borrowed resort towel each, they dried off. After slipping his shirt back on, Jake reached for his son and leaned in to kiss Matisse soundly on the lips. Ryan and Callie looked away awkwardly.

"He's about ready to crash," Matisse informed her husband after she came up for air. She fussed around and made up a plate of food for the toddler before fixing another for Jake, who sat down with Leo on his lap and the plate of food which Leo took to with gusto. The sea air obviously made him extra hungry as well.

Callie handed Ryan a plate and seemed to freeze when his fingers brushed against hers. Her eyes locked with his and he wanted to dive right into their blueness. Her mouth was moving but he couldn't hear what she was saying over the drumbeat of his heart.

"Um." He struggled uncharacteristically to find words. Any words at all.

"Help yourself," she repeated.

What? he thought. *To your lips? Your arms?* He sounded like an old Tom Jones song his grandmother used to play.

Callie was gesturing to the opened containers of food. She pushed a serving spoon in his direction and retreated with her plate to a chair.

"Drinks, anyone?" He found his voice finally, and gave them their choice of cold beverage before settling in the remaining seat.

Jake pushed the remnants of food away and pulled Leo against his chest, patting the little guy on the back. The toddler's eyes drooped and finally closed, and Jake kissed his dark hair. He looked over at his wife before turning to Ryan.

"Matisse and I would like to have a night out, child-free. Is there someone we could get to mind Leo for a few hours?"

"I wouldn't mind," Callie volunteered.

"Actually, we'd like the two of you to come with us. Double date."

Ryan glanced over at Callie. She seemed unsure. "Sounds good to me. Callie?"

"Yeah, I guess that would be nice."

"I'm sure Rosi would be more than happy to look after Leo. She has plenty of experience. Did you have somewhere in mind to eat?"

"Somewhere discreet with maybe a bit of dancing? If such a place exists." Jake winked at Ryan.

Ryan knew exactly where Jake wanted to go. "I can make a booking."

"Great, what about tomorrow night? I had better do some work while I'm here, so maybe that can be a reward for the ladies for allowing us to forsake them for the day."

CHAPTER FOURTEEN

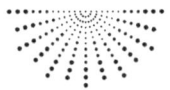

*E*ven though Ryan had visitors, he still made the time for his daily ritual of bringing over her breakfast tray.

It was something Caroline looked forward to every morning. Today, instead of his usual chatter for a couple minutes before he went on with his day, he sat down and stretched out, waiting for her to finish so he could run her back to his house to spend time with Matisse.

"No hurry," he told her. "There was no sign of Jake about when I left."

Caroline tried not to get distracted by him sitting near her while she ate. Practically impossible, especially as his scent of just-showered freshness assailed her senses. Bother, her hands were shaking, just a little. She hoped he hadn't noticed that she had to tighten her grip on the glass of juice. He leaned forward. She stilled, waiting to see what he would do. Was it wrong to anticipate a kiss? She felt lightheaded. Taking the paper serviette in hand he reached up and touched her cheek.

"Jam," he told her simply. That intimate gesture and the smell of mint as his breath touched her face sucked all the air out of her lungs.

At the same moment he apparently realised exactly what he was doing. His ice-blue eyes widened slightly, his breath hitched and he all but reared back and tossed the serviette down. Folding his arms across his chest he leaned back in the seat and turned his gaze to a staff member who was walking about twenty metres away.

Suddenly excusing himself, he almost bumped the table in his haste to jump up and get away.

"Sorry," he mumbled, "I just need to speak to Kafoa for a moment."

Confused, she sucked in a few lungfuls of air, hoping her racing pulse would slow, then swallowed several gulps of juice while she watched him interact with Kafoa.

OKAY, it was an excuse just to get away from her before he gave in to the temptation to pull her into his arms and kiss her. In public. Sweet kisses off the island were one thing, but right here in the daylight? Any of the staff wandering by would be able to see him, breaking the "no fraternising with the guests" rule with gusto. That would not be setting a good example. He'd learned his lesson the hard way years ago.

Shoving his hands into the pockets of his navy work shorts, he called out to Kafoa, trying to come up with a reason to engage the man in conversation. How was work going? Were there any issues he'd noticed on his rounds? How was his family? It wasn't unusual for Ryan to chat with the employees as he went about his day, so Kafoa wasn't perturbed by the sudden appearance of the boss, and if he noticed where Mister Ryan had been sitting, he was too polite to make any comment.

After a few minutes, the conversation ended and the worker went on his way. When Ryan looked back, Callie was no longer sitting at the small table. Hesitating, he waited next to the buggy. Should he go and check on her? Had she changed her mind? Several minutes passed, and just as he was about to knock on her door she appeared with a large bag slung over her shoulder, pausing when she noticed him standing there. Was it his imagination or did she take a breath to fortify herself before she joined him?

"Can I take your bag?" he offered.

"Nope, I'm good." She slid into the buggy seat and he hurried around to the driver's seat.

Jake and Matisse were out on the veranda when he pulled up, and he breathed an internal sigh of relief. Callie jumped out and ran lightly up the steps, dumping her bag to take Leo from his father. She swung the toddler around and pulled him against her for a cuddle. Matisse and Jake embraced in farewell.

"You ready?" Ryan asked as his friend took the seat vacated by Callie.

"Yep, let's get into it. The sooner we're done, the better."

THE TWO WOMEN spent a lovely day together, just hanging out and chilling. Talking. Lots of talking. Room service arrived with lunch, so they never had to leave the house. Bliss.

Matisse pulled out the cache of artwork she had brought with her and Caroline marvelled over the other woman's Impressionistic style. The scenes were easily recognisable from around the island. Views of bures in the crisp early morning light, the beach at sunset. Frangipani and bougainvillea. Every shade imaginable of hibiscus. A group of traditionally dressed Fijians on the dock welcoming arrivals. Someone asleep in a hammock who may or may not have been Ryan. It was hard to tell and she didn't want to ask.

"Wow, these are something else."

"Thanks, I'm glad you like them. You can take one for yourself if you'd like."

"Really?" The generous offer was unexpected and Caroline studied each one carefully before choosing a scene of a bure, not unlike the one she was staying in, with a couple sitting at the table out front.

"Good choice, that's one of my favourites."

"Thanks so much."

Matisse just waved her away as if it were no big deal.

~

"MATE, WHERE ARE YOU?"

"I'm right here," Ryan replied.

"Yeah, no. Something, or should I say someone, has got you practically tied up in knots."

Ryan shook his head.

Jake's raised eyebrow told him he knew different.

"Face it, Ry. She's it for you."

"I don't know, man. Sometimes I look at her and go, yeah, this is it and other times..."

"Ryan, Callie is not Lucy."

He knew that. But Lucy was always lurking in the background. He had thought Lucy wanted what he had to offer.

He had thought she was the one. But she was just toying with him. There was no intention on her part to move to Fiji to be with him. Lucy needed bright city lights, shopping and night life and, well... he didn't. The quieter, laid-back lifestyle suited him just fine.

After she broke his heart, he had thrown himself into his work here on Tokalau. And, honestly, he understood it would be a big ask for any woman used to life in Australia to give it up to move to Fiji. Despite its stunning natural beauty, there was poverty outside of the main tourist areas. It wasn't a first world country. Fiji was all well and good for a week or two, maybe every year, at any one of a number of well-heeled resorts, his included. But to live here permanently with little access to the same amenities that were on offer back home? Not so much.

THE TWO WOMEN took their time deciding what Matisse would wear out for dinner. In the end they chose a delicate autumn-toned floral boho dress with short sleeves. Caroline had only brought one dress to the house with her and she slipped it on, settling the skirt around her.

"Oh girl, Ryan is going to be in so much trouble when he sees you in that."

Heat swept up Caroline's face at Matisse's suggestion.

"Here, let me get the tie at the back for you."

Gathering her hair up in one hand, Caroline stood in front of the mirror. "Up or down?"

"Oh down, no question about it. Those waves are divine."

"Courtesy of the salt air and humidity."

"Better than a salon."

"And cheaper." Matisse dropped her hair and walked over to the corner to slip her feet into wedge sandals.

Rosi came back to the house with Ryan and Jake, and busied herself getting to know her charge while the adults finished getting ready. Caroline knew the Fijian mother had been a part of Ryan's family since he was young and had often looked after him and his siblings. Leo would be in capable hands tonight.

WHILE RYAN and Jake stood waiting in the living room for their dates, Rosi was on the floor playing with Leo. Despite closing in on sixty years of age, Rosi was used to sitting on the ground and had no problem getting down with the toddler. Matisse came into the room, fussing with last minute instructions, and had to be reassured by her husband.

A movement out the corner of his eye caught Ryan's attention. Callie. Tonight she was wearing a long, soft aqua and white dress that took his breath away. The side split wasn't too revealing but the glimpse of her long legs sent his pulse into the stratosphere. Then the v-neckline at the front caught his attention and he could barely stop his eyes from traveling down, forcing himself to stop at the gold disk of her necklace before his eyes slipped down further. Then she turned around. The dress was almost backless. He sucked in a deep breath. His hand itched to make contact, knowing he could set them both on fire.

"Okay, I think we're ready," Jake broke into his reverie. "Let's go."

Rosi distracted Leo so the adults could slip away unnoticed. The solar lights either side of the path were starting to glow as they made their way down to the dock where *Shaw Thing* was waiting. Ryan helped both women into the boat, taking care not to linger holding Callie's hand. Not that he could help rubbing his thumb across her skin. The softness of her touch felt so right against his palm.

Jake untied the mooring rope and pushed off, stepping across the gap to the boat, landing like a big cat on the deck. He wandered to where Ryan was standing at the helm as they rounded the island and started for Denerau.

The orange orb of the sun was heading to the horizon, painting the sky with a spectacular palette. Fijian sunsets never got old. Everyone on board seemed to be taking it in with the reverence it deserved.

It was a beautiful evening to be out on the water and Ryan was almost sorry when they arrived at the marina. Rope in hand, Jake stood in position until he could tie off, then held a hand out for Matisse and Callie to exit. The foursome paused to be entertained by a group of bare-chested Fijian men spinning double-ended fire sticks in the middle of the shopping precinct. His companions were mesmerised by the glow of the fast-moving light trails. After several minutes they were happy to move along.

"I hope you don't mind the walk," he told them, more for the girls' benefit than anything. "It's less than ten minutes from here."

∼

CAROLINE AND MATISSE walked in the centre with Jake and Ryan automatically on either side—not that Caroline thought it was a necessary safety measure. They left the buzz of noise and people around the restaurant precinct and headed away from the marina, chatting as they walked.

The conversation was broken by the sound of singing, competing with the low rumble of a vehicle. Caroline looked back as the noise grew louder. It was a...? Well, she wasn't quite sure what it was. A bure on wheels? A guy with a ukulele was singing his heart out to the handful of people sitting on bench seats facing outwards. Several of them waved and shouted "Bula!" as it rumbled past slowly. Apparently, the blue-painted bula bus was a shuttle that did a loop from the marina to all of the resorts.

A little further along, Ryan shepherded them to the security point at a gated community. A uniformed guard carrying a clipboard stepped out to meet them. Ryan gave his name and the guard scanned the list before checking it off and gesturing them to go on through.

Caroline felt the warmth from Ryan's hand as he placed it on the small of her back, his thumb coming in contact with her bare skin. The gentle caress sent a wave of tingles radiating out to every cell of her body as he steered her down a pathway that led to a low building bearing an illuminated sign that read "Pats". At the doorway, he gave his name again and the four of them were escorted to a table by a large window that by day would no doubt behold a spectacular water view. For now, the inside lights glowed, reflecting on the glass. Ryan pulled a seat out for Caroline, while Jake did the same for his wife.

As soon as they were settled, a waitress arrived and handed out menus, returning a short time later with several bottles of water, which she left in the middle of the table.

"So, what's this place?" Caroline asked, glancing around the room at white cane chairs set around light timber tables. Most of the tables were in use.

"Pats is actually short for Expats. Membership-only club for Expats," Ryan told her.

"It's really good here," Matisse assured her. "Ryan usually brings us here when we visit. A lot of business gets done over meals. And it's one of those 'what happens at Pats, stays at Pats' type of places."

Most eating places in Fiji seemed to feature produce from New Zealand and Pats was no exception, with lamb and beef on the menu. There were also some Indian choices as well as pizza and pasta alongside the local cuisine.

When the waitress came back to take their orders, Caroline asked for the Fijian-style fish cooked in coconut cream. Ryan ordered lamb while Jake went for curry of the day. Matisse hummed and hah'ed before settling on chicken confit, then launched into a passionate spiel to try and convince her husband and his business partner to make Tokalau Island a wedding destination. The conversation went back and forth as they all debated the pros and cons, but in the end the only concession made was that they'd look into it further.

The four of them got on together so well. Even though Caroline was a newcomer to the friendship group she felt welcome, and enjoyed learning more about her dinner companions.

A singer with a guitar arrived on the corner stage and began to set up. Lights dimmed over the small dance floor and, a few minutes later, he started his first set for the night. After they had polished off their desserts, Jake held his hand out to Matisse, and she let him pull her to her feet and lead her out to the dance floor. Caroline watched as Jake swung his wife gently against him. The tenderness between the pair of them was evident even from where Caroline was sitting. It was heartwarming, and to be honest Caroline felt more than a tug of envy at their relationship.

"How about a dance?" Ryan whispered near her ear. The hint of chocolate on his breath enticed her to turn towards him. His eyes compelled her, and she nodded wordlessly as he reached for her hand. The tan chinos and navy, short-sleeved button down shirt he wore sat just right on his athletic frame. She'd had a hard time all night keeping her eyes off him.

Without hesitation she moved into his arms as he tugged her gently. They quickly found their rhythm and she enjoyed being held close. The warmth of his hand splayed across her back sent her heartbeat into double time. Just as well his grip was sure, otherwise she would have melted when he looked down into her eyes. The room temperature seemed to spike all of a sudden, but she couldn't care less. Ryan planted a soft kiss near her ear and another on her cheek and pulled her closer still. One song led to another dance and then more.

RYAN WAS ON A HIGH. Good food. Good company. And Callie in his arms, fitting just as though she was designed to be there. Breathing in the scent of her and feeling the warmth of her body as she pressed against him was playing havoc with his self-control. Callie's long fingers seemed to have a mind of their own as they made contact with the back of his neck, and it was making him crazy. Two could play at that game. He delighted in her reaction when his thumb started to caress the bare skin of her back. The delicious shiver it elicited in her made him chuckle.

"I forgot to tell you how gorgeous you look tonight," he told her. "That dress should be illegal."

"It's not overly revealing, is it?" She seemed aghast that he might think her dress was not appropriate for Fiji.

"That's not what I meant," he murmured in her ear. "I'd like to steal you away from here for some alone time." She pulled back to look at him. Intently. Did he imagine the frisson of want that steamed between them?

He just couldn't resist leaning in for a kiss. The sweet taste of the caramel dessert lingered on her lips. How could he stop at just one kiss?

The smirk from his friend as he danced by with his wife achieved the same end as if he had been hit with a bucket of cold water. Oh, yeah. He was in public. Time to rein it in.

Easier to think than do. Just as well the song ended. Callie seemed disappointed when he pulled back, but it had to be done or else he would make a spectacle of them both in the middle of the dance floor and Jake would never let him live it down.

Reluctantly, he steered her off the floor.

"Just so you know," he told her quietly, "I've not had my fill of dancing with you, but any longer and I wouldn't be responsible for my actions. And I don't want to run the risk of being banned or losing my membership."

The small, "Oh," she made was barely audible, but it spoke volumes anyway.

"I'm just going to grab a drink. Can I get you something?"

"Umm, maybe just a lemon, lime and bitters, thanks."

～

CAROLINE SAT STEEPLING her fingers on the table as Ryan wended his way over to the bar.

Don't watch him walk. Just don't, she commanded herself. But she couldn't obey her own words.

Matisse came and sat beside her as Jake joined Ryan at the bar.

"Callie girl, I thought we were going to have to grab a fire extinguisher there for a minute. You two were almost ready to combust."

Caroline gave a little shrug. "It's not like you can talk. Just saying."

"True," Matisse admitted. "Fiji is still pretty conservative— even here among the expats. Ryan has to live and work here. We're just foreigners. That's our excuse. Ry, on the other hand, should know better."

"What should Ry know better?" Jake asked as he set a bottle of water down in front of his wife.

"Never you mind." Matisse shot him a warning glance as Ryan arrived at the table.

After calling it a night, they headed back to the marina. Jake and Matisse walked a few paces ahead, her hand tucked securely in the crook of his arm. Callie's hand slipped down to Ryan's and she entwined their fingers, leaning into him.

IT WAS A NO-BRAINER to slow his pace so he could enjoy every possible second with her by his side. At one stage, the other two stopped and waited for them to catch up. Both his friends sent knowing grins his way. Looked like he'd be in for a hard time when they got back to Tokalau.

Once onboard *Shaw Thing*, Jake took a seat alongside his wife and they cozied up for the return trip. There was a cool breeze in play, so Ryan went down to the cabin and pulled out a couple of lightweight blankets.

"Incoming," he called as he lobbed the rolled blanket underarm across the deck. Jake quickly flicked it open and wrapped it around his wife's shoulders, hugging her to his side.

"You okay or would you like to go below deck?" he asked Callie.

"I'd rather stay out here with you."

"That'd be nice." The boat glided out of the marina and Ryan turned in the direction of home.

Callie unrolled the second blanket and pulled it onto her shoulders.

"Come here." He beckoned, holding out his arm so she could duck underneath. Then he tucked her in close, but only briefly before kissing her cheek and releasing her.

"I need to concentrate," he told her. "You are waaay too distracting."

"Should I go sit somewhere else?" Concern laced her words.

"No, you are fine. I just need to keep you at arm's length, that's all."

There was very little noise from Callie—she just stood quietly at his side. From time to time, he said something to her and they conversed for a while before falling back into silence.

A FEW BOATS PUTTERED BY, coming into the marina as they made their way out. The Denerau lights faded to become twinkling stars.

Caroline guessed that Ryan could do with another pair of eyes on lookout. For what, exactly, she wasn't sure. Jake was no help whatsoever; he was currently occupied making out with Matisse. Every so often some loving sound effects drifted over. Awkward.

Ryan looked over his shoulder.

"Can't you two at least wait until we get back?"

Jake just waved him off.

The return trip was at a much more leisurely pace. Anything to stretch the evening out was more than welcome as far as Caroline was concerned, and she was disappointed when they finally tied up at the dock at the bottom of the garden near Ryan's house. Ryan took her hand on the short walk up to the house and she enjoyed the caress of his thumb on her skin.

Sneaking in quietly, they found Rosi napping in one of the comfortable lounge chairs, but she woke quickly, giving a report about Leo. Matisse thanked her with a big hug before she and Jake turned in for the night.

Rosi collected her things and followed Ryan out the front door to the waiting buggy. She climbed into the back, leaving the front seat vacant for Caroline. Ryan dropped Rosi at the staff quarters and thanked her again for looking after Leo. "Vinaka."

"Moce. Ni sa moce."

After Rosi had closed the door on her bure, Ryan took Caroline to her accommodation.

Jumping out as soon as the buggy came to a halt, he jogged around to her side and took her into his arms as she stepped out. Her hands flew around his neck as his lips captured hers, releasing pent up emotion. With one step, he backed her up against the side of the buggy. The metal pressed into her back but she didn't care. She was too busy losing herself in the fervour of his embrace. Their surroundings receded into the background. Hands roved across her body and pulled her hips hard up against him. Her lips parted as he took his kisses deeper and she clutched at his shirt to keep herself upright. Ryan showered her cheeks, her eyes, her neck with the most divine kisses. Tipping her neck to allow him easier access, she whimpered as his lips worked their way down slowly.

Before he went beyond the point of no return, she grabbed his face and took control and he was happy to let her.

A SUDDEN FLASH of light out of the corner of his eye brought Ryan back to reality as Callie jumped out of his embrace.

The torch beam glanced off the front of the buggy as Ryan shielded his eyes.

"Is that you, Mister Ryan?" the security guard asked.

Aware that Callie was slowly inching out of range, Ryan stuffed his hands in his pockets to prevent him reaching for her again. Acknowledging the staff member, Ryan engaged him in a conversation, hoping his voice didn't betray his guilt at being caught making out with one of the guests. Even as he pleaded silently with Callie not to leave, he knew it wasn't going to happen. Somewhere behind him he caught a mumbled goodnight. The guard made to continue his rounds.

Disappointment washed over him, but Ryan understood why Callie had left him standing there. He fought himself to avoid glancing in her direction. Not wanting to draw attention to her, Ryan got back into the buggy and drove away without looking back.

CAROLINE LEANED back on the closed door, trying to get her breathing under control. The emotion of the moment had escalated quickly. The sizzling kisses he had trailed over her skin had left her wanting him.

Shocked, she realised she had been a nanosecond away from pulling Ryan into her bure, so she pretended to be grateful for the divine intervention that had brought the security guard past at that exact moment. By the time she crept into her bed, her thoughts were still scrambled.

It would probably be wise to back off as far as Ryan was concerned. He was firmly entrenched here in Fiji. Could she stay if he asked her? Did she even want to?

A Fijian holiday was all well and good, but living here permanently was a whole other thing entirely. Realistically, a holiday romance was all she should expect and at the end of her time, she would go back to her life in Australia and forget about him.

Oh, who was she kidding, she would never forget about Ryan. The way he made her feel. Treasured and adored. Nowhere in her world had she experienced that depth of feeling before. Never had she felt such a connection with a man to the degree she had with Ryan. But she struggled to convince herself it could ever work. Her head was more than happy to convince her it wasn't possible, but her heart told her not to pay any attention.

CHAPTER FIFTEEN

*T*he morning knock on her door had Caroline in two minds about opening it. On the one hand, she wanted to see Ryan again, even if just to catch a glimpse of his blue eyes. But part of her was worried it would be awkward between them after last night.

The knocked sounded again. Well, she would never know unless she opened the door. Pausing with her hand seemingly frozen on the doorknob, she took a deep breath and pulled the door open.

It wasn't Ryan standing there. Caroline was relieved and disappointed at the same time.

Thanking the bearer of her breakfast tray, she carried it inside, pushing the door closed with her foot.

After eating, Caroline smoothed sunscreen onto her skin, took her e-reader and wandered down to the waterfront to settle into one of the white lounge chairs, unsure if she would be welcome over at the house. Thankfully, there was no one around at this end of the resort. Most of the other guests would likely be gathered around the pool.

Reading and relaxing, she decided, was a good idea—when she wasn't distracted by thoughts of Ryan and those kisses. The memory of each kiss chased itself in a continuous loop in her head until stomach rumbles reminded her it was almost time for lunch. Closing the cover on her reading device, she walked back towards her bure. A buggy seemed to be on its way towards her. Ryan? No, it would be one of the workers for sure.

As the buggy got closer, Caroline noticed the white female driver. Matisse. The buggy stopped next to where Caroline was standing.

"Hey Callie, have you had lunch yet?"

"No, I was just thinking about getting myself something."

"Wanna jump in and we can go grab a bite to eat? Rosi, God bless her, has taken Leo, so I have a couple of hours to myself."

"Um, yeah, sure." Caroline walked around to the passenger side and stepped in, clutching at the seat when her friend took off with a jerk.

"Sorry, Callie. My belly is making it hard to manage." After parking near the main building, Matisse hauled herself out from behind the wheel with as much dignity as she could muster.

It was a relief to discover the small eatery was quiet for a lunch time. Maybe the other guests were eating by the pool or out on a day trip somewhere.

"The boys not around?" Caroline asked.

"Yeah, they are helping with something or other in the gardens. I think they wanted to work off last night's dinner," Matisse joked.

The two women chatted while they waited for their order to arrive.

Matisse seemed to zone out for a minute, rubbing at her stomach.

"You don't look too comfortable there," Caroline observed. "You okay?"

"Um yeah... Just some Braxton Hicks. It's fine."

Caroline must have looked sceptical.

"No really, it's all good."

"You sure you're not going into labour?"

"I'm sure it's nothing. Braxton Hicks are common during the third trimester. Just a little discomfort."

Once lunch arrived, Matisse said, "So, Jake and I were hoping to have a Leo-free night away while we're here. It will probably be the last chance we get before this one arrives." She pointed to her baby bump. "We were wondering if we could ask you to look after him for us?"

"Well, I'm not sure."

"Oh, Ryan would be on hand to help as well. Leo seems to have taken to you, and Uncle Ry is always good value."

"So, we would both be looking after him?"

"Well, yes and no. Ryan will be working but checking in during the day."

Caroline was hesitant—it would mean she would need to be at the house. Her resolve to take a step or two back from Ryan would be put to the test immediately.

Matisse told her they would just be going over to the resort on nearby Malolo Island—close enough if, for some reason, they needed to get back quickly. "What do you think?"

"Um… I guess that would be okay." She hesitated. "I suppose I could manage one night."

THE CHECKLIST for Leo's routine left on the kitchen bench seemed thorough. Caroline could only hope his parents had thought of every contingency. Although she didn't have a whole lot of experience with toddlers, she prayed it was enough to see her through. Rosi would be on call, but Caroline didn't want to call on her unless necessary. The woman was busy enough with her regular job on the island. She held Leo in her arms so he could wave off the boat, as Ryan took the helm for the short hop over to Malolo.

"Okay, little Leo, it looks like it's just me and you for the time being."

Taking him back inside the house, she crouched down and tried to set him down in the corner where the toys were scattered. Leo surveyed the room, his little hand latched onto a fistful of Caroline's shirt. Kneeling alongside him, she stretched one handed for a pop-up toy, trying not to pull the toddler over in the process, and encouraged him to play with it.

Plopping down, he reached for the toy. She assumed she would have to help him with the buttons to make the animals pop up from their boxes. But he was a pro and pushed her hand away. Once they were all up, he pushed them down again and went through the routine a few times before he got bored and went looking for the next activity. This happened a few more times and Caroline started to wonder if the little guy was getting too old for some of the toys Uncle Ry had on offer.

Ryan dropped the love birds off at Malolo, wondering how Callie was coping with Leo. He was a cute kid but, man, he could keep you on your toes. Hopefully, between the two of them they could manage. Sure, he had nieces and nephews who visited, albeit infrequently, but he didn't usually have sole responsibility for them overnight. A toddler was probably much more work. Cutting the engine as he arrived back on Tokalau, he tied the boat off before going to check on Callie and Leo.

"Hello," he called as he came in the door.

"In here."

Ryan followed the sound of her voice to the kitchen, where Leo was sitting on the floor happily munching a breakfast cracker even though it was well after lunch. The size of the crumb trail indicated it wasn't his first one.

"How's it going?"

"So far, so good. But it's still early yet. Wait till he realises his parents aren't coming back tonight... then we might be in for some fun and games."

"Will you be okay with him for a couple of hours? I need to go to the office and get some jobs done."

"I guess I'll just have to see, won't I?"

∽

AFTER ALMOST GETTING CAUGHT out by the security guard kissing Callie a couple of nights back, Ryan had thought it might be a good idea to lie low for a while. But he hadn't realised how difficult it would be. Not taking the breakfast tray to her bure and seeing her first thing in the morning to get a fix of her gorgeous dark-blue eyes had practically set him up for withdrawal symptoms. He had quickly become hooked on every little thing about her, and he didn't know how long he would last without that simple morning routine.

Leaning back in his office chair, his thoughts wandered.

Seeing her with Leo ignited a desire to have his own family. With Callie. Even though she wasn't confident with Leo, he knew when the time came she would grow into her own role as a mother. Parenting was a huge commitment, but with Callie by his side they would be an amazing team.

Ryan shook his head. Dreaming of a future with Callie was an enjoyable way to pass the time—but he needed to focus on his work for a while. In any case, there was the little matter of her life being in Australia and his being here. Was she prepared to give up life back there to start anew with him? If not, was he prepared to give up all he had worked for in Fiji? All his parents and grandparents had worked for? He couldn't throw that away easily. But did he want to stay in Fiji if it meant he couldn't have Callie with him? This was uncharted territory for him—he had never thought he would contemplate giving up his lifestyle on Tokalau.

Late that afternoon, the resort chef prepared dinner and boxed it up in a thermal bag for him to take back to the house. One less thing to worry about. And if Leo had run Callie ragged, it was sure to be appreciated. At the door he paused, surprised not to be accosted by noise. Was that a good thing or not? Slipping the dinner bag onto the kitchen bench, he noticed a piece of paper, Leo artwork, attached to the refrigerator, and wondered if the kid was developing a passion for art like his mother.

Going in search of Callie and Leo, the sound of her laughter drew him to the main bathroom. He leaned on the door frame watching as Callie created a crazy hairstyle for Leo who was splashing in the huge tub. Scooping up a huge handful of bubbles, she pretended to blow them only to have Leo beat her to it and she reacted in surprise as Leo laughed and she splashed him in retaliation.

Leo looked over and spotted him. "Unca Ry."

"Hey buddy, looks like you've been having fun."

"Oh yeah, we have," Callie replied.

Ryan took the handful of steps over to the bathtub, almost slipping on the well-watered tiles, and joined Callie on the floor. Leo swished around, pulled a plastic boat out of the water and handed it to his honorary uncle, insisting he join in the game.

CAROLINE WATCHED Ryan interact with Leo. They had a good relationship, judging by the way they were both grinning and splashing around in the water. Seeing them together, it wasn't hard to picture Ryan with his own kids one day. Could she picture herself as the mother, though?

Could what they had be more than just a holiday thing? She wasn't sure, even though every day she was falling for Ryan just that little bit more. His strength and tenderness, his presence, his work ethic. Okay, he was good looking, his kisses were second to none and he lived in an island paradise. But would living here, permanently, wear thin after a while? Could Fiji Time become a way of life? The laid-back lifestyle certainly held appeal. Ryan held appeal. Her thoughts were going all over the place, like Leo's attempts at drawing earlier this afternoon.

Back to now. That was all she could deal with at the moment. The future was clouded like a dirty window—she couldn't see what lay beyond.

"Okay, I think time's up. Leo is all wrinkly," she observed.

"C'mon, sport."

Leo stood up while Caroline took the shower hose and rinsed the bubbles off. Ryan grabbed the fluffy towel, wrapped it around the youngster and lifted him over the side. Once Leo was dry and dressed, the adults teamed up to read him a story or two and get him settled for the night.

"Have you had a chance to eat yet?" Ryan asked when they finally made it out to the kitchen.

"No, I was just snacking while Leo ate."

"Good, because I brought dinner back with me." He unzipped the bag and pulled out the containers. "One distinct advantage of managing a resort and living on site."

"Do you ever prepare your own meals?"

"Not often, to be honest. I'm usually so busy it's easier to eat while I'm over at work, or I bring it home with me. I also eat with the guests once or twice a week."

Caroline quickly set two places at one end of the large dining table and poured some drinks.

Ryan put the plates down and went back to the kitchen, rummaging around in the pantry before producing candles and matches. Then he added some quiet instrumental music in the background.

THE CONVERSATION as they ate was relaxed. In the soft light, Ryan was captivated by Callie. Admittedly, she was a little rumpled around the edges from looking after Leo for the afternoon, but to him she looked just as beautiful. Reaching across the table, he took hold of her hand and rubbed his thumb across the soft skin. His eyes swept over her again and paused on the sweet curves of her lips. Did she know what he was thinking?

Keeping hold of her hand, he pulled her up with him and folded her into his arms. The gentle sway of her body with his and the scent of her skin as he breathed her in made him light-headed. Leaning down, he slowly moved in for a kiss.

A cry from Leo echoed from the bedroom and she pulled out of his embrace with a mumbled apology. Raking a hand through his hair in frustration, Ryan sighed at being disturbed at the wrong moment. No wonder Jake and Matisse were keen for some kid-free time.

After a few calming breaths, he followed Callie to Leo's room. The sight of her cradling the sobbing toddler triggered a good dose of the guilts.

"He wants his mum," she said.

"Guess that's understandable."

Ryan sat next to her and helped console the two-year-old. Once the crying deescalated to sniffles, Callie put Leo back down on the bed, softly patting his back, until he finally fell asleep. Ryan beckoned her quietly, but as soon as she got up, Leo's eyes popped open and he started to wail.

"You go," she told Ryan. "I'll say here with him for the time being."

"You sure?"

"Yeah, I'll come get you if I need help."

Ryan retreated to his room to shower and change. By the time he snuck back to check on the two of them, he found Callie curled up around Leo, both of them asleep. He fetched a light blanket to cover them, barely resisting the urge to stoop down and kiss Callie on the cheek.

◈

THE WAKE UP cry was at about 3 am, according to Ryan's bedside clock. He found Leo howling in the middle of the bed, pulling at an ear, while Callie was fumbling around trying to find the bottle of children's paracetamol. Sucking up the dosage into a plastic syringe, she managed to squirt the liquid down Leo's throat with help from Ryan, who pinned his arms to his sides.

"Can you grab the tube of teething gel? It's just there on the bench."

"How does this stuff work again?" he asked, unscrewing the cap.

"Wash your hands and squirt some onto your finger and rub it on his gums."

Easier said than done. You'd think it would be a straightforward process, but no. The toddler was determined not to let anyone near him. It took some doing, but with Callie's help Ryan got the teething gel where it was supposed to go.

"Here, I'll take him for a while," Ryan told her. "You try and get some sleep." He scooped up the flailing toddler, holding him firmly against his chest. "C'mon buddy, let's go and hang out."

Even though he could tell she wasn't sure it was a good idea, Callie handed over Leo's pacifier. It was only fair he take a turn with Leo—after all Callie hardly knew the kid and he had agreed to the night away for his friends. Digging through the collection of DVDs that his siblings had left on one of their visits, he pulled out a Wiggles music concert and pushed it into the machine. The noise caught Leo's attention and his cries subsided.

Taking one of the recliners, Ryan sat Leo back against him and tried to find a comfortable position, as the four skivvy-clad singers launched into another song.

THERE WAS no sign of Ryan next morning when Caroline padded through the house after she woke up. Yawning, she set the coffee maker going and pulled out something to eat for breakfast. The buggy was still parked out the front, so he hadn't taken Leo over to the resort. Surely they couldn't be too far away. Maybe they were walking on the beach. If they hadn't turned up by the time she'd eaten, she would go and investigate.

Okay, she made sure she looked presentable this morning. The wild-woman look in the middle of the night wasn't her finest moment. She'd been horrified when she went to the bath-room after Ryan left with Leo, and saw her reflection in the mirror. Even though it was the early hours, it was still a shock to the system. Maybe that contributed to Leo's cries... that and teething pain and missing his parents.

Rinsing the plates and other bits and pieces, she left them in the bamboo dish drainer and dried her hands before heading out to the back veranda, scanning up and down. Oh wait. It looked like there was someone in the hammock under the thatched hut not far from the house. Must be Ryan. There was no movement when she approached, and no wonder. Both of them were sound asleep. Leo was sprawled, front down, on his honorary uncle's chest, with one of Ryan's arms draped across the small body. Dang if that wasn't the cutest thing she was likely to see all day.

There was something about seeing this man asleep with a child that tugged at her heart strings. One day, he would make a great father, she had no doubt. It wasn't hard for her imagination to picture him down on the sand building sandcastles, playing beach cricket, walking along at sunset with someone on his shoulders and a couple of other children gambolling behind. And a woman by his side holding his hand. Was that women her? Would that even be possible?

The two figures looked so peaceful she didn't want to disturb them, but at the same time she had an overwhelming desire to lean down and kiss Ryan. Hesitating, she sighed and turned to leave.

"Hey there."

She startled and turned back. "Hi, I didn't think you were awake."

"Barely." He swept his free hand over his face and hair and checked to see if Leo still had his eyes shut.

"How long have you two been out here?"

"We watched the sunrise together."

They talked quietly until Leo started to stir. He rolled over onto his back with Ryan's steadying hand on his arm. Bewildered, he tried to sit up, wriggling into the gap between Ryan's arm and torso, squatting awkwardly. His little hands grabbed at the hammock and he cast his eyes around—no doubt looking for his parents.

The bottom lip started to tremble. It looked like he was about to set up a wail. Caroline spotted the shape of the pacifier in Ryan's top shirt pocket and dipped her fingers in to grab it before she realised what she was doing.

Ryan's eyes caught hold of hers. A burst of electricity seemed to arc between them. Caroline felt her face flush under the warmth of his gaze. Her eyes dropped to his lips and back. They were so deliciously close. Ready. Inviting. Maybe just a little taste wouldn't hurt.

Before she had a chance to act on the impulse, Leo started howling and the moment evaporated.

"Here you go, kid," she told Leo as she aimed the pacifier at his mouth. He took it in and started sucking vigorously. The stream of tears was heartbreaking.

Ryan must have read her mind—he managed to pull a handkerchief out of his pocket and hand it to her. Even that tiny bit of skin contact was enough to cause a frisson of awareness to dance across her hand and continue right up her arm.

Wiping Leo's face, she put her hands out for the little guy, to encourage him to come to her. He stuck his arms up and she reached out and swung him onto her hip, stepping back so Ryan could tip himself out of the hammock.

∾

RYAN HAD BEEN AWAKE a few minutes before he saw Callie walking towards the hammock, and he pretended he was asleep out of curiosity to see what she would do. He could just make her out through slitted eyes. It seemed like she stood there watching him and Leo for a long time.

When she leaned closer, he caught a trace of the scent of her shampoo and fought not to take a deep breath and get caught out. Was she going to kiss him? He sure hoped so. Maybe he could be the male version of Sleeping Beauty and be woken by a magic kiss.

A small sigh escaped her lips and she turned away. But he wasn't about to let her leave that easily. Then when she'd brushed her fingers against him, reaching into his pocket, she froze. Her eyes widened—all that luscious blueness that he wanted to fall headlong into and never surface. And she was going to kiss him. He was sure of it. And if it hadn't been for Master Leo...

∾

THE THREE OF them walked back to the house, with Caroline jigging Leo to see if she could get a smile out of him. Adding a bit of silly talk seemed to do the trick, and he managed a laugh.

"What time are you getting Jake and Matisse?" Caroline asked him as he breakfasted a short time later.

"They have a late check out—so I'll leave here just before twelve."

Once Ryan left for Malolo, Caroline took Leo inside for a bath, to clean him up before his parents arrived.

A clean outfit and a slick hairdo and Leo was soon ready. The two of them sat on the back veranda while Caroline read stories, complete with character voices and sound effects much to Leo's amusement, his favourite toy car glued to his hand. As soon as Caroline heard *Shaw Thing* making its way back to the island, she hoisted Leo onto her hip and hurried down to meet his parents.

Jake tied off the boat as Caroline walked onto the dock. Spotting his father, Leo was doing his best to escape from her arms, calling out to his dad. Stretching as far as his little body could manage, he was transferred over.

"Hey buddy." Jake greeted the boy and hugged him close, kissing him on the head. "Have you been good for Uncle Ry and Callie?"

Jake looked over at Callie who shrugged her shoulders. "He's teething, what can I say?"

"Ryan said he kept you on your toes."

"Just a little."

"We really appreciate you looking after him for us." Jake turned back to where Matisse was waiting for a hand out of the boat.

"Mum, Mum." Matisse hardly set foot on the dock before Leo was reaching over for her to take him. She winced as the toddler landed heavily against her stomach. "Ouch, Leo. Gentle, please."

Jake turned his attention to helping Ryan offload their overnight bags.

The two women walked ahead into the house. Matisse got as far as the lounge before deciding she needed to sit with Leo for a bit. She seemed very uncomfortable but kept assuring everyone she was fine.

Over dinner that night, Jake and Matisse talked about two older couples they'd met who were on vacation from Cairns. It seemed they got on very well.

Caroline was keen to turn in early. The last couple of days had tired her out and she accepted the invitation to stay another night in Ryan's house.

CHAPTER SIXTEEN

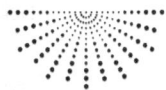

*R*yan was sitting on the back veranda with his first coffee of the day when Jake appeared.

"Um, I think we have a problem."

Ryan arched an eyebrow at his friend, who looked unusually rattled.

"Matisse has been having contractions overnight and her waters just broke."

"Looks like you guys won't be flying home tomorrow then," Ryan said.

"We need to get her to Nadi and a hospital as soon as possible."

"Is one of your choppers available?"

"Oh yeah, of course." Jake bolted inside.

Callie passed him on her way out. "What's with him?"

"Looks like the baby is on its way."

"Oh, that's not good. What are we going to do about it?"

"Jake is going to see if there's a helicopter available to fly them into Nadi."

"So, I guess we'll be minding Leo again?" Callie leaned up against one of the veranda posts.

"Looks like it."

Jake returned, panic-stricken. "No luck. They're too far away to get here in time."

A loud moan reached them. Jake darted off again.

"I'd better go see if there's anything I can do." Callie pushed off the post and hurried after Jake.

Ryan grabbed his phone off the kitchen counter to make a few calls.

~

CAROLINE HESITATED at the bedroom door. Matisse was leaning over the edge of the bed as Jake massaged her back.

"We'll just have to get Ry to take us in to Nadi by boat and ring ahead to have an ambulance on standby," he said.

"Jake Davis. If you think for a moment I'm getting onto that boat and running the risk of having this baby on the way, you've got another think coming," Matisse told him through gritted teeth.

Ryan turned up at the door next to Caroline. "Rosi has delivered her fair share of babies, and I thought I could get her before she left the island for her week off, but I just missed her."

"Guys, didn't you say one of the women you had dinner with on Malolo is an obstetrician?" Caroline reminded them.

"Um, yeah I think so," Jake said.

"Her name is Susan Walsh," Matisse managed to get out between laboured breaths. "You need to get her, please."

"Now!" she added when no one moved.

"Okay. I'm on it." Caroline turned in a hurry and ran smack bang into Ryan, who grabbed at her to stop her from ricocheting into the wall. "Sorry, Ryan." She wanted to enjoy the feeling of being held against him, but there wasn't time. "Did you catch that?"

"Yep, I need to get in contact with management at Malolo."

Caroline listened to the one-sided conversation as Ryan called the neighbouring island.

"Right, hopefully they will have located her before I get there, and have her waiting at the dock." He sprinted from the room before returning with a satellite phone.

"If you need help before I get back, 112 is the international emergency number," he showed Caroline. "You should be able to get hold of someone to help you through." He gave her cheek a quick kiss. "Wish me luck."

She followed him onto the veranda as Ryan ran out the door and down to his boat. Untying the rope, he pushed the boat out with his foot and leapt aboard in one fluid movement, firing up the engine and tearing away from the dock.

Caroline looked at the phone in her hand and prayed she wouldn't need to use it. Just then, Leo set up a wail.

In all the craziness of the last few minutes, no one had given the kid a thought. She scurried into his room and scooped him out of the portacot. "Hey, buddy. How are you doing?" Leo squirmed in her arms to be let down, but she didn't think it would be a good idea. Crossing to the bathroom, she hip-bumped the door shut, made sure Leo was toileted and plotted her next move. Should she mind Leo? What if Jake and Matisse needed her help? Was there someone over at the resort who could look after him?

Some people had their kids in with them when they had a home birth. Would his parents want that? Would seeing his mum in pain upset the little guy? It was bound to be traumatic for such a young one. Caroline wasn't even sure how she would cope, let alone a toddler. There was no easy answer and she wondered if Jake was in the frame of mind to be able to make a decision.

Taking matters into her own hands, she took Leo with her into Ryan's home office, shutting the door so the toddler couldn't escape. She settled him on the floor at her feet while she looked around for the resort numbers, finally finding them listed near his computer.

She punched an extension number into the phone and

listened, hoping for it to connect. It took a while for her to make the person on the desk understand what was going on, but they promised to send someone over as soon as they could.

Leo complained he was hungry, so Caroline quickly grabbed some food from the kitchen and ushered him outside, away from his mother's moans. Soon after, a buggy from the resort pulled up and one of the female staff climbed out of the passenger seat. Caroline recognised the face but had no idea what her name was. Vilisi introduced herself.

"Thank you for coming."

"You are welcome, ma'am. Is this who I'm looking after?"

"Yes, this is Leo." Caroline crouched down next to the two year old. "Leo, this is Vilisi. She is going to be your friend for a while. Okay?"

Leo sized up the Fijian woman. Vilisi bent down to Leo's level and started talking to him.

"I'll just go and grab some stuff for him. Be right back."

Caroline raced inside and pushed whatever she thought might be helpful into Leo's *Thomas the Tank Engine* backpack. By the time she got back outside it looked like Vilisi had charmed Leo and he was more than willing to go with her.

"We will keep him until we hear from you then?" Vilisi asked.

"Oh, hang on a minute." Caroline ran back to grab the instructions Matisse had left her before, and handed it to Vilisi who took it gratefully. Leo seemed happy to take the older woman's hand and walk to the buggy. Vilisi hoisted him up and sat him between her and the driver while Caroline waved them off.

Blowing out a breath of relief that there was one less person to worry about, Caroline walked through the house back to the dock area, as if she could somehow will the boat to appear. First, she walked up and down, then she sat. But she couldn't stay still more than a couple of minutes.

Anxiously she kept looking towards the house. There was no

frantic yelling from Jake. Would Ryan make it back in time? She wasn't sure she could cope if she had to help Jake deliver the baby.

At last, she spotted the boat coming in and hurried down to the dock. Ryan cut the engine as he pulled up alongside and quickly tied the boat off. He held a hand out for the passengers to alight. There were two women.

"Hi, I'm Susan Walsh. I hear there's a baby keen to be born in Fiji rather than back in Australia."

"Yeah, something like that." Caroline gestured for Susan to go ahead of her. "I'm so thankful you were able to come."

"Lucky for Matisse we were just lounging by the pool while our husbands are out fishing somewhere. This is Laura Bradley by the way. She's a nurse, so I thought she should come as well."

Caroline nodded as they hurried up to the house with Ryan following with an overnight bag. It was quiet when they walked inside. Caroline didn't know if that was a good thing or not. Ushering the two women into the room where Matisse and Jake were, she stopped in the hallway to lean on the wall.

"I'm glad you found them," she told Ryan who joined her. "I've sent Leo off with Vilisi for the time being."

"Good thinking. Vilisi will be good with Leo."

They talked quietly until they were interrupted by Susan.

"Hey there, I need you guys to get me as many towels as you can, clean sheets, and if you can find plastic for the bed and maybe for the floor, that would be good. Garbage bags or whatever you can come up with. Extra pillows would be helpful and a large plastic container of some sort. Soap or sanitiser. Shoelaces and scissors—those will need to be sterilised."

"How is she doing?"

"Not too bad." The moaning intensified. "I don't think it will be long now, so if you can gather that stuff together asap, that would be great."

Ryan pushed off the wall and Caroline followed him around the house, looking for the required items.

Sheets, towels and pillows were an easy find. Caroline took them back to the room. The other items took a little longer to round up and they passed them to Laura at the door.

"Thanks, guys." She took the last of the supplies into the room, shutting the door behind her.

"Now what?" Ryan asked

"Looks like it's a waiting game." Callie chose a movie and they settled in.

~

"ANY IDEA HOW MUCH LONGER?" Ryan asked after the movie finished.

"Your guess is as good as mine." Callie yawned and stretched. Ryan tried not to notice the way her top rode up. He almost had to sit on his hands to stop them wandering over to touch her bare skin and pull her close. Callie got to her feet and he wondered what she would think if he confessed what he was thinking. She disappeared into the bathroom while he chose another movie and slipped it into the machine.

They were well into the story when the sound of a newborn's cry reached them.

Callie's eyes were huge as she looked at him. Was everything okay, he wondered? It was hard being patient, but eventually Jake wandered out with a huge grin on his face.

"It's a girl," he told them.

"Congratulations." Ryan shook his hand and gave him a man-hug.

"How's Matisse?" Callie wanted to know.

"I'm in total awe of my wife," Jake told them. "She's doing okay. We're so grateful for Susan. It could have been a different story if we were on our own. The cord was wrapped around the baby's neck."

Laura came to the door. "Jake, we need you back in here."

~

HALF AN HOUR LATER, they were still waiting for more news when Susan came out of the bedroom. Her clothes were stained and she was looking a little dishevelled, but Caroline guessed it was no wonder. Delivering a baby outside the confines of a delivery suite no doubt had its challenges. They both looked at her expectantly.

"Baby is doing well, all things considered. Matisse had a rough time but she came through it in the end. As you can imagine, they don't have anything here for the baby, so I need you guys to go into Nadi for supplies."

Caroline was about to ask what was needed, but Susan seemed to read her mind.

"Laura is just writing out a list for you. The sooner you can get going, the better."

"Can we take a peek at bubs first?" Caroline asked.

"Yes, I don't see why not."

Caroline took tentative steps into the room with Ryan close behind. Laura was shoving a pile of soiled linen into a large plastic bin bag as they walked towards the bed.

Jake held a towel-wrapped bundle in his arms as he sat next to a very pale and exhausted Matisse, who gave them a weak smile.

"Hey, there she is," Caroline commented as she glimpsed the baby, blinking back tears as the emotion of the moment hit her. "Have you chosen a name yet?"

"Yes, it's Sienna Jade," Matisse told them.

"Hey, SJ, welcome to the world, little one."

"Would you like to hold her?" the proud father asked.

"Oh, I don't know." Callie was hesitant but Jake passed the baby over to her anyway.

~

RYAN WATCHED her initial awkward grasp on the bundle and then Callie was apparently lost as she gazed at the infant.

Jake's knowing grin aimed at his friend affected him more than he would like to admit. The sight of Callie holding the baby escalated the desire he'd been feeling since Jake and Matisse arrived, to have his own family.

"Well done, mumma," Caroline was telling Matisse. "You did great."

"Yes, she did," Jake commented, leaning down to kiss his wife.

"Who is minding Leo?" Matisse asked.

"Vilisi. One of my staff. She is really good with kids, so I'm sure he's being well looked after over at the resort." They visited for a few minutes longer, then took the shopping list from Laura.

AN HOUR later Ryan was pushing a shopping trolley around a Nadi supermarket next to Callie as she searched the shelves looking for all the items they needed to buy for Matisse and the baby. Her frustration was evident, so he took matters into his own hands, finding a staff member to help them. Laden with nappies, wipes, lotions and other products, they dumped the bags into the back of his car and drove to the next shop.

The babywear store was way more interesting as far as Ryan was concerned. And Callie? Well, Callie gushed as she picked up various items of clothing. Way too many were ending up in the trolley. Sienna Jade would easily be the best-dressed newborn in Fiji.

"Callie, do you think you may have gone overboard just a little?" he ventured.

"What... no..." She looked at the trolley. "Oh, maybe..." She sighed.

"Matisse could dress Sienna in a new outfit every day for a month at least."

"I guess, but everything is so darn cute."

Ryan thought Callie was so darn cute, but he didn't tell her. "Have you got what's on the list?" he reminded her.

"That's just the bare minimum." He didn't say anything. "Oh, fine then," she muttered. She sorted through the clothes pile and pulled several outfits out and put them back.

"Hey, look at this." Callie held up what appeared to be a bag, but then folded it out to become a small bed. "There's probably no point buying a bassinet for the time they will be here, but this might be just the thing."

"Couldn't we just empty out a drawer or something to use for a cot? SJ won't take up much space." He was teasing but he could tell by her expression she wasn't sure if he was kidding or not.

"Seriously?"

"I'm sure back in the old days they used whatever they could find."

The incredulous look she threw him was priceless, as was the eye roll when she realised he was kidding. She added the item to the trolley along with a sling, and went on to choose a couple of muslin wraps.

When they got to the toy section, he knew he was going to have a hard time getting her to resist the soft toys. Her arms were soon full of teddies and other animals, and he shook his head in mock despair.

"Only one, Cal."

She just smirked at him, dropping the pile back and tossing two neatly into the trolley.

"If this is what you are like now, I hate to think what you will be like when the time comes to have your own kids."

"Maybe the novelty will have worn off by then," she told him.

"Or maybe not," he replied.

She gave him the sweetest smile, and he would've let her buy as many toys as she wanted. Shaking his head but unable to stop a grin, he pushed the trolley to the checkout.

~

CAROLINE HELPED Ryan stow all the bags below deck. They had to make two trips from the car. It was probably overkill, but she couldn't bear the thought of baby Sienna having nothing to start out in life with. Maybe they should've bought an extra suitcase for their friends to take it all home.

Choosing everything had been more fun than she'd anticipated. Caroline had to admit she enjoyed Ryan's reactions to the items she piled into the trolley. But to give him credit, he was way more indulgent than she had expected.

There'd been a Mexican stand-off at the checkout though, with Ryan insisting he wanted to pay for everything. But she didn't want him to fork out for all the excess she had chosen. There was a bit of back and forth before he eventually agreed to split the bill, probably because he didn't want to inconvenience the people in the line behind them any longer.

Splitting the bill seemed too hard for the checkout operator, who had to call the manager to come and deal with it. Ryan patiently explained the issue and Caroline was relieved he spoke Fijian fluently.

~

RYAN STEERED *Shaw Thing* out of the Denerau marina, as Callie took the seat next to him.

"I think we did good," she said, and settled back to enjoy the trip back to the island.

Late afternoon was a good time to be out on the water. The sting of the sun had dissipated, and with it the blinding glare off the water. He loved being out on the boat. Life sometimes got in the way and he didn't get to enjoy it as much as he would like. Maybe he just needed to make more of an effort. But it was much better having someone to share it with.

Callie seemed to enjoy getting out on the boat. He could easily get used to having her alongside him as they cruised along the beautiful Fijian waterways. Her eyes were closed in enjoyment and his own eyes couldn't help being drawn to her.

Maybe he could just idle the boat for a minute or two and reach over and kiss her. Who was he kidding? He'd have to anchor the boat. Sighing, he turned his attention back to steering.

∼

MATISSE WAS OVERWHELMED and cried when she saw all the bags they brought into her room.

The choices soon filled the top of the bed, and she insisted on drawing Caroline and Ryan into a fierce hug.

Laura whisked away the nappies and an outfit, and set about changing Sienna.

"Thanks, guys," Jake told them as he also hugged them both.

Ryan had dinner sent over from the resort restaurant. Matisse managed to make it out to join the group as they sat around the large dining table. Before long, Susan was regaling them with stories of some of the birthing experiences she'd had over her many years as an obstetrician. Then Jake asked Laura about her volunteer work overseas.

"Oh gosh, that was a while ago now, but it's how I met Marcus," she said, referring to her husband.

The more Laura talked, the more Caroline felt she knew the story. It seemed familiar. Then it dawned on her that she'd seen a movie about their time overseas.

As expected, the discussion eventually turned to Caroline's situation and her run-ins with the media. Laura and Marcus had faced more than their fair share of publicity so she could relate to Caroline's predicament and was happy to offer a few tips.

~

RYAN DROVE Callie back to her accommodation later that evening. Susan was staying overnight while Tui took Laura back to Malolo, but Laura would stay the following night. It was fortunate that the women were holidaying nearby and he knew his friends were grateful for their support. Matisse would be more comfortable at the house than at the hospital. He would talk to his staff about organising a big thank you dinner for Susan and Laura and their husbands.

"Thanks for running me back," Callie told him. She leaned over and brushed her lips lightly against his cheek, then stepped out of the buggy and swung her bag up over her shoulder. He should have been happy to let it go at that—but he wasn't. He climbed out from behind the wheel and followed her to the door.

"You not ready to say goodnight yet?" she asked him as he leaned against the door frame while she turned the key into the lock.

"Nope."

"Well, sorry to disappoint you, but I'm totally whacked. I'm going to have to take a raincheck."

He wasn't surprised—he'd seen her drooping over dinner. But he still hoped Callie would say otherwise. She reached up to give him another kiss on the cheek.

"Night, Ry." She smiled sleepily at him.

"Goodnight, sweetheart, sleep well." She gave him a little wave as she shut the door.

CHAPTER SEVENTEEN

*R*yan sat alongside Jake, who was waiting for his appointment at the Australian High Commission office in Suva. It wasn't unusual for babies to arrive early while their parents were holidaying overseas, but there were a few hoops Jake and Matisse had to jump through before they could fly home.

Jake was here to pick up Sienna's passport. They had extended their trip until Sienna was old enough to fly and for the necessary paperwork to be completed.

But they were almost there. Just as well. Jake was getting anxious as news reports indicated a tropical depression was strengthening and forecast to intensify into a cyclone, with the prediction it could hit the western end of Fiji by the end of the week. Understandably, Ryan's friend wanted to be off the island and on a plane back to Australia as soon as possible.

Jake's name was finally called. He walked across to the counter, returning a short time later waving the passport. "We are finally good to go." He strode to the exit with Ryan close behind. Jake was keen to get back to Nadi and across to Tokalau so he could see about booking flights.

"So, what are you going to do about Callie?" Jake asked, now that he could apparently turn his attention to other things.

"Well, I'd send her back to Australia with you, but she's refusing to go," Ryan told him, as he pressed the accelerator so the car reached the maximum speed of eighty kilometres on Queens Road.

"No, I meant long term. Do you see a future with her? You seem to be getting along well."

"Yeah, actually I can see a future with her."

"Matisse seems to think she's good for you, and I agree."

Ryan didn't just think Callie was good for him. He knew without a shadow of a doubt she was. But he wanted her to be the first to hear it. From him. As soon as he worked up the courage to go there again. Lucy had done a number on him, big time. His repaired heart wouldn't be sturdy enough to take another knock if someone else rejected him. If Callie didn't want to be with him... well he hoped there wouldn't be another bridge of heartbreak to cross.

CAROLINE WAS GOING to miss Matisse when she and Jake and their family flew back to Australia. They had become firm friends, and Matisse had extracted a promise from Caroline to come and visit them where they lived at Cape Otway on the south coast of Victoria. It was somewhere Caroline had always wanted to visit but had never found the time. Now she had a reason... and a place to stay.

Ryan and Jake finished stowing luggage into the buggy and the four adults piled in for the short trip to where the helicopter would meet them, taking them straight to the airport to catch their connecting flight to Melbourne. Jake held his daughter carefully while Leo "helped" Uncle Ry drive the buggy.

There were hugs all around and last-minute cuddles of baby Sienna. Who knew how big she would be before Caroline saw her again—if ever? And Leo had grown up so much since his baby sister arrived. It was like he had stepped up now he was the older sibling. He was still full-on, but Caroline would kind of miss that as well.

The thunk-thunk of the rotor blades echoed as the Davis Air helicopter came in to land.

Jake immediately went to the helicopter and returned with a miniature pair of earmuffs to place over his daughter's head. He also carried a headset for Leo so he could hear his father and the pilot over the noise of the engine.

Then they were gone.

CHAPTER EIGHTEEN

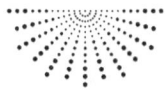

The order came to evacuate the guests, as Ryan had known it would. Tourists on the surrounding islands were heading to the mainland and those who could were flying out. Extra ferry services were running to cope with demand and more flights out of Nadi had been added to the regular schedule.

The cyclone was increasing in both size and strength. As a Category 3 storm it was packing wind gusts of up to 224 kilometres per hour. At the moment it was slow moving, which gave them ample time to get ready. The staff made preparations, nailing timber panels across glass windows, putting outdoor furniture inside. Loose objects that could become missiles were stowed away. The bow-rider had been covered and was currently anchored on Ryan's side of the island next to *Shaw Thing*, where it was more sheltered. The mooring lines had been doubled to help keep both boats secure.

"Water. Torches," he said.

"Yep."

"Batteries. First-aid kit."

"Yes, and yes." Callie was helping make sure all the emergency kit items were accounted for. He could tell she was on edge even though she tried to hide it.

While he would've preferred her to be off the island and out of harm's way, this way he could hopefully keep her safe, confident that the main resort building and his home at least would survive most of what Mother Nature could hurl at them. The bures were another matter. But for all they knew, the cyclone could change course any number of times. Not that he wished destruction on others in the Mamanucas, or anywhere else for that matter.

~

THERE WAS a low murmur in the dining room as staff gathered to get the latest briefing. Caroline took a seat at the back of the room as Ryan stood to address his workers. Everyone had been working diligently, with a sense of purpose. No panic or fear. She guessed the islanders saw many cyclones pass through, though they weren't blase by any means. But she sat twisting her hands in her lap.

"I just want to thank you all for volunteering to stay on. I know you must be concerned about your own families and friends. Now that most of the resort has been prepped, you should have all you need here. Sitiveni and Tui will be in charge whenever I'm not here, so if you have any concerns at all please talk to them."

Ryan answered questions before the meeting wound up, and the small group of staff members headed out to their final tasks.

"I'm just going to take a walk around and see if anything has been missed," he said to Caroline. "Stuff that might become a missile, things like that. You can stay here if you would prefer."

"I think I'd feel better sticking with you. I really need to move around. Who knows how long we will be stuck inside later?"

Donning heavy duty rain gear, they left the building. The sky was ominous, darker than it had been over the past few days and Caroline could see a curtain of torrential rain moving towards Tokalau. The usually glassy blue water surrounding the island started to seethe and boil a deep stormy grey. The wind intensified, pushing against them as they walked—and it was only going to get worse.

Ryan started at the far end of the bures and they worked their way back, building by building, checking everything was secure.

By the time they finished inspecting the site, the rain was pelting. Sideways. And the wind was strengthening as they hurried back to the main building for one last check on the staff before heading to do the final lockdown at Ryan's house.

All staff were accounted for, and had gathered in the main dining area. Furniture had been pushed to one side, bedding set up. Torches were lined up at the ready and a battery operated radio was broadcasting the current trajectory of the cyclone as it picked up speed. Now it was a waiting game to see if the cyclone would make landfall around here or veer off in another direction.

SATISFIED THAT EVERYTHING was in hand at the resort, Ryan made last-minute arrangements with his staff. Ushering Callie out to the buggy, they set off back to his house. Preparations at the resort had taken precedence over his own needs, so he wanted to check everything was secure at his place, hoping they weren't cutting it too fine to get there and back. The wind buffeted them as he sped along the track, swerving to miss fallen branches. At one point, both of them had to work together to clear a section of path that was blocked by a fallen tree—no easy feat in the driving rain and wind.

The adrenaline rush of fighting the elements to get home was something he wouldn't like to repeat in a hurry. Maybe it hadn't been a good idea to leave the relative safety of the resort, but there was no turning back now.

Callie white-knuckled the support bar on the side of the buggy as he gripped the steering wheel tighter. The buggy bounced along the last of the track, almost becoming airborne at one point before hurtling through the gateway and around to the storage area. He grappled with the door before parking the buggy and grabbing a rope to tie it to a support beam for good measure. It took the two of them to get the door shut before he grabbed Callie's hand and they made a run for the house. Once on the veranda, Ryan went methodically around the outside checking and rechecking each storm shutter was secure. Callie was at his shoulder every step of the way.

With the cyclone bearing down on them quickly, there was no way they would make it back to the resort now. They would have to ride it out here on their own. He ushered Callie inside.

After shedding their rain gear, Ryan braced the door. Out of habit he flicked the light switch, but the generator had already been turned off. With all the storm shutters closed, the house interior was pitch black. Snatching up a torch, he pushed it on, then grabbed Callie's hand to pull her along to the safe room in the centre of the house where the supplies were prepared.

Callie clung to his shirt, her fear palpable. He found the battery-powered lamp and turned it on in favour of the torch, then pulled Callie down beside him onto a mattress on the floor, backs pressed up against an inside wall. She wrapped her arms tightly around herself. Knees up to her chest. Eyes closed. Looking vulnerable and small.

THE HOWLING wind grew stronger with each passing minute. Caroline had heard people describe the sound of a cyclone as like a freight train passing overhead, and they were right. The sound hurt her ears and she slapped her hands over them in a vain effort to muffle the sound.

To her left, Ryan seemed cool and collected. This was

nothing new to him, but her body was going into preservation mode. The forces of nature were just as diabolical as the forces of the media and public opinion back home. The building creaked and groaned under the lashing of wind and rain. A loud crash sent her heart pounding. Just a tree, Ryan assured her.

The air inside the room was suffocating. Pressing down.

Fighting for air, she bounced to her feet, hands on knees, sucking in gulps of stale air. Fresh air became an obsession as she looked around the dim room. Stumbling, she banged painfully against the wall, sliding her shoulder along as she tried to keep contact with solidness.

"Callie?" his voice was laced with concern.

RYAN JUMPED UP, his eyes accustomed to the dull light so he reached Callie within seconds and pulled her close. She trembled in his arms and he tried to soothe her fear, rubbing a hand gently up and down and across her back, murmuring words he hoped would bring her comfort. His grip on her firmed so that, he hoped, she felt protected in the shelter of his arms, his lips finding the sweet curve of her neck where her pulse fluttered erratically.

His finger lifted her face to his and he sought to distract her with a searing kiss. Shocked into stillness, she whispered something unintelligible before her arms flung around his neck and she returned his kiss. Fear turned to passionate fervour and he moulded her body to his, taking his kisses deeper. The tiny whimper that escaped her lips was all but drowned out by the wind and the pounding of his own heart. Angling his head, he gently sucked her bottom lip into his mouth, then scattered kisses across her cheek. Callie eased away, before burying her face into his shirt, her arms tight around his body.

"You okay now?" He leaned close to her ear so she could hear him above the windstorm beating against the house.

There was a small nod. Time lost meaning as they stood together, holding each other. A loud crash was followed by another. Not being able to see outside made the sounds scarier. The very foundations of the earth vibrated beneath them. Callie burrowed against him and his arms tightened.

CHAPTER NINETEEN

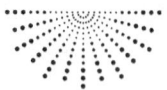

The wind dropped to a whisper. Calm. The Eye. Then it shook them from the other direction. The shudder of the walls increased. Would the house stand, or collapse into nothing more than a pile of firewood?

Finally... it abated. Ryan panned the torch around until the beam fell on the radio, right where it should have been. It crackled to life as he switched it on and he listened intently to the storm information as it came to hand.

"Looks like we just caught the edge of the cyclone," he told Callie. "Seems like it skirted around us to the south and is headed in the direction of Tonga."

"If it's just skirted us, I'd hate to think what a full-on assault would be like."

Heavy rain, a tropical downpour, beat against the roof of the house. Exhaustion demanded they sleep, but the adrenaline rush was still seeping away. Fully clothed, they fell onto the mattresses and lay awake in the dark, listening to the retreating wind and rain.

It was hard for Ryan to sleep, so close to Callie, but he wasn't about to take advantage of her. Even when she rolled over with a little moan and her hand brushed against him.

Lying on his back, fingers linked behind his head, he stared up into the inky darkness. The emotion of the day had taken a toll on both of them, and he couldn't help reliving that scorching kiss they'd shared earlier. It had done its job—to distract her—but had sent his system into overload. He was in danger of his brain short circuiting.

Restless, he turned away from Callie, taking out his frustration on the pillow before finally succumbing to sleep.

THE FIRST THING she noticed when she woke was the quiet stillness. The wind had howled and reverberated for so long she was sure she had suffered some damage to her hearing. This morning, her ears felt like they were stuffed with cotton wool.

Caroline rolled up onto one elbow. The spot beside her was empty and she guessed Ryan was checking on the damage.

Outside, the Fijian sun was back in place, blinding her after the dark interior of the house. Maybe yesterday had been a bad dream and now she was really awake.

Yeah, nah.

Out front, a large palm tree had fallen across the driveway. Debris littered the grass. Palm fronds and other foliage. Some pieces of metal roofing from who knows where. Stepping carefully down the rain-soaked steps, she looked all around. Some trees were leaning at an alarming angle. Others had been stopped from falling completely when they hit other trees.

"Oh no." The tree that she must've heard smash down late yesterday appeared to have glanced off the edge of the storage shed and was now blocking its doorway. There was no sign of Ryan. Maybe he had already gone across to the resort to check the damage there. The house was still intact, on this side at least.

Retracing her steps, she went through to the back of the house. The heavy door was propped open, allowing some much-needed light and air to start circulating into the living area. The two boats were still tied up at the dock. They hadn't sunk or been pushed up onto land, so that was a good sign.

Ryan appeared around the corner of the building, wiping his hands on a rag. The cap on his head had been spun around backwards. As soon as he noticed her standing at the edge of the veranda, a smile lit his face. He jogged the last few metres and leapt up the steps in one bound.

"How's things?" she said.

"All things considered, not too catastrophic… the generator is back up and running… the house has fared well. The storage shed is a bit battered, but it'll survive."

"Have you heard how things are over at the resort?"

"No, not yet. I thought we'd grab something to eat before we head over… we'll have to hike it, though, until I can get a crew back here with a chainsaw. The boats will need a thorough inspection before we can put them into action."

SWEAT TRICKLED down his back and he used the edge of his sleeve to wipe his face as they walked back to the main part of the island, anxious to see what damage had been done. There was no way they could've escaped without experiencing some of the wrath of the cyclone. They walked quietly, both lost in thought, processing events from the night before.

The gardens were the first port of call and Callie's dismayed cry at the flattened plants, debris, and downed trees echoed his own emotions. One of the older huts had collapsed and the pond was an overflowing, muddy mess. The boardwalk was still in one piece, although he'd had visions of the planks peeling off one after the other, like in a cartoon. There was a lot of work ahead of them here, but it was the least of his worries as they continued on the path towards the main building.

The whine of a chainsaw rose on the breeze, and the crack of a felled tree split the air followed by the thump as it hit the ground. A hive of activity greeted them. Workers were carrying branch after branch. Already there was a growing pile of debris on the beach above the high tide line, directly out in front of the reception building.

Sitiveni spotted his boss and hurried over. The two men discussed the clean-up progress as he gave them a tour, pointing out the areas in need of repair.

It was as if the cyclone's edge had touched down on the eastern side of the island. Five of the bures had lost their roofs completely and were in the process of being tarped from the resort's emergency supplies. Another two or three had minor damage. The pool was full of debris. The staff quarters had copped a battering, with damage to several of the units there. The just-repaired clothes lines at the back of the staff quarters were already full of drying linen. A hodgepodge of furniture stood in the sun.

Inside the main dining room, beds on the floor had been neatly made and lined up along one wall. Everyone seemed to have been allocated a place for their gear to be stored. The floor had been swept and freshly mopped. It was eerily quiet here with everyone outside working.

WHILE RYAN and Sitiveni sat and worked out a plan for repairs and rebuilding, Caroline found Rosi and was soon put to work stripping all the bed linen from the bures and putting the soft furnishings out on each of the small verandas. Broken shutters and smashed lights seemed to be the most common damage. There was a growing pile of destroyed bure decor. Bowls, vases, light fittings, mirrors—as well as smashed artwork which Caroline painstakingly rescued.

The clean-up was hot and draining but there was no point complaining. Tokalau had fared well compared to reports that were coming in from other areas around Fiji.

Late afternoon, a crew with chainsaws made it over to the other side of the island to help Ryan clear the toppled trees. A stack of cut timber stood to one side of the track and another next to the storage shed.

Caroline rubbed the back of her gloved hand across her forehead and blew a puff of air at an errant wisp of hair, stifling a groan as she stretched to relieve some of her aches and pains. Most of her body hurt, but she was determined to keep at it until Ryan called time. It was the least she could do for all the weeks of relaxation and rejuvenation she had enjoyed.

The light gradually slipped from the sky and the crew drove away. Ryan looked as shattered as she felt as they trudged towards the house. A lukewarm shower was better than nothing when she doubted others were so lucky. Afterwards, dressed in a clean pair of shorts and a t-shirt, she padded out to the kitchen, a towel wrapped around her wet hair.

Pulling the refrigerator open briefly, she investigated its contents to see if her scrambled brain could figure out something to eat or if she should just call it quits and head for sleep. In the pantry she found a white and pink packet of the ever-present breakfast crackers, so she added a thick smear of the first spread she could find, which turned out to be mango jam, and took her plate to the table with a cup of tea.

Movement out of the corner of her eye caught her attention, but she hardly had the strength to lift her head in acknowledgment.

For his part, Ryan shuffled like an old man and did nothing to hide the yawn that overtook him.

"Thanks for your help today," he muttered as he also investigated the contents of the refrigerator and came to the same conclusion Caroline had, spreading jam on some breakfast crackers and coming to join her. He propped his elbow on the table, cradling his head.

"You guys needed all hands on deck, so it was a no-brainer. Are you happy with what you got done?"

"Yeah, everyone really worked hard. I'm not sure how long it will take to get the roofing materials we need. Everyone will be clamouring for the same stuff."

"Have you heard if there is any offer of international aid on the cards yet?"

"There's talk that the Australian defence force will send one of its big ships, either the *Canberra* or *Adelaide* with their helicopters. They'll have something like six hundred personnel along with tonnes of equipment and supplies for the provinces that were hardest hit."

"I guess your family would be worried about you?"

Ryan nodded. "I managed to get a call through, so they know there's some damage but are just relieved everyone is okay."

The next day, Caroline went with Rosi and some of the others over to the staff quarters, which was in a private area not far from the main resort. Several of the roofs had been tarped here, Rosi's cabin among them. Caroline helped her to clean it out. Because Rosi was one of the longest serving staff members, her quarters were twice the size of many others. There were two bedrooms and a decent-sized living area with a compact kitchen. Most of the decorative hangings had been completely ripped from the walls and there were many rectangular marks where photos should have been.

The two women went in, armed with heavy duty gloves, cleaning supplies and assorted storage containers, and started salvaging what they could.

Debris littered every surface. They picked through the mess before Caroline swept it out to the doorway. Waterlogged cushions were laid out in the sun, along with anything else that had copped a drenching. They cleared the table and pushed it against the wall so they could sort through all the bits and pieces Rosi had collected over her many years working on Tokalau.

While they worked, the older woman told stories of Ryan and his siblings growing up. It touched Caroline to see that Rosi still had a cardboard photo frame made by Ryan when he was maybe four or five, containing a photo of him with a young Rosi. The frame had survived virtually intact, but the same couldn't be said for some of the other photos. Carefully, Caroline rescued the pictures from the smashed frames and put them aside.

They boxed up the surviving kitchenware, then pulled the clothes out of Rosi's cupboards and threw them into canvas bags to be washed. It took a while to clear everything out, to put into storage until the roof and other repairs could be made. The older woman was always softly spoken and despite the circumstances she was still able to laugh. Rosi was stoic and Caroline couldn't help but be drawn to her calmness. Despite the hard work, she enjoyed spending time with her.

~

ONCE REPAIRS on Tokalau were well in hand, Ryan had the staff move on, via boat, to some of the nearby villages. The days started at first light and they were long and arduous. At night they returned to the resort, not wanting to place extra burden on scarce village resources.

He was impressed that Callie worked alongside everyone else and never complained, putting in just as many backbreaking hours.

They cut and hauled away tree debris into piles. Made makeshift repairs to houses, helping clean them out and rescue whatever contents they could.

Everyone was exhausted by the end of each day, but the overwhelming need in some of the areas they visited kept them going back. They couldn't help everyone, but they could make a difference for some villagers.

The regular sound of a Davis Air helicopter reverberated as it made its way back and forth, assisting wherever needed… to rescue people, drop off supplies, or transport building materials. Jake had wasted no time pressing his small fleet into service.

~

AFTER A FEW WEEKS, everyone was ready for a well-deserved break, especially as both Christmas and the New Year had passed by in a bit of a blur. Jake had somehow managed to get extra food supplies flown in for them and there was a celebratory dinner one night at the resort.

Callie was well and truly accepted as part of the team and Ryan made no pretence about hiding their relationship anymore. Most of the staff had figured it out anyway.

He was starting to see a future for him here on the island that included Callie. Hopefully a family was in the mix as well. By all accounts there wasn't much back in Australia for her, and he was planning to ask her to stay on… indefinitely. It was hard to imagine life without her now. The shared looks and stolen kisses made the recovery process easier to cope with.

Callie just had a way of bringing a peaceful calm to his psyche, and he was making plans to whisk her away somewhere for some exclusive one-on-one time.

CHAPTER TWENTY

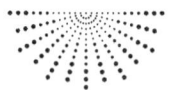

*C*aroline had never been sailing before. *Maiden Fiji* was a sleek wooden boat Ryan and an expat mate from another island had been refurbishing for months. It had escaped damage in the cyclone and Ryan was taking Caroline out for a sail for a couple of days. Some time to themselves.

"Is this how you've spent your days off? Fixing her up?"

"Mostly… this had been a joint venture from the start, and now she gets taken out on chartered trips."

"She's impressive, that's for sure."

Ryan reeled off facts and figures about *Maiden Fiji* that Caroline didn't really understand, and she hoped she responded with enough enthusiasm. It wouldn't match his, though. Before too long she was pressed into service as crew, and hoped she was pulling her weight as Ryan hoisted the sail.

Below deck, Caroline found the galley and where the drinks had been stowed and took a couple of bottles back up to Ryan, unscrewing the lid of his favourite beverage before handing it over.

"Thanks, sweetheart." He winked and kissed her cheek before taking a swig. Ryan urged her to go and relax on the front deck. Reluctantly, she found a spot in front of the cabin. It felt a bit weird at first, by herself, but the warmth of the sun and the cooling breeze lulled her into a pleasant stupor.

After enjoying a pleasant time under sail, they motored around some nearby islands. Dropping anchor, Ryan rowed them ashore for lunch in one of the many picturesque bays that they had all to themselves. There were so many of them, she suspected if they visited a new one every other day they would be busy for several years.

~

IT TOOK Ryan some coaxing before he persuaded Callie to use a rope to swing off the boat into the water.

He whooped and hollered as he sailed out over the water and dropped into the refreshing liquid. Rinse and repeat. Her delighted laugh as she watched just encouraged him to ramp up his antics enough to convince her to have a turn for herself. First up, he took her hand, and they jumped from the side of the boat into the water a couple of times, then she took the rope and stood hesitating for the longest time before she finally mustered the courage to jump. He wasn't sure if the scream was one of delight or edging on terrified, but the grin on her face and thumbs up as she broke the surface told him it was the former.

They swung on the rope about half a dozen times each before Callie called it quits, then he joined her, lying back on deck to dry off. The afternoon sun was drifting slowly to the horizon, taking the temperature reading with it. An unexpected burst of rain sent them scuttling below deck. The shower quickly passed and Ryan emerged to weigh anchor and head for the final port of call where they would spend the night.

When Callie joined him a short time later, his eyes nearly fell out of his head... and he had to remind himself to breathe. The lightweight, loose-knit, pale blue pullover she had donned due to the cooling breeze was slipping off one shoulder—whether by accident or design, he couldn't be sure. For some reason the sight of her in that top and the long flowing white linen pants and bare feet was more alluring than the tankini she had been wearing for most of the day. The thick blonde mane of hair, now dry, tumbled over her shoulders. His fingers itched to thread themselves through her tresses and pull her in as close as he could get her, to taste her sun-kissed skin.

"Ryan?" She hesitated, and he realised he had been staring at her.

"Um, hey. Sorry I was zoned out for a second. Do you want to have a turn at being the skipper?"

"Can I?"

"Sure you can." He beckoned her over and took half a step back so she could slip in front of him and take the wheel.

"What do I do?"

Ryan was more than happy to invoke the classic "guy with his arms around the girl" move on the pretext of helping her. The gentle scent that still permeated her hair tingled his olfactory senses. Struggling to string together enough words to make it sound like he had a clue what he was talking about, his traitorous eyes kept drifting to the tantalising glimpse of silky skin with just a hint of pink across the edge of her bare shoulder.

Where his eyes drifted, his head and lips wanted to follow, and he couldn't decide if he should keep fighting the urge to kiss her or give in and take his chances. Callie at least seemed oblivious to his inner turmoil. When she accidentally brushed against him—or did he accidentally brush against her?—his nerve endings exploded into some sort of demented craziness. By the time they reached their destination he was ready to dive overboard to cool off. Instead, he steeled himself and suggested they enjoy a drink or two along with the sunset.

THEY SAT on the edge of the boat, dangling their legs over the side. Caroline didn't really think she had actually sailed the yacht, but it had been fun to pretend, especially as she enjoyed having Ryan wrap his arms around her and guide her movements as her hands held the wheel. Every one of her senses came alive when his words gently caressed her cheek. The enticing combination of his fresh outdoor scent mingled with the slightest hint of coconut had mocked her determination to restrain herself from turning around and planting a few delicious kisses on his lips, his cheeks and wherever else took her fancy, but she had managed to hold on to her composure… just.

Another boat motored into view as they enjoyed the last remnants of the sun. Her companion frowned at the intrusion when it anchored less than a hundred metres away, off the port side where they were currently sitting.

"It's a free waterway, Ryan. You can't stop other people from using this bay to stop for the night."

There was a significant pause before he answered. "I know. I'm being selfish and wanting to keep this spot just for us."

RYAN FELT guilty about lying to Callie. There was more to it than simply wanting the bay for themselves. He had noticed the boat a couple of times today. While he wasn't about to say they were being followed, there was a sense of unease settling in his midsection. He didn't know if there was any cause for concern yet, so he didn't see the point in alarming Callie unnecessarily. But it was too strong a coincidence to dismiss outright.

Jake had warned him the media were hunting everywhere for Callie. Maybe they had finally figured it out. Or maybe it was his overactive imagination getting the better of him.

He and Callie hadn't flaunted themselves any time they were out and about in Fiji, but they hadn't stayed out of sight either. Anyone at any of the places they had visited while she was at Tokalau could have recognised her and contacted the media. Scrambling to his feet, he waited until Callie put her hand in his and hauled her up beside him. Those soulful eyes locked onto his and he automatically leaned down... oh crap... what was he thinking? The crew on the other boat would have an unobstructed view of them making out if he succumbed.

Forcing himself upright, he blew out a frustrated breath as he looked away from the disappointment etched on her face.

"I hope you're hungry." He tried to distract her and used his body as a barrier to obscure her from the other boat as he steered her below deck.

~

SLIDING INTO THE DINETTE, she watched as Ryan moved easily around the small galley, chatting as he prepared their evening meal. The main cabin area, which Ryan called the saloon, was compact but not as cramped as she had expected.

"Do you get out on this boat much?"

"Nowhere near as much as I would like. It's a working vessel. Sailing for pleasure is a rarity." He glanced over to where she was seated. "I'm usually too busy back on Tokalau to justify time away."

That comment surprised her, given that he had taken her here, there and everywhere in the last few months.

"I should feel honoured that you spend so much time with me, then... it's a wonder you are not in trouble with the rest of the staff for shirking your responsibilities."

The grin on his face said it all. "I've just been learning to delegate a little more. Sitiveni and Rosi have been telling me I need to, for years... I guess I've never had a real incentive up until now... and so I'm learning to work smarter the rest of the time." He flung the tea towel over his shoulder and picked up a plate in each hand, placing them on the table before sliding in next to her.

~

"So, you can have the main bedroom through there," he pointed.

"What about you?"

"The seat here converts to a bed, so I'm all good."

"Okay—if you're sure?" Caroline found her bag and headed to the room. There was no need to use the handheld shower as she had been in the water on and off all day, so she didn't feel like she needed to wash off. And it was only for one night.

A small twelve-volt fan helped circulate the air. The open hatch did little in the way of allowing a breeze in—but thankfully the air didn't feel stale. After pulling on a pair of shorts and a t-shirt, Caroline crawled into bed, kicking the sheet to the end. The day with Ryan had been blissful.

Yawning, she laced her hands behind her head as she lay on her back, going over every detail of the day. The feeling of connectedness with Ryan was growing. It was fair to say she was well on her way to falling in love with the guy. Maybe she was already there. The feelings swirling through every part of her body were something she had never experienced before. Warmth and light flowed in and around her. Happiness seeped into every pore of her being. A feeling of being wanted, cherished… loved.

Was their relationship about to ramp up to another level? She fervently hoped so. In fact, she could probably seek him out now and do something about it herself… but was Ryan interested in more than just a holiday fling? She knew she was after more.

As tempting as it was, she stayed in her cabin until the gentle movement of the boat finally lulled her to sleep.

BREAKFAST WAS a simple meal of cereal and fruit. Earlier, when he had gone up on deck, Ryan had noticed the other boat was still there. Callie told him she was keen for a swim over to the nearby island to explore. If he had his way, he would up anchor and hightail it away from here as soon as possible. But as soon as Callie batted those gorgeous blue eyes at him, his answer was always going to be yes.

Without alerting Callie, he made sure their boat was effectively a shield between them and the other vessel when they dropped into the water off the starboard side. If there was a long lens on board the other boat, he hoped he and Callie would be out of range. There was a rocky outcrop to provide some cover for them, so he used that as the end point in a race for the shoreline. His stroke slowed as he allowed her to pull ahead just a little and he made the race seem closer than it should have been.

To be honest, he wanted to be behind her when she got out of the water in the white bandeau and high waisted bikini that had sent his pulse into overdrive the second she appeared on deck wearing it. Did she have any idea the effect she was having on him in that outfit? The saucy grin she shot him as she waded out was all it took, and he knew the answer.

THEY SLOW-WALKED along the water's edge, comfortable silence wrapping around them. Caroline inhaled deeply. Pulling in the refreshing Fijian air and the tantalising scent that was purely Ryan.

Suddenly he pulled out of her grasp. "Wait here. I'll be back in a sec."

He jogged up the sand to the tree line. Initially confused, her eyes followed him. There was a lone frangipani tree with a handful of blooms. He circled around, and reached up to pluck a flower to bring back and present to her. Pure white with a yellow centre. The smell of these flowers would now forever be associated with this moment, in this place, with this man, and his blue eyes locked on her with adoration.

Carefully, she took the stem and lifted the flower to enjoy the fragrance. Then she pretended to stick it behind her right ear only to swap at the last minute and sweep it behind her left ear. Taken.

Ryan's grin couldn't get any wider if it tried, and he scooped her up in an exuberant hug. Her hands encircled his neck and she tipped her head in for a kiss... or two. Grinning, she walked backwards, tugging him willingly with her, grabbing his hand and lifting it up so she could duck under and have his arm across her shoulder. Her arm wrapped itself tightly around his waist as they walked back the way they had come.

HER LIGHT PLAYFULNESS WAS INTOXICATING. Ryan revelled in the fact she had decided she was in a relationship with him. Happiness bubbled inside his chest from deep down as she twirled around under his arm and landed against his chest. Letting her arm go, he grinned as she laughed with him.

They neared the spot where they had first come ashore and Callie pulled out of his grasp.

"Race you back." She grinned and took off running, the frangipani falling to the ground.

Ryan splashed after her and dived into the water, matching her stroke for stroke as her hair streamed out in the water. She pulled ahead a little and he made a grab for her leg. Callie twisted and tried to fend him off. The water was barely chest-height when she scrambled to her feet, splashing in a vain attempt to keep him at bay. Lunging at her, he wrapped his arms around her as she squealed.

They laughed and mucked around until he managed to pull her up against him. The wet-lashed look did him in. It was time for another kiss. One hand snaked around her in the water and the other slipped up to cradle her face. If she could look at him like that every day he would be a very happy man.

The kiss went straight from light to passionate in a nanosecond. Callie was his everything. The woman he wanted by his side. The taste of her salted lips sent him into a spin.

There was movement. In his peripheral vision. Off in the distance. A thought dropped into his overstimulated brain. The other boat.

His head jerked up just in time to catch a glimpse of what he thought was a very long camera lens.

Ryan swore and in one motion had turned them both around, so his back was to the other boat, pulling Callie up tight up against him and holding her firmly. This was not going to end well.

"Ryan, what's wrong?" Callie pulled back as far as he would let her, to search his eyes.

The frustrated breath he blew out betrayed him. "I think there's a photographer on the other boat... pretty sure there is a long lens trained on us."

The colour drained from her face and the defeated look she had worn when she first arrived at Tokalau was back in place. Panicked gasps of air shook her body and he pulled her in close again, hoping to infuse her with some courage. Closing his eyes, he tried to think of a way out of the mess.

"We will have to make a swim for it. I will be alongside you and hopefully obscure their view. We'll head for the stern— sorry, the back—and climb on there. If I get on board first I can grab something to shield you." Maybe if he splashed enough while he swam it would make it harder to get a clear photo... just until they had the sailboat as a cover.

They set off. For several agonising minutes their boat didn't seem to be getting any closer. They kept swimming.

He clambered aboard, raced below deck, pulled a couple of sheets off the beds and rigged them up where Callie could climb aboard. It was crude but hopefully would do the job. Peering over the side, he spotted her treading water and signalled her. Callie struggled to haul herself back up into the stern of the boat.

Ushering her below deck, he flung a towel around her before throwing a t-shirt on himself. Hurrying around the deck, he made preparations to start the engine and get as far away from the other boat as he could, praying the other vessel wouldn't follow.

So far so good, the other boat didn't appear to be following them—but he decided to take a roundabout route just in case. Lucky he knew this area so well. There were so many islands to hide between and behind. Ryan managed to phone his friend to let him know they would be returning the boat much later in the afternoon.

The anchor splashed down. He hurried to check on Callie, who he had urged to stay below deck.

The main cabin was deserted and he walked through to the stateroom. Callie, still in her swimsuit, was curled up on the bed, facing the wall.

Sitting gingerly near her, he reached a comforting hand over and gently rubbed her back. "Hey, how are you going?"

Her head shook and she wouldn't look at him. His stomach dropped. All he wanted to do was tell her that everything would be just fine, but in truth, he didn't know that. "I think we lost them, for now."

She hadn't moved but he knew she was awake.

"I'm so sorry, Callie… I didn't know if the boat was following us or I was being paranoid."

"You knew?" she accused him hoarsely, rolling over to face him. The tear-streaked face broke his heart. And knowing his carelessness had contributed just added to his guilt. "Why didn't you tell me?"

"Because I wasn't sure and I didn't want you to worry unnecessarily… then… I got distracted."

"This is what I was afraid of… being found," she whispered.

"I know, and I feel bad that I didn't keep you safe like Lloyd asked me to."

Callie's arm crossed over her head as she stared unseeingly at the roof above.

"As soon as we get back, I'll contact him and see what he wants us to do next."

"I guess we will have to wait and see what the fallout is first." She propped herself up on her elbows. "Where are we, anyway?"

"Just hiding out, north of Yanuya Island, not that I expect you would know where that is. It's about ten nautical miles from where we started yesterday… a bit over twenty kilometres. I'm hoping the other boat gave up and went back to Denerau."

Gulping back tears, she held her hands over her face.

"The coast is clear for now. Would you like to come back up on deck?" The shoulder shrug of uncertainty was all the response he got. "Okay, I'm going to get us something to eat. I know you probably don't feel like anything but there will be food available if you change your mind."

Padding around, he fixed some sandwiches, set a couple of bottles of juice on the small table and sat despondently. The food was tasteless. They had shared such a beautiful moment together —just to have it cruelly snatched away. Now, he didn't think she liked him very much because he had let her down. Dropping his head onto his propped hand, he sighed in frustration. A warm hand touched his arm, as Callie slid in next to him and picked at the plate of food he had put out in the hope that she would join him.

"Just so you know, I don't blame you. I'm still in shock… I had almost forgotten I was a person of interest… back home. Being in Fiji has been just what I needed, without even knowing what it was I actually needed… and you… you have been a gift…" Callie was talking to her plate of food, pulling little bits of bread off and dropping them next to the plate. "This time with you has taken my breath away… for good and unfortunately not so good."

Ryan just sat and let her pour out the emotion she was struggling to contain.

"I don't know what's on the cards now… and I feel like the last few months has been a dream and I'm about to wake up and still be stuck in the middle of the whole Sommerfield fiasco."

"Except you are forgetting you have someone prepared to stand by you. We'll get through this… together… whatever it turns out to be."

Her hand reached over and squeezed his. "Thanks, but you might want to find out what sort of mess you would be stepping into before you sign up."

"Doesn't matter. If it affects you, it affects me. We are a team now." Closing the gap between them, he brushed his lips her forehead.

CAROLINE DASHED AWAY TEARS. Having someone, Ryan, offering to support her through this next phase of whatever it was going to be was… more than she dreamed of. But she wasn't sure she could allow him to sacrifice the time and energy and privacy which would be inevitable if he was with her. All she could manage was a wobbly smile as he took his plate to the small sink and headed upstairs.

The boat got under way again. Caroline needed fresh air… and Ryan. The miserable pile on her plate that used to be a sandwich held little appeal and she tossed the contents into the bin.

Grabbing a dress, she pulled it on and made her way to where Ryan was standing at the helm. Wrapping her hands around his waist, she leaned in against his back, just to feel the solidness of his presence.

"Hey, come here." He beckoned and she slid around in front of him and he pulled her back against his chest. One arm holding her securely and the other on the wheel.

CHAPTER TWENTY-ONE

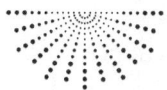

*B*y the time they arrived back on Tokalau, Ryan had decided calling his godfather could wait until the morning.

Callie curled up next to him on the lounge at the house and they watched a movie until she fell asleep.

The first call came early the next morning. From Jake. Ryan took the call as far away from Callie's bedroom as possible, so he didn't disturb her.

"Just giving you a heads-up. You and Callie are all over the front of the papers this morning."

"Yeah, we expected as much."

"What were you thinking, making out in public like that?"

"To be fair, we weren't exactly out in public. There was only one other boat around… it just so happened there was a photographer on board." He paused before asking, "How bad is it?"

"Well, at the moment you are the mystery man and admittedly they don't have an exact whereabouts."

"Yeah, I think we gave them the slip."

"But as soon as someone identifies you, it'll be game on."

"I know, but I'm not sure what we can do about it."

"Matisse wants to know how Callie is going?"

"Not great, to be honest."

"Well, give her our love and let us know if you think of anything we can do from this end to help."

While Ryan was grateful for his friend's offer, at the moment they were flying blind.

He'd hardly got off the satellite phone when it rang again.

His parents.

And his father didn't waste time with pleasantries.

"Is that you by any chance splashed over the front of the papers in a passionate lip lock with that Sommerfield girl? One of your mother's friends rang to find out what was going on, but of course it was the first we had heard of it. Had to go and buy a paper to see it for ourselves. A bit of warning would have been appreciated."

Ryan rolled his eyes, trying to stay calm.

"Okay, Dad, I'm sorry you didn't hear it from me first. We met a few months ago when she came to Tokalau. Because of the nature of the media interest in her, we were being discreet, but unfortunately we got caught out."

"I suppose this was all Lloyd's doing that she is even there in the first place?"

"Well, he is her lawyer and she needed to lie low for a bit, so of course he sent her my way. It's not unheard-of for him to do that, remember."

"You should have stayed away, son. It will be nothing but trouble."

"I'm well aware of the trauma that has been heaped on her over the last couple of years. But apart from all that crap, Callie is really someone special, and she has come to mean a great deal to me… so I would appreciate it if you kept your narrow, uninformed view of her to yourself."

There was a harrumphing noise on the other end of the line.

"Dad, she is nothing like what the media have made her out to be."

"Well, if you are sure…" He obviously wasn't convinced.

"You are just going to have to trust me on this and reserve your opinion until you have spent time with her in person. I'm hoping she will agree to become a permanent part of our family."

"That serious, huh?"

"Yes, that serious. Once you get to know her, you will fall in love with her as I have..."

"Caroline Hammond—man, you must be crazy!" This from one of his brothers. As he expected, there was a continuous stream of calls from his siblings, concerned for his wellbeing because he had taken up with the infamous leader of the Sommerfield Seven.

About now, he was wishing they weren't such a tight-knit family. He knew they meant well, but man, they had all been sucked in by the media hype. It was starting to rile him, but he knew that wouldn't achieve anything.

It just strengthened his resolve to stand by Callie from here on in. She needed someone else in her corner.

CAROLINE PADDED out into the living area. There was no sign of Ryan... but then she saw him outside on the phone. While she couldn't hear what was being said, the wild gesticulations on his part gave her some clues. Watching on, she saw him shake his head as he finished the call, looking at the phone in frustration. Turning back, he headed inside, the scowl changing to a smile when he saw her.

"Good morning, gorgeous." He dropped a chaste kiss on her cheek and continued on to put the phone back in its cradle.

"Hey, you okay?"

"What? Oh, yeah... the photos have hit the fan back in Oz, so I've had a few phone calls... family members expressing their 'concerns' about me being photographed with you... to put it mildly."

Her heart dropped, along with her head. "I'm so sorry you got caught up in all this."

"Hey now, don't you worry about it. I'm up for the challenge. So far I've not been named, but I'm sure it's only a matter of time." By now he was standing in front of her.

"Callie, look at me." His fingers lifted her head. "Whatever happens, we are in this together, okay?"

When she nodded, he pulled her in against his chest. It was easy to believe from inside the circle of his arms that everything would be okay, but it was hard to see how.

"Jake called. He and Matisse send their love and they will do whatever they can to help."

The phone rang again and they both turned in its direction.

"I'm guessing that might be Lloyd, I haven't had a chance to make contact with him yet."

RYAN'S HUNCH proved correct and he greeted his godfather while walking outside with the phone.

"I suppose you've seen the papers."

"I have. I figured you two might get along, Alistair, but... not quite that well."

"Yeah, well... not going to apologise. So, you were doing a bit of matchmaking were you?"

"Yes and no. I could've sent her someplace else until things died down, but then I thought you might actually be good for each other."

"Then I guess I should be thanking you for being so perceptive. Callie is something else."

Lloyd's chuckle echoed down the line. "That she is."

Tokalau still wasn't ready to welcome tourists back, but every day was a step closer. They had fared better than many places. Bookings were still strong and they were able to reassure most potential guests that they would soon re-open for business.

Tui caught his attention two days later. A boat nearby seemed to be headed for their dock. Day trippers were unheard of at Tokalau as it was a privately-owned resort, but this didn't seem to be worrying whoever was on the vessel. Ryan had already briefed the staff, giving an abbreviated version of what had been going on, so everyone was on the lookout for anything out of the ordinary.

Tui and Sitiveni went to investigate. Ryan thought it prudent to stay out of sight. Someone, somewhere must have identified him from the earlier photos. There was a lot of arguing going on, that much he could tell. The crew seemed to be Fijian and there were a couple of westerners with them. Reporters? Maybe. It just seemed rather odd for a boat to suddenly turn up out of the blue. The boat left the dock and sped back the way it had come. Tui was shaking his head as he walked back with Sitiveni to find Ryan.

"They were looking for you and Miss Callie, boss," Tui told him. "We told them you weren't here, but they weren't convinced. We got rid of them for the time being, but I don't think they will give up that easily."

It was getting late in the afternoon and Caroline was planning to take advantage of a cooling breeze to sit in the hammock out the back of Ryan's house where she could enjoy the view at the same time. About to swing herself into the hammock, she heard the sound of a boat engine. On this side of Tokalau it was highly unusual. She automatically went on high alert, changed direction, and scurried back inside the house.

There was a pair of binoculars on the coffee table and she

snatched them up and focused them on the boat. Sure enough, there was a guy out the front with a humongous lens on his camera, scanning the shoreline. Lifting the camera to his eye he aimed towards the house. Caroline gasped and jumped back. Had she been seen? How close would they dare come to the dock where *Shaw Thing* was tied up? Another man joined him at the bow as the boat slowed alongside the waterfront.

"Hey, Callie," Ryan said as he walked in. She desperately signalled him to be quiet.

"What's wrong," he asked walking over to her.

"Visitors." She gestured.

"Oh crap."

OVER THE NEXT FEW DAYS, a cat and mouse game ensued. At all hours of the day, a boat would cruise around the island. The boats changed in shape and size but the same two men on board gave them away every time.

The absolute last straw came when she and Ryan were out in the garden early one morning. It should have been a safe place, but the irritating high-pitched sound of a drone made them realise it wasn't. Ducking for cover, they huddled together. The noise had attracted Sitiveni working nearby. The drone operator made the fatal mistake of coming in low and the Fijian swatted it like a giant mosquito. It crashed to the ground and he used a shovel to finish it off.

CAROLINE SOBBED, tears obscuring her vision and running freely down her face and onto her clothes as she tried to pack her suitcase. She was done. They were going to win.

Island life here had been disrupted for far too long and the only way the others would get any respite was if she left the island. It would break her heart to do it but there was no other option.

Ryan and Tui and the others didn't need to be looking over their shoulder the whole time. They had all gone above and beyond for her, but enough was enough. She cared about them too much. It was time to go back and face the media storm and get it over and done with. Maybe if she gave them what they wanted, did an interview or something, they would leave her alone. She could pick up the scraps of her life and move to some other isolated part of the world where she wouldn't be recognised and harassed.

"What are you doing, Callie?" Concern laced Ryan's voice.

Thankfully, her back was towards the door. In the three steps it took him to cross to where she was standing, she wiped her eyes and tried to settle her emotions. "What does it look like, Ryan? I'm leaving Tokalau."

"But I don't understand."

Exactly, she thought to herself. *There is no way you could understand.* "It's clear that the media are not going to rest until they get the photos… and whatever else they want. Everything and everyone on Tokalau is compromised while I am here. So I'm leaving you guys in peace."

"No." His vehement response caused her to snap her head up… briefly… and then she went back to her task.

"It's for the best, Ryan."

"But what about us? I thought we had something worth pursuing."

Caroline paused, struggling to keep herself together. The shrug she gave was half-hearted.

"I don't want you to leave, Callie."

"Just think of it as a holiday romance that has run its course… and we can both move on."

"I'm not going to give up on us so easily, Cal… I want you by my side."

"Don't make this harder than it needs to be, Ry."

Turning, he threw his hands in the air, frustrated, pacing around the bedroom. "I have enough contacts in Fiji that you could move from place to place…"

"Living on the run is not the way to go, Ryan. I'd be by myself a lot… I know how hard you work. I might as well be back in Australia as here."

"What are your plans then?"

"To be honest, I'm not sure… Lloyd will pick me up from the airport and we can decide from there how to deal with it."

EARLY IN THE MORNING, Ryan stowed her luggage in the back of the buggy and drove her to meet Tui at the main dock.

It looked like everyone was there, dressed in their brightly coloured clothes to see her off.

Sitiveni grabbed her gear and took it down to the boat. Then the singing began.

Isa Isa vulagi lasa dina. Nomu lako au na rarawa kina.

The harmonies of the traditional farewell song touched her so deeply. Caroline had fallen in love with this island and the people who worked here, and she had no idea if she would ever make it back. By the time the singers reached the echoed words of *Isa Lei*, Caroline was emotionally wrecked, rubbing at the goosebumps on her arms.

At song's end, Rosi pulled her into a fierce hug. "I will pray for you, Miss Callie."

"Thank you for your kindness, Rosi. I will never forget you." Caroline's voice broke and she hurried to the end of the dock. Ryan handed her into the boat and untied the mooring lines before stepping in himself.

Choking back tears, Caroline returned the farewell gestures of the Fijians until the boat rounded the edge of the island and disappeared from sight, then slumped into the nearest seat. She was vaguely aware of Ryan and Tui talking together at the helm, but she was in a numb daze.

Her heart and head were at war. Her heart was begging her to go back to Tokalau and her head insisted leaving was the right thing to do.

CHAPTER TWENTY-TWO

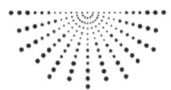

*T*he boat berthed at Denerau marina. Caroline stood on the dock waiting for her luggage to be offloaded. Tui handed up the bags to Ryan who set them down.

"What? Wait a minute." She was confused. "There's an extra bag," she said, pointing. "That one is not mine."

"It's mine," Ryan answered, turning back to farewell Tui. The two men back-slapped each other and Ryan's colleague wandered off in the direction of the cafes.

"I don't understand."

"I'm coming with you."

"No, I can't let you do that."

"Too bad, I'm coming whether you like it or not."

"What about the resort?"

"They can manage in the short term and my parents will go and cover for me if need be."

Caroline tugged at his arm until he stopped and turned to her. "You have no idea what you will be getting into."

Ryan just shrugged and kept walking.

~

ONCE THEY HAD CHECKED in and made their way through customs, Ryan steered Callie to a seat in the departure lounge. She'd hardly said a word to him since they left the marina. Was she angry with him or just overwhelmed at what might lie ahead? Maybe a bit of both, but he was determined to help in any way he could. Lloyd had given him an idea what might be on the cards. It was daunting, but Callie needed him, even if she wouldn't acknowledge it yet.

Glancing up, Ryan noticed a guy in the next row of seats over, facing them.

Was he imagining it, or was the man checking them out? No, it had to be his overactive imagination, surely?

Ryan kept casting his eyes over. When people came and sat opposite, obscuring his view, Ryan pretended to stand and stretch, shifting enough to catch a glimpse of the stranger, who was now on his phone.

A trickle of unease slid down his spine. The stranger wandered around the seating area as if he was looking for a place to talk out of earshot of the other passengers.

STACKING THEIR SUITCASES ONTO A TROLLEY, Ryan lined up with Callie. Lloyd, out in the arrival lounge, had already warned them it wasn't going to be pretty. Every news channel had sent a camera crew to the airport to cover Callie's arrival back into Australia. Someone had leaked her return to the media.

While he had no definitive proof, the guy who had been eyeing them off at the airport was the likely source. On the plane, the man had walked the aisle as if he was looking for someone. He barely glanced their way. Maybe he was just stretching or headed for the toilet at the rear of the cabin. But Ryan doubted it.

Callie shrank into herself as they made their way to the door. "It's okay, Cal, you've got this." Ryan's tone was calm and measured. "I'm right here and I'm not going anywhere. Lloyd will meet us on the other side. You don't have to say anything. Hang on to me, okay."

She nodded mutely, grabbing onto his shirt for dear life, sucking in a jagged breath just before the sliding door opened. The barrage was instant—microphones shoved in their faces, questions flying at them. He felt Callie sidle up as close as she could to him, head down, her loose hair obscuring her face. Lloyd came alongside Callie without a word as they tried to make their way out to the waiting car. The media scrambled alongside like a wake of vultures. Lloyd wrenched the back door open for Callie, who stumbled as she got in and slid to the middle. The two men threw the luggage into the boot.

"No comment. No comment," they chanted over and over.

Ryan climbed in next to Callie and grabbed her shaking hand. She stared straight ahead and Ryan could tell she was struggling to keep it together as the cameras crowded the windows on both sides of the car. As soon as they left the airport precinct, Ryan put his arm around Callie and pulled her trembling body against his.

Jayne Miller, Lloyd's wife, was on hand at the house when they arrived and pulled Caroline into a hug. Caroline sagged against her.

"Oh Caroline, was it bad?"

Caroline nodded, wiping at her face with the back of her hand.

"Let's just get you set up in your room." Jayne turned to the man by her side.

"Ryan, honey, it's so good to see you again. I just wish it was under happier circumstances." She pulled him into a hug and kissed his cheek.

Caroline ran on autopilot. Up to her room to shower and

change. There was no chance of sleep as her thoughts ran ragged in her head. Why had she come back to Brisbane?

Every media outlet would be desperate to get *the* exclusive interview, but could any of them be trusted not to do a hatchet job?

~

THE MILLERS HAD HOSTED Ryan's family many times over the years. Today was a casual barbecue with his parents, who were en route to Fiji because Ryan wasn't sure when he would get back to Tokalau.

Tugging Callie's hand, he pulled her to his side and wrapped her in a hug. She grabbed onto him. There was a cooling summer breeze this afternoon in Brisbane, and Callie was wearing a three-quarter sleeve, loose, navy, boho-style blouse with pale blue stonewashed jeans. The navy blue made her eyes seem so much more vivid and even though she was nervous, he could still lose himself in their depths.

"Don't look so worried. Everything will be fine, you'll see." He dropped a kiss on the end of her nose and took her hand firmly in his.

~

OF COURSE SHE WAS NERVOUS. It wasn't quite taking her home to meet the parents, but it was close enough. Lloyd and Jayne were in her corner, but it remained to be seen if Ryan's parents would join them there. And as if that wasn't enough to deal with, two of his siblings and their families would be coming along as well.

Had they already judged her based on what had been reported in the press? Caroline was grateful Ryan had gotten to know her before he found out what the media had to say. He had been steadfast, but if his family thought otherwise, would they pressure him to end their relationship?

~

"DAD, MUM, THIS IS CALLIE." His arm around her waist held her easily against his side. "Callie, these are my parents, Ross and Joana Shaw."

The three of them regarded each other for what seemed a long time, but in reality it was probably just a couple of seconds, before Ross reached out to shake her hand and leaned in for a quick peck on the cheek.

"Hi Callie. Nice to meet you rather than just hear Ryan sing your praises over the phone."

Caroline's face flushed under the older man's assessment. Joana followed his lead and gave Caroline a quick hug. "How are you holding up? I imagine coming back hasn't been easy."

Ryan was glued to Callie's side, not letting her face his parents alone, and making it clear they were a couple now—whether the others liked it or not. Lloyd and Jayne were effusive in their praise of Callie. Ryan's thumb made strokes back and forth on the back of her hand, and he hoped the motion would soothe her taut nerves. She had barely started to relax when his oldest sister arrived with her family in tow.

"Ry, good to see you, little brother." His sister pulled him into a hug, whispering in his ear, "I'm going to give her the benefit of the doubt, for the time being." She turned her attention to Ryan's side. "You must be Caroline... I'm Kalesi, the oldest in the family."

"Kalesi... isn't that a Fijian name?" Callie asked.

"Yes, and so are the names of our sisters... Mereana and Laisa. The boys got the regular names... Alistair, Declan, Mitchell... and Brock." She indicated the younger version of Ryan who had just arrived.

The brothers did the whole man-hug, back-slap thing and

Ryan leaned down to side hug Brock's wife, and kiss her cheek. "Hey, Niah, how's it going? You keeping this guy in line?" He tilted his head in his brother's direction.

"I do what I can," she replied good-naturedly as a small person tugged at her skirt.

Swooping down, Ryan scooped up his niece. "Woah, Miss Tesha, where have you been, I've missed you heaps."

The five-year-old laughed. "Uncle Ry, we just visited you at Easter."

"But that was forever ago, and you've grown so much you are almost as tall as me." Tesha squealed as he tipped her upside down and swung her by her legs.

∾

IT WARMED Caroline's heart to see Ryan interacting with his nieces and nephews. It looked like he was the 'funcle'—the fun uncle. Tesha had an older sister. There were three other cousins who all seemed to adore Uncle Ry and it seemed mutual.

Niah was very welcoming, and she and Caroline were chatting away like old friends in no time. Kalesi was more reserved, as if she was sizing up Caroline to see if she passed whatever criteria she had set for Caroline to date Ryan. The family were just looking out for him and that was understandable.

∾

NIAH HAD EASILY GIVEN Callie the tick of approval, but the rest of the family seemed to be reserving judgment, Ryan thought to himself later that night.

Tacit approval was better than nothing. He hoped they would come around, in time.

CHAPTER TWENTY-THREE

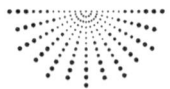

"*Y*our sisters have been in touch with me via their solicitor," Lloyd told Caroline after he called both of them into his study. "It seems your father has late Stage Four liver cancer and has been admitted to a hospice in Melbourne. Your sisters thought you should know, in case you wanted to visit him."

Caroline shook her head. It was her father, and she knew she should feel some compassion and try to see him before... well, before he passed away, but...

"I think you should make the effort, Callie." Ryan laid a hand on her shoulder as she sat stiffly in the chair across the desk from her lawyer and friend.

He was right, but at the same time he had no right to interfere with her family life. The scant details she had given him in no way painted an accurate picture of her father and what she had gone through in the last two years.

It would be a long way back to any sort of relationship with her father.

~

OVER THE NEXT WEEK, Caroline wrestled with Ryan's words. Should she visit her father? Could she cope? Would he even want to see her?

Her sisters had made contact. If not for her father, maybe she should do it for her two younger siblings.

In the end, Ryan organised flights and accommodation for them both. There was no way to talk him out of coming with her. To be honest, she felt relieved that he would be with her.

"WELL, that went about as well as I expected," Callie told him as they exited the hospice building a few days later.

"I'm so sorry, Cal. You tried and that's the main thing. It would have played on your mind if you hadn't."

"I don't think so... but at least my sisters are talking to me again, so that's a positive."

Eleanor and Tania had apologised for keeping their distance and not being there for Callie when she needed them.

Family should stick together, but this one had fallen apart. Maybe there was still time to mend bridges.

RYAN SUGGESTED they stop at a cafe for coffee and a bite to eat. It turned out to be a mistake.

A couple of the customers recognised Callie, took exception to her being in the same space as them, and were very vocal about it. The language that came out of one woman's mouth as she stabbed her finger inches away from Callie's chest was, in a word, disgusting.

Ryan couldn't understand why the woman was lashing out. Sure, Rex Sommers was charismatic and everything he touched business-wise seemed to turn to gold—but that didn't mean the man was above reproach.

There still seemed to be a slice of the community convinced the man was innocent and the seven women had fabricated their accusations for the attention, and possibly monetary compensation. He was pretty sure there were better ways to get noticed than to make false accusations against someone like Rex Sommers. The legal process had taken a huge toll on Callie and he knew she'd had no idea what would unfold when she decided to blow the whistle on her boss. He imagined it was the same for the other women in the group.

Ryan reached out to grab the woman's hand and push it aside, but she turned on Ryan then, calling him all sorts of names for daring to associate with one of the reviled Sommerfield Seven.

It was hard to stay calm when he could see how devastated Callie was, as if Callie was solely to blame for Rex Sommers' imprisonment—no matter that the jury had found him guilty. This woman would not accept that he had been convicted in a court of law.

The other cafe customers were watching the drama unfold. Some were filming on their phones and would no doubt share the footage on social media. He wanted to rage at them and smash their phones, but that would only attract more attention and Callie didn't need him to lose it in public.

Amid the scuffle, Ryan pulled Callie to her feet, shielding her as best he could from the onslaught. The enraged woman lashed out and Ryan blocked her attack with his free arm. One of the wait staff and a couple of male patrons managed to restrain the woman until police arrived. Callie did not want to press charges and he had to respect her wishes.

THE MANAGER APOLOGISED PROFUSELY, but all Callie wanted was to get out of the place. She ducked her head, trying to make herself invisible as they left the cafe. There were people lined up against the window, peering in at the side show.

~

PUSHING PAST, Ryan wrapped his arm around Callie and hustled her away. An older, well-dressed woman stood in the way. Ryan tried to steer Callie around her, but the woman stopped them. He felt Callie stiffen and braced himself for more vitriol.

"Ms Hammond, I just wanted to thank you for doing the right thing. No matter what just happened in there, you need to know that there are many more people around the country who applaud your courage. Not everyone believes what is in the mainstream media. We can think for ourselves. You keep your chin up, you hear." The businesswoman walked by and crossed to the other side of the street.

Callie was shaking and he hurried to get her to the relative safety of the hire car.

The cafe outburst had shocked him. Was this what she had been dealing with? Alone? As he escorted her to her hotel room, it hurt to see her shattered.

Covering her face with her hands she turned away from him, but there was no way he would abandon her now. Pulling her into his arms, he held her. Tried to soothe her. Initially, she sank into him. He kissed the top of her head and rubbed his hand across her back.

Then, it was if she had fortified herself and she pulled away from him.

"I can't put you through this every time we go out together. It would be best if you just went back to Fiji and forgot about me. You don't deserve the hatred splashing over onto you because you are with me."

"Callie, you are not getting rid of me that easily. Yes, it was uncomfortable, but you don't have to face this alone. I want to help you get through this."

"Please, Ryan," she pleaded, taking a step back, her hands out as if to stop him. "Don't make this harder than it already is."

"You can't chase me off, Cal. I'm here for the long haul." He took a step forward, expecting her to back away. But she didn't. Taking her hands, he pulled her into his arms and kissed her. Maybe his actions would convince her. Pouring all of the passion he felt into the embrace, he drew her closer.

In a moment, her passivity snapped and she returned his kiss, fiercely, deeply, as if she was starving and she needed to get her strength and sustenance from him for whatever lay ahead. Matching her kiss for kiss, he realised he wanted her for now and for always. They could weather this rough patch and move on to a better life. Together. Her name flew from his lips as he pulled her as close as he could manage. He felt his shirt being tugged from the waistband of his trousers.

He wanted her, but not like this, when she was vulnerable and hurting. It took all of his willpower to put her aside.

Her eyes had fluttered closed and her extremely-kissed lips were inviting him back for more. Running his thumb across the pink marks on her skin where his face had scraped hers, he sighed and kissed the spots tenderly and pulled her against his chest.

He hardly recognised his voice. "You try and rest for a bit… and we can catch up later for dinner if you are up to it. I'll let Lloyd know what went down so he's not caught by surprise, and we can go from there and hopefully figure out our next move." Placing a finger under her chin, he lifted her face to his. "Will you be okay?"

There was a small nod, but then she shrugged her shoulders and put some distance between them, crossing her arms and rubbing her hands over them as if she was trying to erase the ugly cafe scene.

They both hesitated, unsure. Ryan cast one last look at her before leaving her room.

~

CAROLINE STAGGERED ACROSS THE ROOM, collapsing onto the bed. The jolt of hitting the mattress unblocked her emotional reservoir and sobs wracked her body. Hailstones of emotion pummelled her as she gave herself permission to give way to the stress and the hurt. The shock and disbelief.

Her father. Her sisters. Rex Sommerfield. The other whistle blowers. Her lawyer. The media circus. The cafe. The business-woman. Ryan.

Every thought was like crashing down a set of rapids in a leaky kayak. When she thought of Ryan, it was like she had reached a section of calm water before the next set of white water hit. She was white-knuckling it all the way, praying she would reach the safety of the bank before she capsized.

Finally, Caroline succumbed to an exhausted sleep.

~

CAROLINE COULDN'T EXPLAIN IT—BUT when she woke up a couple of hours later, she felt... not better, exactly, but different. A seed of determination was starting to germinate. Her story, for better or worse, needed to be told.

"Are you sure you want to go through with this?" Lloyd asked on a conference call with her and Ryan after dinner.

"Yes. I need a chance to explain myself. To set the record straight. There's so much rumour and innuendo flying around."

"You could just be setting yourself up for more anguish," Ryan added.

"I know that, but it's something I think I need to do, to try and settle myself. People will perceive it however they will, and I can't control that. It's for my benefit... to have my say, to have it on record… not to convince the public that what I did was right."

"Okay, well, there's been a number of different shows that have been in contact."

"Let's do this."

Lloyd set up the interview. It would take place in Sydney. And Ryan would be there for support.

CHAPTER TWENTY-FOUR

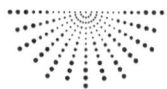

*C*aroline stood at the graveside flanked by her sisters, arms around each other. She was there to support Eleanor and Tania, not out of respect for her father. There had been no deathbed reconciliation as she had hoped. That was obviously only something for the movies.

The harsh words that had been flung at her still cut deeply. Still, for better or worse he had been her father, and her younger siblings were feeling the loss more keenly.

Her own eyes were dry, and she stared at the coffin as it made its slow descent into the ground. The celebrant said his final words and it was over.

Hugging each of her sisters in turn, with a promise to catch up, she walked away from the small group of mourners, Ryan by her side as he had been since they left Fiji.

Reaching out, he took her hand and held it firmly. The crisp Melbourne breeze swept around them, as if the city was keen to bypass early autumn and move straight on to winter, and she pulled her coat tighter. Lloyd and Jayne fell in beside them and Jayne took her other hand and squeezed it reassuringly. It was a sombre procession to where the hire car was waiting. A gaggle of reporters were being kept at bay by police, just outside the cemetery gates.

After saying goodbye to her lawyer, who was more of a father to her than her own had been, Caroline and Ryan were whisked away by Jake and his helicopter, to take them back to visit with his family at Cape Otway.

THE REMOTE LOCATION was just what she needed. There was a bench seat not far from the clifftop house, and that was the spot she gravitated to, more than anywhere else. The wild untamed expanse of the Southern Ocean was so different from the blue waters around Tokalau, but no less stunning.

Slowly, she was clawing back some equilibrium. Spending time with Matisse and the kids was like soothing gel on a nasty sunburn. Jake's extended family had embraced her as one of their own, and she enjoyed spending time with them at his parents' nearby property. In particular, Claire Davis, Jake's mother, had been a God-send to help her process her thoughts and feelings, and was instrumental in helping Caroline find some sense of perspective.

EVERY DAY, Ryan could see a little more light in Callie's eyes. Slowly, she was returning to him. The aired interview didn't really change public opinion. People still either supported Callie or they didn't. But she was satisfied with the end result, and that was all that mattered.

Even though he was desperate to get back to Fiji, he was determined to wait until Callie could return with him. His parents were happy to hold the fort, but they weren't getting any younger and the job wasn't getting any easier.

Jake and Matisse were gracious hosts and they all enjoyed

one another's company. The two men worked on several projects together related to the Tokalau resort, and conference-called his parents regularly to check in. His parents also had regular Face-Time chats with Ryan and Callie and they were steadily building a relationship.

CAROLINE FELT she was finally ready to start on the next part of her life. The last few chapters had been incredibly hard going, and she was hoping what was ahead might make up for it. Her country of birth was losing its hold on her. There was not a lot to keep her in Australia. Who knew if she would ever be able to fully escape the Sommerfield Seven tag and live a regular life?

Was it too much to hope for, to go back to Fiji and become part of Ryan's world? Having someone to share her life with. Who didn't blink an eye at her history of bringing down one of the biggest high-flyers in the country.

LEO AND SIENNA were visiting their grandparents for the day. Matisse was busy painting in her studio. Caroline liked to just sit in the room while her friend worked, reading, or even trying her hand at some amateurish painting.

Light streamed through the large picture windows and the ocean view was even more stunning from this level. It was easily one of Caroline's favourite rooms in this house. There was a bookshelf along part of one wall and a bank of storage racks filled with blank canvases. A large table was crammed with all manner of paints and brushes and other artistic supplies. Several easels held work in various stages of completion. Currently, Matisse was hidden behind an enormous canvas.

Caroline made them some lunch which she placed on a small table at the far end of the room. It was a few minutes before Matisse joined her, wiping her hands on a cloth hanging from the side of the easel.

"Where did you say Ryan got to, again?" Caroline asked Matisse, not having seen either of the men today.

"Jake was wanting some help with a project down at the cabin. Rewiring some lights, I think." The cabin was where Matisse first lived when she arrived in the Otway area.

The two women chatted for a while before Matisse drifted back to her work-in-progress. Caroline followed her to check out the commissioned piece destined for an office foyer in Melbourne.

IT WAS late afternoon by the time Matisse called it quits. She and Jake had planned a family dinner at his parents' house. Caroline and Ryan had been invited but had decided to have a night to themselves.

"You haven't been down to the cabin yet. How about we meet the guys down there?" Matisse suggested.

"Sounds like a plan."

The track to the cabin was a little rough in places and Caroline grabbed the handle above the door of the four wheel drive to steady herself. Matisse pulled alongside Jake's dual-cab ute. He was already walking down the front steps towards them, and kissed his wife through the open driver's window.

"You ready to go now?" Jake said.

"Yeah, in a minute. I thought Callie would like to see the cabin."

"Sure, you can head in now if you like, Cal. Ryan's finishing up. I just need to speak to the missus for a sec."

Caroline slid out of her seat, sure Jake's words were code for "I haven't seen my wife all day and I'm desperate to make out with her."

Pushing the cabin door open, she saw tea-lights glowing in

jars dotted all around the room. A table covered with a white cloth and set for two stood in front of a large window. Fairy lights had been strung outside along the veranda rail and from the gutter. Beyond the cabin, there were more lights crisscrossing between the trees. Magical.

Caroline vaguely noticed the sound of a car driving away from the cabin but she hardly paid any attention. Soft music started playing and she turned towards the sound.

Ryan walked over and held out a hand to her. "Dance with me?"

Nodding, she let him pull her into his arms, and started to sway to the music with him. "So, is this what you were doing with Jake all day?"

"Mm-hmm—you like it?"

"It's gorgeous. You've gone to a lot of trouble."

"You are more than worth it, sweetheart."

His grey, oh-so-soft knit sweater begged for her to snuggle up against his chest. The collar of his white button down peeped out of the neckline and the bottom of the untucked shirt stood out against the blue jeans he wore. The man was a walking advertisement for *Men of Australia* magazine, all the way down to his tan lace-ups. They danced through three or four songs before Ryan led her to the table and pulled out a chair for her. Shaking out the napkin, he placed it on her lap and disappeared into the kitchen.

A three-course meal was produced. Caroline wasn't sure if it was all Ryan's handiwork, but at this particular moment she didn't care, except that every mouthful was delicious. Roasted pumpkin soup followed by marinated lamb and vegetables, and a chocolate brownie dessert complete with raspberries and cream. They toasted each other with an Edenvale Pinot Noir. Caroline appreciated that he respected her preference for non-alcoholic drinks.

Hands down, this was the best meal she had shared with Ryan. With anyone, come to think of it.

The heated looks he sent her way were spellbinding and sent her circulatory system into overdrive. His thumb traced delicious circles over the back of her hand.

"Come outside, I want to show you the cabin from there." He pulled her gently to her feet.

"What about the dishes?"

"They can wait."

The night air quickly cooled her body and Ryan pulled her close, comforting her with his body heat.

Once they reached the light-festooned trees, she turned to take in the warm glow from the illuminated building.

"Wow," she breathed. "This is breathtaking."

"So are you, Callie." The tug on her hand pulled her around to find Ryan down on one knee.

Her free hand flew over her mouth and she was instantly fighting a tsunami of tears.

Ryan's hand held an open box cradling a blue gemstone flanked by diamonds.

"Callie, I didn't realise how much I was missing out on until you came into my life. You have added so much more than I could ever have imagined. The love I feel for you continues to grow every day, and there is no one I would rather share my island home and my future with. Will you marry me?"

Caroline only had to get one word out, but emotion clogged her throat. Nodding her response, she finally whispered yes as he slipped the ring onto her finger.

"I chose tourmaline because the colour reminds me of the waters around Tokalau on a beautiful sunny day, and seeing as we first met on that water, I thought it was a fitting choice."

"It's perfect." She found her voice, thick with want and need.

Ryan kept hold of her hand as he got to his feet and pulled her in for their first deeply passionate kiss as an engaged couple.

EPILOGUE

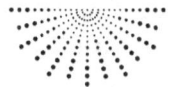

*I*t was fitting that the Event Coordinator's first wedding in Tokalau's new chapel should be her own.

While the photographer snapped a few more frames, Callie stood in front of the mirror in the bridal suite, a beautiful space built from scratch in the same style as the other bures on the island.

The staff had worked tirelessly over the last few months to bring this project to life. The finishing touches had been put in place earlier this morning by Jake and Ryan—the plinths for the floral arrangements had arrived at the last minute and had taken longer to put together than they expected, so it was almost down to the wire.

But Callie's outlook had gradually become more Fijian. No hurry, no worry.

The local women who were part of her team had been tasked with supervising the wedding so Callie could enjoy her day.

The island had been closed to visitors for the past week, so their wedding guests could enjoy all the serenity Tokalau had to offer. Ryan's family almost filled the building, along with a few of his friends. Callie's streamlined possessions had already been moved into the main house from her accommodation shared with Rosi.

A smiling Tui drove her to the little white chapel over-looking the water. A larger buggy carried her attendants. Both Eleanor and Tania had enjoyed extended stays on the island over the last few months, getting to know their older sister all over again. They now joined Matisse in the bridal party, along with Niah. They all wore ankle length, capped-sleeved dresses, in shades of blue synonymous with Tokalau resort, flowers woven into their hair.

Lloyd was waiting to escort her down the aisle. It was only fitting as he had been instrumental in getting her to Fiji in the first place. Callie kissed him on the cheek and smoothed his tie into place. "I can never thank you enough for sending me here to Tokalau."

"Yes, it was one of my more inspired decisions, that's for sure." He tucked her hand into the crook of his arm. "I am thrilled that two of my favourite people are getting together."

Matisse as matron of honour was holding onto Leo's hand before he walked the rings down to the front. He was dressed similarly to the groomsmen and would no doubt steal the show. Miss Sienna, dressed in her wedding finery, was already inside in the arms of Rosi, who sat proudly in the front row dressed in a chamba sulu in the same eye-catching floral print as the bridesmaids.

Callie had gone for a soft and simple flowing gown with a keyhole back, and she would ditch the silver sandals as soon as she could. Flowers adorned her flowing hair and she carried a matching bouquet of tropical blooms.

Floor-to-ceiling glass windows at the front of the chapel framed a picture-perfect view of shades of blue. White chairs tied with Tokalau-blue ribbon sat either side of the woven mat that ran down the centre the building. At the other end of the mat, Ryan was wiping at his eyes as he waited for her to come towards him to start their life together.

He was wearing a grey suit. The only other time she had seen Ryan in a suit was in Melbourne and even then it was on loan from Jake. But this suit fit him to absolute perfection and he took her breath away. But she imagined the jacket and tie would be shed at the first available opportunity, so she wanted to enjoy every second of time seeing him dressed up.

Beside him stood Jake, and Ryan's brothers. There had been a lot of debate about the groomsmen wearing sulus with sandals for the ceremony, but they had settled for black trousers with shirts that matched the bridesmaids' dresses.

As a name, "Caroline" was much too formal for the lifestyle she was now enjoying and she was more than happy for everyone, not just Ryan, to call her Callie. "Caroline" was a reminder of a past she was keen to leave behind as she moved forward into the next chapter of her life. Married. To Ryan.

RYAN AND CALLIE stood on the dock, suitcases already stowed in *Shaw Thing*. The casual beach marquee reception had been as perfect as it could be. A mix of traditional local fare and a healthy dose of Australian cuisine from a serve-yourself buffet. Of course there was a display of dancing and singing from a group of Fijian performers.

Now, staff and guests gathered in a semi-circle. The harmonies of *Isa Lei* always gave Callie goosebumps—she never tired of hearing the farewell song when guests were departing the island.

But, unlike the last time she had left the island with Ryan, she knew this time she would be coming back.

Her husband stood behind her with his arms wrapped around her as the last of the harmonies floated into the sunset sky.

THE END

A NOTE FROM THE AUTHOR

Dear Reader,

I hope you enjoyed the love story of Caroline and Ryan.

If you can spare the time, I would greatly appreciate it if you could leave a review on your favourite platform. For an indie author like me, it helps other readers to find my story.

To see photos of the places my stories are set, and connect with my writing journey and future stories, please sign up for my newsletter at

alisonjoywriter.com

Thanks for reading,
Alison

ABOUT THE AUTHOR

As a teenager, Alison Joy wrote stories in her head at night before she fell asleep. She still does, but finally decided to get some of the stories out of her head and onto paper, then computer, and finally published. She enjoys being able to say what goes on in her characters' lives, who falls in love with whom, unexpected journeys, and changing things if she doesn't like it.

A long-term resident of Queensland's capital city, Brisbane, she is a recent convert to e-reading. Nothing will beat a physical book, of course, but for storage practicalities—especially when travelling—the e-reader rules.

As well as reading, she also enjoys photography and is a procraftinator from way back.

alisonjoywriter.com

 instagram.com/itsa.joy

ALSO BY ALISON JOY

Brushstrokes of Love

Still grieving the loss of her fiancé, Matisse leaves Sydney to spend six months living in an old loggers' cabin near Cape Otway on Australia's wild southern coastline.

She hopes the solitude will help her focus on her painting, but she hasn't counted on the distraction of property owner, Jake Davis, and his canine sidekick, Charlie.

Jonno was the love of her life, but is there a chance for Matisse to find love again?

For Love and Charity

How far would you go to raise money for charity?

When nurse Laura Maxwell volunteers on the remote Pacific island of Levati, clashing with the doctor in charge is the last thing she expects. She has no idea why he aggravates her so much.

A clinic run into the jungle with Doctor Marcus Bradley ends in disaster. Kidnapped by rebel forces, they must put aside their animosity if they are to survive.

The media frenzy surrounding their eventual release dubs them "The Kidnap Couple" and Marcus convinces Laura to continue their fake relationship in order to exploit the publicity machine and raise much-needed funds for the medical charity so close to his heart. Reluctantly agreeing, she finds herself pulled deeper into a mire of half-truths.

Despite her growing feelings for Marcus, all Laura wants is her old life back. But will a life without Marcus Bradley be enough?